MW00772999

TIMEBLINK: DRAGONFLY

MJ MUMFORD

TINY✳BLUE
DRAGONFLY
PRESS

This is a work of fiction. Names, characters, places and incidents either are the product of the author's imagination or are used fictitiously. Any resemblance to actual persons, living or dead, business establishments, events, or locales is entirely coincidental. The publisher does not have control over and does not have any responsibility for author or third-party websites or their content.

TIMEBLINK: DRAGONFLY

All rights reserved. This book or any portion thereof may not be reproduced or used in any manner whatsoever without the express written permission of the publisher except for the use of brief quotations in a book review.

Cover by
Elizabeth Mackey

Copyright © 2024 by MJ Mumford

ISBN 978-1-7773362-6-4 (ebook)
ISBN 978-1-7773362-7-1 (paperback)
ISBN 978-1-7773362-8-8 (hardcover)

For my husband, Alistair
who has supported this wild and wonderful dream of mine every step of
the way.

"From now until the end of time no one else will ever see life with my eyes, and I mean to make the most of my chance."

Christopher Morley
Travels in Philadelphia

Are You Ready for Dragonfly?

This story picks up moments after the dramatic ending in book two, *Flight 444*. As such, if you haven't already read it, you may wish to start your timeblinking journey with *Flight 444* where key characters and events lay the groundwork for this series finale.

Of course, for the most immersive experience, you might also consider going all the way back to the beginning wth *TimeBlink* and find out how Syd first discovers her power of time travel.

Wherever you happen to be in the timeline, the author wishes to thank you for your interest in this genre-defying series.

Please note that Dragonfly *includes content that may be unsettling for some readers. For details, please visit the* **Guidance** *page at mjmumford.com.*

Chapter One

In the shadowy realm of consciousness, voices swirled around me, crackling with energy like dry twigs in a campfire.

Voices that seemed near, yet far off.

Children, adults. A barking dog. All of them steeped in panic.

My mind retreated to the darkness—a comforting haven that I didn't want to leave.

Don't wake up.

Don't give in.

Despite my resistance, the physical world slowly crept in, imposing itself upon me. Tugging at me. Pulling me to the surface.

Don't go there.

Keep the pain away.

Resist. Resist.

But reality demanded my attention, assaulting my senses one by one.

The scent of freshly mown grass. Pine trees. Wet clay.

The drone of a small outboard motor chugging away in the distance.

1

Blades of stiff Kentucky bluegrass prickling my neck, my arms.

A cool, damp cloth settling over my forehead.

A small hand stroking my shoulder.

A voice, clearer now. Familiar.

"Shouldn't we call an ambulance?" It was my friend Rose.

"No, no. She has a history of fainting spells. It will pass. It always does." My sister, Kendall.

"Is Auntie Syd going to be okay?"

"Oh, Connor. Of course she is. Please don't be upset."

"It wasn't my fault."

"I know. It was nobody's fault."

"Devin was supposed to be watching him, I swear. It was his turn."

"It was not!" came Devin's voice, distantly.

"Was too!"

"Boys! That's enough. I'll say it again: it was nobody's fault. I don't want to hear another word about it."

Devin, closer now: "The lady said she knew Auntie Syd. And she had the same necklace. The one with the dragonfly on it."

My eyes shot open.

Connor's face surged into view. "She's awake! Auntie Syd, are you alright? Do you want some water?"

Kendall nudged Connor away. "Okay, everyone. Give her some room."

Everything went quiet. Even the sparrows and crows seemed to sense the trouble at ground level and stifled their chatter.

I grabbed the wet cloth from my forehead and flung it aside. Struggled to sit. Dizzy. God, I was so dizzy. Kendall and Rose steadied me, their hands supporting my back.

"Christopher," I choked out before my throat closed, the memory of his disappearance slamming into me like a tidal wave. My vision blurred, tears flooding my eyes. I was powerless to hold back the sobs that followed, stiff and jarring in the quiet.

My baby was gone.

My sweet, innocent Christopher now existed in an entirely different timeline.

And without the talisman, my bridge to him had collapsed.

Chapter Two

Agent Jimmy Lopez

Agent Jimmy Lopez adjusted the contrast on the twenty-six-inch surveillance monitor and rubbed his chin. "Looks like a new guest has arrived."

"Probably her sister's husband," Agent Tom Jenkins said from the soundboard next to Lopez. The agents, members of the FBI's Antiterrorism Division, were hunkered down in a rented home at Sandalwood Lake, their vantage point giving them a clear line of sight into the Brixton property across the water.

As Jenkins monitored the audio feeds, he added, "He's apparently bringing the hot dogs and steaks."

"Which sister? Syd has a few of them."

"Kendall. Husband's name is…hang on a sec, let me have a look at my notes…it's Brett Parks. Realtor. And a pretty successful one at that."

"Okay, so Mr. Parks, the rich realtor, is bringing the wieners."

"Affirmative."

"Cut it out, will ya? *Affirmative*, my ass."

Jenkins laughed. "Hey, give me a break. I'm new. Just trying to do everything by the book."

"I don't care if it's your third stakeout or your thirtieth. When you're with me, you're free to speak like a normal person."

"Sure, boss," Jenkins said. "Hang on. The doorbell just rang at the Brixton property. Want to put your ears on?"

Lopez swiveled on his chair and snatched his headphones from the console then rolled over to his camera perched on a tripod at the window. "Might as well get in on the fun."

Three months prior, the tech team had installed five listening devices inside the Brixton cabin, one on the grand deck overlooking the lake, and a surveillance camera at the front door. So far, the sophisticated equipment had proved to be nothing more than a fancy decoration. None of the footage or recordings Lopez and Jenkins had captured thus far had provided any evidence to indicate that Brixton or any of her friends were anything but average people, much to Lopez's frustration.

He lowered his eye to the viewfinder just as the sister, Kendall—who'd been sitting on the deck with the rest of the guests—excused herself to go answer the door. Inside the house, the voices on the headphones were as clear as if he were standing in the same room.

"I'm Sam, a friend of Syd and Jarett's—but they're not expecting me. It's a surprise," the agents heard the newcomer say.

"Fun! Well, it's nice to meet you, Sam. They're outside on the deck. Follow me."

Lopez grunted when Sam stepped through the patio doors and onto the sunny deck. "Hm. This guy looks familiar. Take a look."

Jenkins came over to the high-powered fieldscope set up next to Lopez's camera and peered through the eyepiece. "Huh."

"Huh, what? Do you recognize him?"

"Neg—no, can't say as I do." Jenkins pulled back from the fieldscope. "First time I've seen him."

After taking several close-up shots, Lopez zoomed back just wide enough to see the whole expanse of the deck.

"What's this, now?" he muttered as the new guy, Sam, climbed onto a deck box and fiddled with an exterior pot light over the door. Then he went on to the next one. "Shit!" At the third light, Sam extracted the tech team's only outdoor bug on the property and slipped it into his pocket.

"What's going on?" Jenkins asked, who'd hurriedly repositioned his eye on the fieldscope.

"We won't hear anything outside the house now. Our new friend Sam knew exactly where to find our only exterior bug and took it upon himself to remove it," Lopez grumbled. "Well, shit. I just remembered where I've seen him before. At the Port Raven PD."

"He's a cop?"

"Maybe. Or an investigator. Or the lunch dude. Lucky for us, we can find out pretty quick."

Lopez made an adjustment to the camera and took another burst of photos. When he was finished, he said, "Send those to Lancaster for an ID."

"Will do, sir."

With his eye still glued to the viewfinder, Lopez said, "Our mystery man has everyone's attention now. And... great. Ms. Brixton is having a Grade-A meltdown. This is a disaster." He sat back. "We can officially kiss our cover goodbye."

"But we'll stick around, right? Maybe they'll say something inside the house."

"Not likely, now. This Sam fella probably knows there are interior bugs, too."

"It doesn't mean he'll be able to find them all."

"Regardless, they'll be on alert now. The only way we'll

likely get anything more is if one of the kids spits out something juicy."

"That's happened before, right? Whole operations being brought to the ground by one loose-lipped kid?"

Jenkins was right. Lopez himself had busted a fledgling terrorist faction back in '97 thanks to a young boy bragging to a schoolmate about his father's cool vest with 'lots of wires and stuff'. He shuddered. The child's innocent observation had saved hundreds of lives that day.

"Yeah, we'll sit tight. We may have lost the audio surveillance, but let's assume they don't know we've also got eyes on them. At any rate, I'm not leaving before we have an ID on this Sam person."

"Want another coffee while we wait?"

"God no. My ulcer is killing me. You mind grabbing me a glass of water?"

"Sure, boss."

Lopez shook his head at his protégé's nickname for him, finding it endearing despite himself. Watching Jenkins head into the kitchen, he hoped the young agent wouldn't adopt the same all-work lifestyle that had left him fifty pounds overweight and perpetually irritable.

He turned back to his camera to pass the time. At least today's efforts had yielded a flurry of activity to keep him from falling asleep—which he often did during surveillance, especially surveillance that he considered low stakes. These people weren't terrorists, for God's sake. Witches or magicians, perhaps, but not terrorists.

Jenkins returned a few moments later and handed Lopez a glass of ice water. "Here you go, sir."

"Thanks. Grab your ears and have a seat. And cross your fingers one of those kids has a tasty nugget of intel for us."

They had just settled in for another long stretch of waiting when something—or rather, some*one*—caught Lopez's attention. A woman had appeared in the shadows near the Brixton property, maybe twenty-five or thirty yards down the wooded path. He hadn't seen her arrive; it was as though she'd materialized out of nowhere, but that would be impossible. She must have come from the forest between the Brixton and Anderson properties.

"Hey, I need your eyes," he said to Jenkins, who pulled off his headphones and hurried over to the fieldscope.

"Where are we looking?"

"There, to the south. Just past the fallen cedar tree. What do you see?"

Jenkins found the spot right away. "A woman, middle aged. Shoulder-length brown or black hair. Who is she?"

"I have no idea. She literally appeared out of thin air."

"Weird. Why is she just standing there?"

"She's not just standing there. Look at her body language."

The novice agent repositioned his eye on the fieldscope. "It's pretty dark, but it looks like she's trying to keep from being seen."

"Correct. Anything else?"

"Apart from looking a little creepy? Not really."

Lopez took a series of photos, but deep shadows from the surrounding trees obscured much of the woman from view, so he didn't expect them to be very clear.

Jenkins's voice brightened. "I wonder if she's a family member. Maybe she's there to surprise them? Like Sam?"

Lopez nodded. "It's one possibility."

"And...there goes Syd's kid, Christopher, wandering off again. Syd must get tired of chasing after the little guy."

"He does love playing on that fallen tree."

"The bigger kids are totally oblivious. They must have been told fifty times to keep an eye on him." Jenkins took his eye away from the fieldscope. "Sir, I just had a thought. What if he falls into the water when they aren't looking? Would we have time to drive to the other side of the lake?"

"Nope. It'd be quicker to call Syd anonymously. Or any one of her buddies. We have all their numbers, remember."

"That'd blow their minds. *Hey, your toddler just fell in the lake. Better get on that.*"

Lopez chuckled. Being an FBI agent came with its perks, and he'd used them all in his thirty-seven years of service— mostly for noble purposes, but admittedly, also for some less virtuous endeavors. He remembered one particular 'act of god' call he'd made early in his career to put a scare into some neighborhood punks who'd been taunting his dog in the yard. Not the best use of Bureau resources, but it had been *very* satisfying at the time.

Jenkins returned to the fieldscope, his shoulders relaxing. "Never mind. I don't think we have to worry. He's heading straight for that woman."

"See? No panic necessary. But keep your eye on them," Lopez said, sitting back. He reviewed the photos he'd just taken, realizing he'd been right about the poor quality. It would be hard to ID the woman if it came to that.

"*What the fuck?*" Jenkins yelled, stumbling back from the fieldscope like he'd seen a ghost. Lopez flinched. He'd never heard the kid swear before. "They're gone!"

"Who's gone?" Lopez snapped, leaping up to get a look in the scope.

"The Brixton boy! And the woman! I swear, I had them in sight!"

Lopez scanned the area they'd been watching. Seeing nothing, he turned to his colleague. "Did she take him into the forest maybe? Or down the path?"

Jenkins swallowed hard. When he spoke again, his voice was steadier. "No, I'm telling you, the woman bent down as if to talk to him, and they just...*vanished*."

Strange as it sounded, that would line up with the woman's abrupt arrival Lopez had witnessed moments ago. "Look, you're pretty shaken up. Sit down before you fall down," he said, pointing to the chair at the soundboard. "We'll figure this out."

Jenkins took his seat and slipped his headphones over his neck without putting them on. "Should we call Ms. Brixton?"

"And tell her what? That her kid and an unknown woman vaporized right in front of us like a couple of gad-damn Star Trek characters?"

"I mean, well...yeah. We could do it anonymously."

Lopez shook his head. "We don't even know where they went."

"But at least they could start looking."

"Just give it a minute or two. Someone will notice the kid missing."

Lopez went back to studying the scene through the scope, wincing when the pain from his ulcer stabbed at his left side. What had his doctor said? Maybe it was time to quit his high-stress job and ease into an early retirement. Maybe take a part-time job at a hardware store. Lopez had scoffed at the idea; he was up for mandatory retirement next year anyway. He shook his head and forced himself to take some relaxing breaths. In. Out. In. Out. There. As the pain lessened, he could think straight again and was able to see the whole picture clearly: he had simply looked away the very moment the woman had arrived, and Jenkins had done the same thing a few minutes later when the woman and the boy had vanished. It was the only explanation that made sense.

Lopez abandoned the fieldscope and plodded back to his chair behind his camera, sitting down heavily. "What's your take on all this?"

Jenkins shrugged. "I honestly don't know, sir. I've never witnessed anything so bizarre in my whole life." He raised his hands to demonstrate how vigorously they were still trembling before lowering them to his lap. "There's no rational explanation for it."

"But if you had to guess?"

"Honestly? They were there one moment and then *poof,* gone the next. If this was a movie, I might say they were time travelers…"

Lopez barked out a laugh. He hadn't worked with Jenkins very long, but he'd come to admire the younger agent's calm and objective approach in a range of high-pressure situations. Jenkins' leap to a far-fetched notion like time travel only illustrated how rattled he was.

"I wouldn't put that in your report."

"Aren't we supposed to provide *all* our thoughts about what we observe? Isn't that the whole point of surveillance?"

"It's a big part of it, yes," Lopez said, crossing his arms, staring out at the placid lake. He grunted. "I was so damned close."

"Pardon me, sir?"

"I'd been *so close* to wrapping up this useless investigation and going home."

"You really think *The 444 Five* are innocent, huh?"

"Hell yeah. And I'm pretty sure the top brass knows it, too. You know what I think? I think they stuck us with this case to keep us out of their hair—the rookie and the old horse on the brink of retirement."

Jenkins shook his head in surprise. "There's no way. You're one of the best, sir."

Lopez snorted. "Apparently the 'best' have no value past fifty-seven years of age. Ah, well. At least my wife'll be happy. I installed some shiny new hardwood flooring in the living room three years ago, and much to her consternation, I still haven't replaced the trim. Maybe I'll finally get around to finishing little tasks like that once I've got my gold watch."

"So, this whole thing is a *make-work* project?" Jenkins asked, sweeping his eyes glumly over the mountain of high-tech equipment.

"Probably. I mean, the NTSB already put the crash down to human error. The odd coincidence of *The 444 Five*'s survival is the only reason we're here...and there's no chance in hell we'll ever prove they're terrorists. We've been sidelined. I'm sure of it."

Jenkins could only shake his head in dismay.

Lopez felt sorry for the kid but couldn't help himself from elaborating. "Hell, just yesterday I'd all but convinced the director of just that—that these people have been telling the truth all along. The only question left is how they ended up in that cornfield. And you know what? I don't really give a damn. Our job was to find a link between Ms. Brixton's group and the crash, and I'm *positive* there isn't one."

The problem was that no matter how sure he felt about their innocence, a gut feeling wouldn't fly at the Bureau, not with today's events to complicate things. Time-travel hogwash aside, Lopez could just imagine the director's reaction to the news of this Sam person dismantling the exterior bug. On one hand, it could present an opportunity for Lopez to wrap up his career on a high note—potentially exposing a larger conspiracy at play. It wasn't every day he caught someone blatantly interfering with government surveillance equipment. On the other, he'd been eager to wash his hands of this whole affair and high-tail it home.

Now, the investigation was bound to reach a whole new level of scrutiny. And he wasn't happy about it. Not one bit.

Chapter Three

In the slowly dissipating afternoon light, I eyed the postcard-perfect executive homes across the lake. Some were white, others soft gray. One, with a façade made entirely of glass, disappeared like a chameleon amongst the trees.

Today, a peculiar glint caught my eye from the living room window of Bob and Mildred Duncan's craftsman-style home. I pictured Mildred snapping a photo of the lake on her ancient cell phone, which would be just like her. She loved to show off her photos whenever we encountered her on a walk around the lake. But then I recalled her mentioning that some highfalutin film company had rented their house to shoot a bird documentary all summer. Perhaps the odd flash I'd seen coming from her window was part of that.

I sighed.

"We'll find him," Kendall said, but I wasn't so sure.

In the short time since Christopher's disappearance, I'd become absolutely certain of two things: one, that his abductor was Collette Scott, none other than Morley's late wife who had died in 2015 and who'd somehow timeblinked past her death date to commit this crime; and two, that she was somehow, unbelievably, able to timeblink in ways that neither I nor Morley had ever been capable of. I'd waited at the fallen tree where Christopher was last seen—well past the four-minutes and forty-four seconds of a normal timeblink— and when he still hadn't returned after ten minutes, it was clear he wouldn't be coming back, period. He was on Collette's clock now, and I was powerless to do anything about it.

Lainie and Isla were inside keeping the kids occupied while I remained on the deck with Kendall, Sam, Jarett, and Rose, going over the details of Christopher's disappearance.

Kendall offered me another tissue, which I gladly accepted, though I didn't know how many more tears I could produce.

"I'd forgotten about the four-forty-four rule of timeblinking," she said.

"It doesn't apply in this situation, anyway."

"Why not?"

"Because he's on Collette's *return* timeblink. Like Sam is on mine."

"And I can't go back to 2019," Sam added soberly.

I gave him an apologetic look. "Even if you wanted to return to 2019, I have no idea how to get you there. You're stuck in this timeline for good."

Kendall wasn't convinced. "But you said yourself that Collette timeblinked beyond her own lifetime, which you always thought was impossible. Maybe she also knows how to return Christopher to his natural timeline."

"It's wishful thinking," I said.

She had a point, though. The talisman had belonged to Collette first. I'll bet she knew all sorts of things about its power that Morley and I had never discovered.

Rose spoke up. "I have a question. Why on Earth would this woman take your little boy to 2014?"

"I honestly don't know, but it's the year she and Morley

looked after that foster child I told you about. *Tristan*. It's so obvious to me now that it was Christopher."

"Are you sure? Wouldn't Morley have recognized his own son?"

"Not necessarily. Prior to that, he'd only ever seen Christopher as a baby. Remember, Christopher is almost four now." I sighed. "Besides, I only took him three times. Morley couldn't bear the pain of saying goodbye to Christopher each time we left."

Empathy gathered behind Rose's eyes. "It was probably for the best. Who knows what effect timeblinking might have on someone so young."

"That's another reason Morley asked me to stop bringing him. God, it was so reckless of me, taking a tiny baby on time-blinks like that."

Kendall smiled tenderly. "You wanted Morley to spend time with his son. Any of us would've done the same thing."

"I know I would've," Rose said.

Sam raised his hand. "Same."

Jarett spoke for the first time since we'd reconvened on the deck. "You're only *speculating* about the kidnapper's identity at this point. What if it wasn't Collette?"

"I'm almost a hundred percent sure it was her. She had the—" I caught myself before saying 'talisman.'

He cocked his head, waiting for me to finish.

"Devin said she had shoulder-length brown hair and that she knew me. Not only that, but she used to come into the pub with Morley before she died. What if she found out Morley and I had had a child together and wanted to punish me for it?"

"Again, you're speculating."

"It's the only explanation that makes sense."

"Okay. So, say it really was Collette. There might not even be a connection between Christopher's abduction and Tristan's foster care stay with her and Morley."

It was a possibility, but I doubted it. The timing and Christopher's age aligned too perfectly.

"I appreciate you all trying to help, but none of this will matter if I don't regain the power of timeblinking."

Kendall patted my knee. "It'll come back. Have some faith."

Faith would not magically produce my dragonfly talisman. And without it, my only hope was that Collette would come to her senses and return my son to his rightful place. If not—if I'd truly lost the talisman forever—my little boy might be gone forever, too.

Sam's voice wrenched me out of my thoughts. "I know this is an unusual circumstance, your son having been abducted by someone from a different, uh...time dimension, but if there's anything you need from me from an investigatory perspective, let me know."

Kendall cut in. "Just for the record—you're not going to report this, right?"

Sam huffed under his breath. "What would I say? A time traveler kidnapped Syd's little boy? I'd lose my badge. Then they'd throw me in a psychiatric hospital."

"I wouldn't be so sure," Jarett muttered. "Syd's one of *The 444 Five*. They'd probably welcome the time-travel explanation at this point."

"I'll give you that."

"No!" I spat. "I've already told you. Not a word about this to anyone. There's no point. I'm the only one who can get Christopher back."

Jarett added, "I have to agree with Syd. The authorities are powerless to help. No sense in calling attention to the matter...and creating a media firestorm in the process."

"Okay," I said. "We all agree to keep this between us?"

Everyone nodded.

"Good. But before anything else, we have to figure out

what we're going to tell Brett about Christopher's disappearance. He'll be here any minute."

"We tell him nothing," Jarett offered. "Keep him in the dark."

"You don't think he's going to notice Christopher's not here? And what about Connor and Devin? This is the biggest thing that's ever happened to them. Surely, they'll mention their missing cousin to their dad."

Kendall cleared her throat. "Umm...you don't have to worry about Brett."

"What do you mean?" I asked.

She wrinkled up her face at me. "I'm sorry, Syd. But I told him about timeblinking years ago, back when we found Isla and Finn."

I shook my head incredulously.

"Syd, he's my husband. Of course I'm going to tell him big news like that. But don't worry, he swore never to tell anyone."

I rolled my eyes. "So did you."

"Ouch."

"Who else have you told?"

"No one. Honestly. Anyway, he's just like the rest of us. He doesn't know how you actually do it. Just that you *can*."

"*Could*. Past tense. I *once* had the ability to timeblink."

Jarett cut in. "Well, at least we know we can talk candidly around Brett now. But that still doesn't help us with Connor and Devin. Do you think you could convince them to keep quiet about all this?" he asked Kendall.

She took only a moment's pause. "Absolutely. We tell them the police ordered us to keep it a secret. They already feel responsible for Christopher's disappearance. They won't want any extra guilt hanging over their heads."

"Okay, good," I said. "The sooner you tell them, the better. Emphasize the *tell no one* angle...not their friends, not their teachers, not their gaming buddies. No one."

"Gotcha," Kendall said, jumping to her feet. "I'll take them for a walk around the lake and fill them in."

"It might help if you mention I'll be conducting the investigation," Sam added.

I gave him a quick smile. Having friends in law enforcement was coming in handy.

Kendall headed for the door. "I'll go round up the boys."

And then I realized we had another problem. "Wait! Can you take Isla and Finn with you? They need to hear the same story."

"Oh my god. Isla. She's probably having a nervous breakdown right now thinking back to her own abduction."

"My thought exactly. Be gentle. But firm. She needs to believe the police are all over it and that our good friend Sam is extra invested in bringing Christopher home."

"That's the truth," Sam said.

Once Kendall had disappeared into the house, Rose asked, "Are you okay, Syd?"

"I'm holding up."

"That's my point. You're taking all of this extremely well for someone whose son was just abducted to another time realm."

My voice cracked. "I need to get him back, Rose. That's all I'm focusing on right now."

"I get that. But remember, we're your friends, and we want to help."

Jarett nodded. "She's right. You don't need to do this alone."

"Thank you. From the bottom of my heart. I'll ask for help if I need it."

Rose gave me her no-nonsense look. "Promise?"

A lump in my throat prevented me from speaking, so I gave her a thumbs up. I was thinking back to when Isla had disappeared from my life. I'd never felt so abandoned. It seemed as if my family and friends—and even the investigators to an extent—hadn't been able to stand to look at my miserable, broken face. It would have made such a difference to have the same level of love and support that surrounded me now.

Rose's soothing voice pulled me out of my thoughts. She was speaking to Sam. "Do you think the FBI will find out about Christopher's disappearance?"

"Not unless one of us reports it."

"Or one of the kids alludes to it inside the house," Jarett said. "Bugs, remember."

Rose shook her head incredulously at Sam. "I still can't believe the FBI bugged our houses. Thank goodness for your friend at the FBI. Do they honestly think we had something to do with the plane crash? They determined its cause months ago, for goodness' sake."

"You have to look at it from their perspective," Sam explained, spreading his arms. "Yes, the investigation concluded it was the ground crew's negligence. They were responsible for the cockpit window coming loose mid-flight and the cascade of problems that created. However—"

Rose finished his sentence. "They can't explain why we're still alive when they have irrefutable proof that we boarded the plane."

"Yep. Plain and simple," Sam said. "They had no choice. They had to default to blaming it on terrorism to cover their asses."

Rose jumped in again. "And to avoid public scrutiny, no doubt. Still. I hate the idea that we're going to be monitored for the rest of our lives, because that's what's going to happen, right? They'll never have concrete evidence to prove our innocence."

Sam shrugged. "Possibly. I can't say for sure, though."

Rose turned to me. "What if we told the FBI the truth? That at one time we had the ability to time travel and now we don't?"

I shook my head. "You think we're being watched *now?* Can you imagine the frenzy *that* would create?"

"On the contrary," Jarett said. "They'd probably stamp the word 'deranged' on our files and move their efforts to *actual* terrorist activity."

I sighed. "Well, I'd rather be thought of as a whack-job than a terrorist any day."

Just then, the deck door opened, and Kendall marched out with a woeful-looking crew in tow: her twin boys, followed by Isla and Finn.

"Eli's still napping, and Lainie's happy to stay with him," Kendall said to Rose before addressing the rest of us. "Brett just arrived with the food. Anyone still hungry?"

I stood up. "Have you told him what happened?"

"Yes. The basics."

"Okay. I'll fill him in on the details. We'll start dinner while you're out."

"Oh Syd," Isla said. "Please don't bother yourself with the food. I'll take care of it when we get back."

I shuffled over and gave her a big hug. "Thank you, but I need the distraction right now."

She nodded grimly and followed Kendall and the boys down the stairs. My heart nearly broke. A mere hour ago, Christopher would have been part of their tight little group, but now he was gone, possibly forever.

Chapter Four

Agent Jimmy Lopez

"Thanks for coming in, Detective Douglas," Agent Lopez said, closing the door. He took a seat at the table across from Sam, who was certainly no stranger to the interrogation room at the Port Raven Police Department—only, he'd always been the one asking the questions in it.

"You can call me Sam."

"Okay, Sam. First of all, sorry about the room." He twirled his finger in the air. "This isn't an interrogation. Just a friendly chat. It was the only private space available in the whole building."

"Fair enough," Sam said. "I'm all ears."

Lopez leaned forward and crossed his arms on the table. "We'd just like to ask you some questions about a local boy who went missing at Sandalwood Lake. A boy you appear to know."

To Lopez, it seemed like Sam flinched a little, but he couldn't be sure, so he let it slide. When Sam didn't respond, Lopez went on. "We're just wondering if you were aware of it."

Sam relaxed, but only a little. "No, this is the first I've heard of a missing child. Especially one I know personally. And if he's local, why does the FBI know about it before me?"

"Well, Detective Douglas, the funny thing is, we actually stumbled across this incident by accident while we were investigating another case."

Lopez watched Sam's eyes narrow and willed himself not to so much as twitch a muscle under the other man's curious stare. He couldn't risk looking nervous or even slightly unsure of himself.

"Okay, fire away. Who's the missing kiddo?"

Lopez took a quick, confident breath. "His name is Christopher Brixton. Three years old, son of Sydney Brixton, 36. Do you know them?"

Sam's eyebrows shot up. "Christopher is missing?"

Aha. Sam's second untruth. "Yes. Since Saturday. Out at Sandalwood Lake."

"Why didn't you inform us right away? It's in our jurisdiction."

"Detective Douglas," Lopez started.

"Sam."

"*Sam.* Before you say anything more, you should know that we have eyes on the Sandalwood property."

Sam pursed his lips. "And?"

"And…we know you were there when the boy went missing."

"I see."

Lopez stood and fastened a button on his suit jacket, which strained against his belly. He strolled over to the two-way mirror and studied his reflection, looking at Sam over his shoulder. "As I'm sure you're aware, our surveillance is pretty tight, Sam. But I'll be honest, it didn't pick up the most important details. Like evidence of where Christopher might have gone, or"—he turned around—" if someone *has* taken him, who that person might be."

Sam sprang to his feet, knocking his chair to the floor with a clatter. He gestured to the room around him. "What is this, really? Are you accusing me of child abduction?"

Lopez put his hands up again, "Easy, Sam. That's not what this is about."

"Then what *is* it about, Agent Lopez?"

"Please. We're on a first-name basis here. It's Jimmy."

"Cut to the point, Lopez. Why am I here?"

"You're here, Sam, because a little boy went missing three days ago—the son of a member of *The 444 Five*, no less. For some bizarre reason, you—Detective Sam Douglas of the Port Raven PD—were there when it happened. And even stranger? Neither you nor the boy's mother have reported it to the authorities."

"I *am* the authorities," Sam said, bristling.

"Fair. But I checked, and you haven't filed any official paperwork, nor have you informed your superiors. There's no statement from Ms. Brixton or any potential witnesses. Nothing."

Sam grunted. "I thought I would do some poking around first. Get the jump on it before the media got a hold of it. You know how it is, right? Syd's in shock. She doesn't need to be thrown into the spotlight again. First, her missing twin is found, then, the mystery of why she and four other passengers made it off a plane untouched before a hundred others were incinerated in a crash. Another missing family member wouldn't look good. I was trying to protect her."

"Ah, okay. You were trying to protect her. You know that's not your job, right? We have people in blue uniforms for that."

"So?"

"So, you're saying you kept it off the record to spare Ms. Brixton the trouble of heightened celebrity?"

Sam shrugged. "Pretty much. And to keep the perpetrator in the dark. Syd thought it was a good idea."

Lopez pointed at Sam's toppled chair as he settled back

onto his own. "Why don't you take a seat, and we'll hash this out, point by point."

After a pause, Sam plucked the chair off the floor and sat down on it heavily. Lopez thought he looked like a trapped animal plotting his escape.

"I'm still trying to wrap my head around it," Lopez said, removing a small notebook from a pocket inside his blazer, flipping through it, and finding the page he was looking for. "Why would you deny Ms. Brixton the resources of an entire investigatory unit to help find her son? You're one of the lead detectives, Sam—and a damned good one—which makes me all the more curious about why you'd risk your standing for what? A cute blonde?"

Sam tightened his lips into a thin line and pushed some air through his nose. "You're out of line, Lopez."

The agent went on. "You also know the importance of getting on top of these things right away, with a team behind you. Not going off alone, vigilante style. Aren't you due to step up the next rung on the ladder soon?"

Sam shrugged.

"Look, I'm not out to get you. I'm pretty sure you're one of the good guys. Granted, you yourself went missing for five years and recently reappeared. Most of your buddies are pretty tight-lipped about where they think you were and what you were up to, but a couple of them are just as perplexed as I am and aren't happy about looking the other way. Not to mention this other little point of curiosity we can't quite explain connecting you and Ms. Brixton."

Sam folded his arms. "Such as?"

"Dates, Sam. Isn't it interesting that less than a day after *The 444 Five* end up alive and well in an Iowan cornfield, you show up at your family home after a five-year '*vacation*'?" He put the last word in air quotes.

"Coincidence."

"All right. We'll circle back to that one. How do you know Ms. Brixton?"

Sam shook his head, stopping short of rolling his eyes.

Lopez sighed. "Looks like I'm batting zero here. How about we move on to more serious matters, then? Like the question of who tipped you off about the surveillance at Sandalwood Lake? It was obviously someone in my organization."

"Nope. Pure hunch."

"You removed one of our devices, allowing you and your group to speak freely on the property. How did you know it was there?"

"Like I said: intuition."

"All right, how do you explain this: every guest at that Flight 444 reunion party was surprised to see you, which means none of them invited you. How would you have known that the party was happening, aside from hearing it from someone who'd overheard their plans?"

"Come on. Are you really saying none of my friends could have *faked* their surprise?"

"Sam, Sam, Sam. I would hate to start digging around and discover a rat in my organization thanks to y—"

"For fuck's sake, Lopez. Spit it out. What do you want from me?"

"The truth, Sam. That's all. I'm tired of this case. I need your cooperation so I can leave your beautiful city and go home to my poor, lonely wife and my aging French bulldog and my Friday night poker games with the guys. I'm too old for this bullshit."

Sam took a deep breath and exhaled slowly. "Okay then. If what I've told you isn't good enough, what 'truth' are you really fishing for?"

Chapter Five

I shuffled to the door in my slippers and dressing gown and greeted Jarett as energetically as I could manage, which ended up being barely more than a grunt. Not that he could likely hear it.

"Metallica?" he shouted over *Helpless* booming from my subwoofer and several smart speakers placed strategically around the room. "How did you even hear the doorbell?"

I pulled my phone out of my dressing gown pocket and killed the music. The silence startled me. *Garage, Inc.* was the fourth heavy metal album I'd played in the last two hours.

"What?" I asked, crossing my arms.

"Good to see you, too, Syd. Nice housecoat. You do know it's two-thirty in the afternoon, right?"

"Did Rose send you? Or was it one of my sisters this time?"

"Nope. Came of my own free will."

He was still dressed in his police uniform, a sight that always sent a tingle down my spine, and not in a good way. It brought back memories of the evil, child-abducting firefighter I'd once lived with.

"You didn't have to come. I'm fine, you know."

26

He kicked off his shoes, picked them up, and motioned for me to follow him to the deck. It was the only place we knew we could speak candidly.

Once outside, Jarret pulled two Adirondack chairs together, and we sat face to face. He was practically vibrating when he leaned forward and interlaced his fingers on his bouncing knees, obviously excited about something.

"Well?" I said.

"First of all, why do you insist on hermiting yourself way out here in the middle of nowhere?"

"Hermiting?"

"Why aren't you basking in your luxurious penthouse in the city? You know, the one that's close to grocery stores, banks, gas stations…your family."

"What's left of it."

Jarett frowned. "Stop that."

"Excuse me? Stop *what*?"

"Being such a defeatist."

I glared at him. He went on unfazed.

"Look, we've only known each other for what, four months? But I could tell right away what you're made of. You've got a knack for handling situations that would make most people run and hide."

My shoulders slumped. Isn't that what I was doing now? "Christopher's been gone for eleven days, and I'm no closer to figuring out how to find him."

He sat back and rubbed at his beard. "No progress on the timeblinking front, I take it?"

I shook my head, wondering if it was time to go against Morley's wishes—to tell Jarret that the talisman was the whole reason timeblinking was possible. In Jarett's eyes (and the eyes of everyone else in my cozy little group), I'd simply lost the ability to timeblink like an elderly person might lose their ability to walk. He didn't know that without the talisman, my timeblinking days were over and I was just another heartbroken mother whose child had gone missing. Though, I'll bet mine was the first to be taken to a whole different dimension.

As if reading my mind, he said, "Are you sure you don't want to tell me how it all works? Maybe a fresh pair of eyes would spot some vital piece you've overlooked, then we could go get your little boy."

My heart swelled. He seemed almost as desperate to get Christopher back as I was. "I would have told you by now if I thought you could help."

"Have you told Isla yet?"

"What, that I used to be a time traveler? Yes. I laid it on her a few days ago. She kept pestering me about going to the police to give them our formal statements about Christopher's disappearance, but I told her—several times—that Sam is a Port Raven detective and that because he was here when it happened, witness statements weren't necessary." I chuckled. "That's Isla, though. Always wants to do things the proper way. So, yeah, I had to come clean before she blew the lid off things."

"How'd she take it?"

"Like anyone does. She was super skeptical. Thought I was pulling her leg. Then everything fell into place when I told her timeblinking is what saved our lives on Flight 444."

"She really had no clue?"

"No. She believed the FBI's story. The one they're spinning to the rest of the world: that we never got on the plane to begin with."

"Which is why the media has dropped us like a hot potato. Not the most exciting story anymore, is it?"

"Not unless you're a conspiracy theorist. Those guys are still in a mad scramble trying to figure it out. Fortunately, they never will. Not without the...not with my superpower gone."

"Is there *anything* I can do to help you get it back?"

He couldn't. It was up to me to find the talisman, which, as far as I knew, was in one of three places: somewhere in the plane wreckage (thus, in the possession of the FAA, the NTSB or even the FBI Counterterrorism Division), the bottom of the lake that Lainie and I splashed down into, or, if it had come off sometime during the skydive, it could be resting in a cornfield miles in any direction from our landing point. If I'd had even the slightest inkling of where it had dropped, I would have purchased a commercial-grade metal detector and gone to Iowa to look for it myself, but the scope of the search was just too wide for one person. Would I resort to that strategy at some point? Probably, considering the investigators weren't willing to tell me if a dragonfly pendant had been found at the crash site. You'd think they'd be getting tired of my incessant emails to them, but no. They shot back the same reply every time: because it's an active investigation, no personal effects could be released to the survivors or the victims' families until the file had been closed. It's all bureaucratic bullshit, and it's beyond cruel to deny a woman a simple yes or no answer about whether a special piece of jewelry from her late fiancé had been recovered or not. To pour even more salt into the wound, they never missed an opportunity to remind me that the investigation could take months, or even years, to wrap up.

"Just as I was coming to terms with never seeing Morley again, *wham*, Christopher disappears. Now I *have* to get the power back."

"I bet it'll return when you're least expecting it."

I nodded and took my focus to the lake. While I lost myself in the view, two mallards scooted under the dock and popped out on the other side.

"Have you thought about going back to work?" Jarett asked, pulling my attention back. "It could help take your mind off things a few hours a day."

"Yeah. I talked to Daniel yesterday. He put me on the schedule three days a week starting next Friday. Ugh. Who knows if I'll be ready by then."

"I'm sure you'll be fine. What story did you give him, anyway?"

"He thinks I'm experiencing delayed grief from my dad's death. I hated lying to him like that, but I had no choice. The truth would've landed me in psychiatric care."

"You mean he wouldn't have believed that your son was abducted by a time traveler?"

I laughed weakly. "He's heard a lot of excuses from his staff over the years, but that one would be a first."

"Anyway," Jarett said, leaning forward again, "the whole reason I came here was to give you some good news."

"What're you waiting for? Lay it on me."

He bit his bottom lip. "I've been approved for that transfer. Here. To Port Raven."

"Jarett, that's fantastic news! When do you start? Where will you live?"

"Whoa, whoa! One thing at a time."

"Okay. When?"

"It's all going to happen pretty quick. They fast-tracked a senior officer's retirement, so my first day will be on the sixteenth. Less than two weeks from now."

"That *is* fast. You must be so excited. No more ninety-minute drives to go golfing with Sam."

"Or to see you. Y'know, so I can keep an eye on you."

I blew out a raspberry. "I'm a big girl, Jarett. I can look after myself. So, have you found a place yet?"

"Yes, but it won't be available until October first. I'll be staying with Sam and Lizzy in the meantime. Going to move a bunch of my clothes and such there on the weekend of the fourteenth."

My eyes went wide. "Do they have room for you with all their kids running around?"

"Yeah, their house is massive. And it's only for two weeks."

"Um, just a thought, but I've got a three-bedroom, 3200-

square-foot condo in the city you can stay at. By yourself. And you could *walk* to the station from there."

"I thought of that but didn't want to impose."

"For shit's sake, Jarett, don't be a doofus. Take the condo. You'll thank me for it later."

He looked up at the sky and rubbed his beard comically, pretending to think about it. I grabbed my cushion and threw it at him. He caught it before it hit him in the head.

"Fine! I'll stay at your place. But I really think you should move back there yourself. What do you say? It'll be fun being roomies."

"Maybe," I said. But I'd been avoiding it for a reason. Christopher's imprint was all over that place, even more than here.

"Alright. Think about it. Listen, I had another motive for coming here today. An invitation. I wanted to give it in person so you couldn't say no."

I raised an eyebrow.

"But now that I'm here, I see I probably could have done it over the phone. You seem in much better spirits than the last time I saw you, despite looking like a tornado just pulled you out of bed."

My hands flew up to my hair, discovering a frizzy, lopsided ponytail. "I'm surprised you didn't run away screaming when you saw me," I said, trying to tuck some loose strands behind my ears before giving up. It didn't matter. I'd run the gamut of emotions over the past week and a half, and Jarett had seen them all. Right after Lainie went home to Buffalo, two days after Christopher's abduction, I'd found myself completely alone in the house with no one to distract me, and I'd crashed. Even Jinx was gone. Kendall took him when I admitted I hadn't walked him since Christopher disappeared. I shudder to think about what I would have done without Jarett, Kendall, and Isla taking turns staying with me that first week. I'd been a mess.

"Sam and Lizzy are throwing a dinner party on Saturday," Jarett said brightly. "And they've invited us to come."

"Oh…"

"*Oh?* That's all you have to say?"

I sighed. "I don't know, Jarett. I'm not really up for socializing right now. I'd ruin their party with my mood."

"Maybe I overstated the scale of the 'party.' It'll only be the four of us—their kids will be with their cousins. Come on, what good is hermiting yourself in the woods all this time?"

"*Hermiting* isn't a word."

"Don't change the subject. It'll be good for you. And you have three whole days to prepare."

"You make it sound like I'm Cinderella getting ready for the ball."

"Sure, if that's the mindset you need to get your butt out of the house for a night."

"Can I think about it?"

"No."

I groaned.

"Look," he said, "you'll hardly have to make any effort. Just run a brush through your hair and put on some clean clothes—hell, *any* clothes would be an improvement at this point—and I'll take care of the rest. C'mon. You even said you needed a distraction to keep your mind off things."

"Ugh. You're right. I *would've* said no over the phone."

"But since I drove all this way to put the charm on you…?" He batted his ridiculously long eyelashes at me, and my heart fluttered. I pushed the feeling away. Grieving mothers aren't allowed to feel pleasure.

"Fine. I'll come. I've been wanting to meet Lizzy anyway."

"Hallelujah, my plan worked. Welcome back to real life."

I rolled my eyes. "But if I can't handle it when we get there, promise you'll take me home?"

"Of course. But you'll be fine. Remember, it'll just be the four of us. It'll be fun."

32

"Enough, already. I said I would come."

He gave me a pouty look that made me feel like a jerk, so I reached over and patted his knee. "Thanks for looking out for me."

"I'm happy to do it. Honestly, Syd, whatever you need."

"Well, in that case, I do need your help with something." I jumped up and started down the stairs in my flip-flops and housecoat. "Come on."

He followed me to a five-foot-wide crater in the middle of my lawn, about halfway between the house and the shoreline.

"What the hell?" His eyes were as wide as the hole.

"I've been busy."

"I'll say." After he did a lap around the hollowed-out earth and gawked at the mound of soil next to it, I pointed to a potted tree tucked next to the house.

"Meet Christree."

"*Kristy?*"

"No…Chris-tree. I'm planting it in my baby's memory."

"Syd, that's—"

"I know! Amazing, right?"

"I was going to say *morbid*. You'll get your boy back."

I didn't want to talk about it anymore and motioned for him to follow me. Once we were standing in front of the five-foot-tall specimen, he grasped the tag and read it aloud. "White Gold Cherry. This rare self-pollinating variety is celebrated for its vibrant gold to orange-red fruit in mid-June and its abundant white blossoms in the spring."

"Christopher loved cherries. I wanted to honor him." What I didn't say was that it was also a nod to Morley's memory, for the white-gold engagement ring I'd presented to him on my last timeblink. I imagined the flush of snowy flowers that would appear every year, making it impossible to forget my absent family.

Jarett scratched his head. "Have you chosen the best location? Won't it block the view of the lake in a few years?"

"It's a dwarf variety."

He consulted the tag again. "Says here the mature size is eight to fourteen feet tall. Even at the smaller end, it'll get in the way."

"All the better. A constant reminder of my baby boy. Now, are you going to help me drag it over there so I can finish the job?"

He rubbed at his forehead with his fingertips. "Is it what you really want?"

"A hundred percent."

"Okay, then, step aside."

"Thank you."

"I'm sure you'd do the same for me," he said, getting to work. "Plus, I'm a sucker for sad, lonely hermits."

Chapter Six

I was in no mood to make small talk with Sam and Lizzy, but Jarett would be arriving at the condo in less than fifteen minutes—after a long drive from Seattle, no less—making it impossible for me to bail out now.

After seven outfit changes, I'd finally settled on my high-waisted black dress pants, a cream satin blouse, and a delicate, extremely uncomfortable pair of mid-heeled black patent slingbacks that I hadn't worn since my boss's daughter's wedding several years ago. My only solace was that I'd be kicking them off in the front hall of Sam's house in the suburbs a short while later.

Standing at the full-length mirror in my bedroom, I released the last bouncy blonde ringlet from my curling iron (which surprisingly still worked, given I hadn't used it since that same wedding). I felt ridiculous, like a kid being forced to dress up for her sister's confirmation ceremony.

I was tired, too, given the emotional ride I'd been on the last twenty-four hours. I'd finally given in to the prompting from both Jarett and my sisters and moved back to the penthouse yesterday, and it had damn near killed me.

Of course I'd made a beeline to Christopher's bedroom

the moment I'd arrived. I'd picked up his unwashed clothes and sobbed gutturally at the sight of the dried ice cream that had dribbled onto his t-shirt the day before his abduction. I'd curled into a ball on his bed amongst his stuffed toys and treasures and smushed my face into his pillow and breathed in his essence. I'd hugged his favorite T-Rex to my chest and bawled for three hours before finally passing out from exhaustion.

In retrospect, I probably should've resented my neighbors for not coming to check on me. God knows I would have knocked on *their* doors had I heard the same relentless wailing. But then again, the lack of neighborly concern was probably just another of those weird quirks about living in an executive penthouse where the majority of the tenants tended to keep their heads down and their standards high. Either that or my suite really was *that* soundproof.

"Ugh, I don't want to go," I said to my reflection, catching a quick flash of light over my shoulder. I whirled around, half expecting to see Christopher appearing out of thin air. But only darkness greeted me. I hurried over to the door, peering up to where I'd seen the flash. Or where I *thought* I'd seen the flash. It had been small and quick, like the sun glinting off a dime.

I turned to look out the floor-to-ceiling window next to my bed. The sun was low against a band of pink and orange clouds, still bright enough to bounce off something shiny. Unfortunately, owing to the tall doorways throughout the condo—each an absurd nine feet in height—I would need a ladder to investigate whatever it was that might have caught the light.

I tottered out of the room in my fancy shoes and made my way to the front hall closet where I kept an apartment-sized ladder. As I opened the door, my phone buzzed. Good. Jarett was here early. He could help me with the ladder.

When I swung the front door open a couple of minutes later, my stomach flipped. Jarett looked like a million bucks.

Over the few months I'd known him, he'd typically been dressed in shorts or jeans and one of his boldly patterned button-down shirts or, if he was heading to the golf course with Sam, a pair of chinos and a polo shirt. I'd also seen him in his official police uniform maybe half a dozen times—a sight that invariably sent a jolt of displeasure down my spine —but tonight, he'd outdone himself. He was decked out in what was obviously a custom-tailored suit that could have easily cost him a month's pay. His neatly manicured beard added a touch of ruggedness that played off the crisp lines of his suit, enhancing his natural good looks. If Kendall had been here, she would have punched my shoulder and said, *"Aha! I told you he was hot!"*

Noticing my jaw hanging open, Jarett filled the silence with an explanation. "I know, a bit over the top, but it's a special night." When I was still at a loss for words, he swept his eyes over my outfit and added, "You clean up well, yourself."

After an unladylike gulp, I said, "I'll take that as a compliment."

"You should. I don't hand them out very often," he joked, winking. "Ready?"

"Not quite. I need a favor."

"What's up?"

"*You*, in a minute. Grab that ladder and come to my bedroom."

"Hot damn, that's the weirdest invitation to someone's bedroom I've ever gotten," he said, starting down the hall with the ladder.

"Very funny. But it's not what you think."

"If it's to help you change a lightbulb, it's exactly what I think."

"Wrong again."

Once we'd reached the bedroom, I instructed him to position the ladder in the doorway, explaining the strange flash of light I'd seen earlier. Intrigued, he climbed up to take a look. "Whoa!"

"What, *what?*" I blurted.

He brought his finger down in front of me. It was black with grime. "You don't like dusting, do you?"

"Oh my *god*. Don't be a jerk."

He took his attention back to the door frame. "It's okay, you're in good company. I think Dubya was president the last time I dusted. Oh, wow, look what I found," he said, lowering his hand once more. I gasped and snatched the object he was holding then stumbled backward, collapsing onto my bed.

"Are you okay, Syd?" he said as he hurried down the ladder and came to sit next to me. He put his arm around my shoulder, trying to console me as I sobbed. "What's wrong?"

After I collected my breath enough to speak, I held the object out in front of us. "It's Morley's ring."

"Oh," Jarett said simply.

"I gave it to him the night we got engaged."

For me, that night had only been four months ago. For Morley—had he still been alive—it would have been five years. I slipped the ring onto my thumb and studied it in the room's soft light. Despite its thick, squat composition, it really was a stunning piece under all of the dust.

"Why was it up *there?*" Jarett asked, nodding to the door.

"He...he must have..." I caught myself before spitting out my suspicion (always had to be wary of *the ears*) that Morley had put the ring there the night of our return timeblink, right before we all left for the hospital. That was the last time I could remember seeing him wearing it.

I shook my head at Jarett, pretending to zip my lips. He nodded in quiet understanding then reached over and pulled several tissues from a box on my nightstand.

"I'm so sorry, Syd. He was a good man."

I dabbed at my eyes with one of the tissues he'd handed

me. "I'm glad we discovered it, though. He must have put it there knowing I would find it someday."

"It's a good thing you don't like dusting," Jarett said, rubbing my back in gentle circles. "Imagine if you'd found it three years ago. Or even six months. You wouldn't have known its significance."

I shot him a look that said *too much information!* He shrugged at me apologetically and mouthed, *"Sorry,"* as a wave of fear swept through my body. I hoped it hadn't been a mistake to invite him to stay here until his apartment was ready.

I blew my nose, catching sight of my reflection in the mirror propped up against the wall. "What a mess. I don't want to go anywhere now."

Jarett got up to kneel in front of me. "You shouldn't be alone tonight. Not after this."

"I knew it was a bad idea, thinking I was ready to face the world."

"It's not the world. It's just Sam and Lizzy, and they know you're a little fragile right now."

"They? You mean Lizzy knows about—" I mouthed *Christopher?*

Jarett leaned into my ear, his warm breath sending ripples of electricity right through me. "Sam thought he should fill her in. Not about timeblinking. Just that Christopher had gone missing and that Sam was appointed the lead investigator. Nothing more."

As Jarett leaned back, I fiddled with Morley's ring on my thumb, the only finger it fit well enough not to fall off. In my heart, I knew Jarett was right. It would be good for me to get out of the house, away from Christopher's things. Away from the memories of my lost family. All of it because of a missing dragonfly necklace.

Chapter Seven

After a twenty-minute drive spent in welcome silence, Jarett and I stood outside Sam's door in Balimead, an upscale suburb that had been built in the early eighties. The evening had turned cold, and the house was tucked into a grove of old-growth cedar and arbutus trees that shielded it from the road and the neighbors' properties. I wrapped my shawl tighter around my shoulders as the chill and silence started to sink into my skin.

Jarett noticed my discomfort. "Crazy how cold it is, huh? And dark. I wouldn't want to live here."

"You almost did live here."

He chuckled. "Yeah, thanks for rescuing me. Don't get me wrong. The properties around here are gorgeous, but jeez, they're so far out of the way." He glanced over his shoulder at the long, steep driveway to the road, then studied the towering woodland crowding the property. "I hope I never have to attend a domestic in this neighborhood. It's so secluded."

Before I could comment, the door swung open and Sam greeted us, drying his hands on a dish towel and slinging it over his shoulder. "Welcome to Casa Douglas, your home-away-from-home for the next few hours. Glad you could make it in the blink of an eye."

Jarett and I exchanged shocked glances with each other before turning back to Sam, who shrugged apologetically. The day Christopher had been taken—the day Sam discovered the FBI had ears on us—he'd come up with a "safe phrase" we could use to warn each other that someone outside of our group might be listening. Great. Just when I thought I could let my guard down, it seemed Sam's house was now off-limits, too.

"Something smells delicious," Jarett said, staying composed despite our friend's unsettling warning. He motioned for me to enter the house ahead of him.

"That'll be Lizzy's famous braised short ribs. I hope you two are hungry."

"Starved. I didn't eat lunch" Jarett said as we stepped inside.

I wasted no time getting out of my dainty shoes. My feet were already killing me. "I'm hungry, too. Funny—I wasn't until we got here."

"Aha. That's why Lizzy's ribs are so legendary. The smell of them alone has made at least one of our vegetarian friends cross to the dark side."

"Well, if it isn't our lovely chef now," Jarett said over Sam's shoulder as Lizzy sashayed into the foyer to greet us, flipping a flowery silk scarf over her shoulder as she came. I was momentarily stunned by her beauty. She was tall and slender yet generously curvy in all the right places, and her smoky eyes and thick, dark, upswept hair made me wonder if she was of Spanish descent.

"It's my go-to recipe for special dinners. No-fail short ribs. Put them on in the morning and forget about them all day, so no, I haven't been slaving over a hot stove like my darling husband makes out." She reached her hand out to me. "You must be Syd. Great to finally meet you." I shook her hand and said hello, and before I even knew what was happening, she'd slipped her arm around my shoulder and was guiding me into the living room. As we walked, she looked over her other shoulder at the men, who were speaking quietly between themselves. "Sam! Did you remember to put the wine in the fridge?"

"Yes, dear," I heard him say.

"What would you like to drink, Syd?" Lizzy asked, showing me to a giant, light gray sectional couch. My heart clenched. It bore the same type of juice, chocolate, and blueberry stains as my own couches at the condo and lake, where I allowed the kids to play freely.

"I'd love a glass of water. Thank you so much for all this."

"Like I said, it was a piece of cake. Oh! We're having that too, later!" she laughed as she excused herself to the kitchen. Normally I would have felt intimidated by someone with such confidence and grace, but her energy was delightful, and I found myself completely at ease.

"Beer?" Sam said, walking backward in the direction of the kitchen, pointing two finger-guns at Jarett, who'd come to sit next to me.

"Twist my rubber arm. Syd's my DD."

"You bet. Back in a flash."

"So, I'm your designated driver, am I?" I said once Sam had left the room. "That's news to me."

"I'm kidding. It was just a good opportunity to remind Sam that you don't drink. I'll have a token beer with him and call it quits."

"Well, thank you. I don't mind driving, but you've got to give me warning. I might have chosen different footwear."

"Honestly, I'm good with one beer. This is your night, Cinderella."

I laughed. "I feel more like one of the ugly stepsisters next to Lizzy."

"You're kidding, right?"

"Not at all. She's stunning."

"You're not so bad yourself."

"Wow, you're full of compliments today, aren't you?"

A couple of hours later, when we were stuffed to our gills with a superbly cooked meal and enjoying our after-dinner drinks in the living room, an awkward tension settled over the room when Sam brought up Christopher's abduction.

"Sorry to report I haven't had any more leads on your little guy. How about you? Have you remembered any new details that might help in the investigation?"

I opened my mouth to speak but closed it quickly. He'd issued the warning not to say anything incriminating, so why was he pressuring me to talk?

Lizzy saved me the trouble of coming up with a reply. "It's awful. Just awful. As a mother, I can't even imagine what you're going through."

She had said little about her children, only mentioning being grateful for the peace and quiet while they stayed overnight at her sister's place. And I was grateful for her discretion.

Tears pooled in her eyes but didn't fall. "Please know I'm here for you, Syd."

"That's very kind."

"I mean it. If there's anything I can do to help take your mind off things, just call me. We could go for a walk or do a yoga class or meet for coffee. Anything. You name it."

I nodded and thanked her but was terrified to say much else. What had Sam told her? Did she know her husband was a time traveler from 2019? Or did she honestly believe he'd been under witness protection for five years? I doubted the latter was true. Another woman may have fallen for that story, but now that I'd spent some time with Lizzy, it was clear she was too smart for that. She would have called bullshit on Sam being sequestered somewhere for five years—that he wouldn't have agreed to leave his family like that. Oh, she knew about timeblinking, no question about it.

Jarett spoke next, skillfully steering the conversation away from the subject of my abducted son. "We really appreciate your hospitality and would love to stay longer, but I gotta get Miss Cinderella home before her coach turns into a pumpkin."

"Oh, sure, blame me," I teased. "Are you sure it's not because you have to work tomorrow?"

"What happened? I thought you had the day off," Sam said.

"I did. It's a last-minute favor for a buddy. The one who took a bunch of my shifts so I could spend time with Syd."

By *spend time with me* he meant *play bodyguard during Suicide Watch 2024* when everyone was paranoid I'd off myself after Christopher disappeared. It hadn't been necessary, their worry. How would Christopher get home if I was dead? I kept trying to tell them that, but my words had fallen on deaf ears.

Lizzy got up from her chair. "Well, if you must leave, don't forget your chocolate cake."

"Won't your kids eat it?" I asked.

"Yes, but I made enough to feed an army."

Sam laughed. "It's no use resisting. You're going home with cake whether you like it or not."

As Lizzy hurried to the kitchen, her delicate scarf slipped from her neck and pooled on the floor behind her, but she hadn't noticed. Sam was busy chatting with Jarett, so I got up and collected the scarf before someone stepped on it. I'd been right. It was silk. Smooth and luxurious in my grasp. I draped it over the back of Lizzy's chair and went over to join the men, who had both gotten up from their seats and were drooling over photos of a luxury golf course in Dubai on Sam's phone.

I smiled at Lizzy as she walked back into the room carrying two foil-wrapped packages shaped like swans, like they make for customers at fancy restaurants. But when she got to within an arm's length, I caught sight of something that sent me reeling backward. I grabbed for Jarett's arm as I melted onto the couch.

"Syd! Are you okay?" Lizzy asked in a panic. Her voice sounded echoey, far away.

My heart was pounding so hard I could feel my earlobes pulsing. I couldn't speak. Not because I was rendered mute, but because I couldn't say out loud what had caused my shock. No. I couldn't breathe a word about it to my friends, especially not here, where the invisible "ears" were listening.

It was a silver talisman. Not just *any* silver talisman, but one featuring a beguiling dragonfly rising out of a darkened patina—a perfect match to my own. And it was hanging around Lizzy's neck.

"What's going on?" Jarett asked, wrapping his arm around my shoulder, hugging me tight. "You're shaking. And white as a ghost."

I closed my eyes and took some deep breaths, willing myself not to appear like a complete nut job in front of my new friend.

But *was* she my friend? Did she know about the talisman's power? And if she did, was she involved in Christopher's disappearance? Oh my god. Was *Sam*? I shook my head violently to rid my mind of these thoughts. I'd drive myself crazy if I let myself get carried away like this.

When I opened my eyes, Lizzy and Sam were kneeling in front of me, their eyes pinched with worry. I could feel my chin quivering. They'd been so gracious and kind, and here I was, ruining everything.

But I couldn't ignore it. The fact remained that Lizzy was wearing a dragonfly talisman that looked identical to mine, and it was staring me in the face. I was powerless to tear my eyes away from it.

"Syd, look at me," Jarett said, guiding my chin gently toward his face.

"I'm okay," I said, taking a few more breaths, but it wasn't helping. I was still trembling.

"We should go," Jarett said to the others. "Can you help me get her to the car, Sam?"

"Absolutely. Are you sure she'll be okay?"

"I'm fine. Please don't worry," I said weakly.

Despite my protests, I let them guide me to the door where Lizzy helped me into my shoes and draped my shawl around my shoulders. "I'm sorry," I whispered. It was all I could manage.

"Don't apologize. You've been through hell. Have a nice cup of tea when you get home. And a piece of cake."

A few minutes later, Lizzy leaned into the open window of Jarett's idling BMW where I was buckled in and ready to go. With detached awe, I watched the talisman dangling almost tauntingly a few inches from my face, and the more I stared at it, the more certain I felt that it was *the one*. My talisman. The one Morley had given me as he lay dying in the rain.

"I hope you feel better soon," Lizzy said, pulling me out of my thoughts. It was all I could do to stop myself from ripping the thing right off her neck and ordering Jarett to peel out of there. But even amidst my panic, I knew it wouldn't be prudent to snatch the talisman and run or even to ask her politely to hand it over. What if, by the oddest coincidence ever, it wasn't mine after all?

One thing was certain: I couldn't reveal that the talisman —or one just like it—was what made timeblinking possible. Especially to Sam. I was still unsure about the way he'd told us we were being watched while at the same time pressing me to recall details about Christopher's abduction. It didn't make sense.

Unless he's in on it.

Lizzy patted me on the shoulder and stood back while Jarett raised my window, shutting out the cool evening air. I was glad for the warmth of the car.

Once we'd driven up the hill and pulled onto the main road, my whole body relaxed, despite my racing mind. "Do you mind stopping at Point Alice first? I need to get something off my chest."

Chapter Eight

"Why here? It's pitch black."

Jarett had never been to Point Alice Park, a windswept cape that—during the day—provided glorious vistas of Alice Bay and the Strait of Juan de Fuca beyond. It was popular with picnickers, kite flyers, and hang-gliding enthusiasts, and it was one of my favorite destinations for a run. At night, the park was mostly deserted, save for the odd cluster of brazen teenagers bringing illegally acquired beer down to the rocky beach, where they would inevitably be shooed away by the cops. Sometimes it would be right away. Other times, they'd luck out and get to stay for an hour or two.

Relieved we were the only ones there, I instructed Jarett to park at the tip of the loop where we lowered our windows so we could listen to the surf.

"This sound always calms me," I said, closing my eyes and letting the cold breeze sweep over my face. The lower temperature was probably what had deterred the teenagers from coming down here tonight. Either that, or the cops had recently chased them away.

"So, you're feeling better now. What happened back there,

anyway? Was it about Christopher? Or did it have something to do with Morley's ring?"

My breath faltered. I hadn't thought about the ring the entire time we'd been out. Worried it might slip off my thumb, I'd put it in my purse before we left the condo. A shiver went up my spine. Losing the ring now would trigger a whole new spectacular breakdown.

I tightened my shawl around my shoulders and peered at the black abyss in front of us. "No. Nothing to do with the ring. Although, another piece of jewelry was involved."

"Oh, yeah?"

Was I really about to confide in him? I hadn't even told Kendall about the talisman. Maybe this wasn't such a good idea.

"Sorry, Jarret. How rude of me, keeping you out so late. You have a long drive back to Seattle."

"It's only ten-fifteen."

"But you have to work at three a.m."

"Don't worry about me. I'm no stranger to keeping weird hours. Come on, give me the goods, Syd. What's going on?"

I sighed. "I might not be able to handle this alone."

"*This* being Christopher's disappearance?"

"Mostly that." I flicked a brief look his way before my attention turned back to the sea. "But also life in general. I'm tired of doing it alone."

Jarett stayed quiet.

"All I know is that I'm at a crossroad. On one side is my promise to Morley that I would never tell anyone how time-blinking works."

"And on the other?"

"The knowledge that if I don't tell someone, I might never get Christopher back. I just don't know if I can do it without help."

"Do you mean *my* help?" he asked tentatively. "Are you, Syd Brixton, Ms. Independence, saying you actually agree with me? That if you let me in, I might be able to help you get the power of timeblinking back?"

I groaned and sank deeper into my seat. "Can you roll up the windows? I'm freezing."

Jarett turned the car on, closed the windows, and cranked up the heat. "Syd, you must know by now that I'm on your side. Whatever it is you need me to do, I'll do it. No questions asked."

"Even if it means killing a psycho-bitch time traveler from hell?" I laughed bitterly, as a couple of tears slipped down my cheek.

I could feel Jarett's eyes on me, trying to gauge if I was joking or not. "If it means keeping Christopher from being harmed, you know I would."

I let out an unbridled sob. Just one. "It sucks that we have to sit in a car to have this conversation. I'm so tired of having to watch everything we say and do *in our own homes*. Isn't privacy a human right?"

"Unfortunately, not when it comes to suspected terrorism."

I turned to face him. "I might have found my power."

His eyes went wide. "Might have?"

"Yeah. I'm not a hundred percent sure. I mean, I'm ninety-nine percent sure, but thankfully that one percent of doubt prevented me from doing something stupid tonight."

Despite Jarett's utter stillness, I could practically feel his energy flooding the small space.

"Back at Sam's," I said, licking my lips tentatively. "At Sam's, I was pretty sure I saw the thing that makes time-blinking possible."

He kept his gaze steady on me as his foot tapped softly against the floormat.

"At the end of the evening, Lizzy's scarf fell off and—" I cast a pleading look at Jarett. "Do you promise to keep this between us?"

He reached over and found my hand, squeezing it gently.

"Syd. We've been through hell and back together. You can trust me. I promise never to breathe a word of this to anyone."

I tutted. "That's exactly what I promised Morley, and now look."

"Your little boy is missing. Wouldn't Morley—the father of your child—insist you do whatever is necessary to get Christopher back?"

"Yes, I...I just don't know if betraying his confidence is how he would want me to do it." I almost added, *especially with you.*

He released my hand and shrugged. "Okay. How would Morley have you do it?"

I ignored his question, steeling myself to push ahead with what I'd come here to say. "Did you happen to notice Lizzy's necklace?"

Jarett gave me an impatient look, as if trying to determine what a piece of jewelry had to do with anything.

"It's identical to the necklace Morley gave me right before he died. The one that gave me the ability to timeblink."

Jarett's eyes went wide. I gave him a moment to digest the news.

"Crazy, huh? A silly necklace."

Jarett bit his bottom lip, as if remembering something. "I thought I recognized it."

"What do you mean?"

"It's a butterfly, right?"

"Dragonfly."

"Right, yeah. I've seen it on Lizzy before. In fact, I don't think I've ever seen her *not* wearing it. Not in the whole four months I've known her."

"Why didn't you tell me?"

"Tell you what?"

"That Lizzy has a dragonfly necklace!"

"Why would I?"

51

"Oh, I don't know, maybe because it's the same dragonfly necklace I was wearing the entire time we were in 2019? Or because it's the one I've been emailing the NTSB and FAA about since the plane crashed?" I said, looking at him incredulously.

"That's not fair. How was I supposed to know? Even *you* aren't totally sure it's the same one. You just said that!"

I let out a weary breath. "Sorry."

Jarett stared at me for a few seconds then leaned back in his seat. "Surely there's more than one dragonfly necklace in the world."

"Not like that one. Fuck. What am I going to do?"

"Figure out if it really is your necklace."

"Talisman," I said. "Morley always called it a talisman."

"Okay. How do we figure out if it's your talisman?"

"Without drawing attention to ourselves? I have no idea."

Chapter Nine

A t two-fifteen the next afternoon, I pulled into a parking spot in front of Jarett's apartment and got out of the car to absorb the charm of the East Green Lake neighborhood. There was a coffee shop on the main level of Jarett's building, a bike shop on the other side of that, and a small, independent grocer within easy walking distance away. Although the village was located only a few blocks west of Interstate 5, it was surprisingly quiet and devoid of too much traffic. However, there were plenty of people walking, cycling, or jogging, making me wish I'd brought my running gear so I could go for a head-clearing jog around the lake after our meeting.

There was a tap on my shoulder, and I nearly jumped out of my flip flops as I whirled around. "Jeez, Jarett! Give me a heart attack, why don't you?" I said, clutching my chest.

Jarett laughed. "Sorry about that. I was waiting in the lobby. Saw you pull up. I can't believe your luck with the parking. My guests usually have to stalk people walking to their cars to find a spot."

"I'm oozing with luck these days."

He chuckled lightly, gesturing for us to start walking. "You obviously found my place okay."

"So easy. Love your neighborhood."

"I'll miss it, but I'm ready for a change."

I smiled, realizing I was excited for his upcoming move to Port Raven.

At the Twiddlebird Café a few minutes later, we found a secluded table for two in the window. My heart twinged with sorrow when I remembered the last time I'd sat in the window at a restaurant. It had been with Morley the night I proposed. The night before he died.

"They have the best clubhouse sandwich in town here," Jarett said, pulling my chair out for me to sit down. "They put onion jam on it. Talk about next level."

"I just might have to try it."

"You won't be disappointed," he said, sitting down. "By the way, it was a good thing our evening was cut short last night. I would have been dead tired on my shift today, which, as it turns out, was a total shitshow."

"Ooh, what happened?"

He smiled tightly and shook his head.

"Yeah, yeah. You're not allowed to say. Were you able to get some shuteye afterwards?"

"Yep. Had a forty-five-minute power nap as soon as I got home. What a wimp, hey?"

I was glad for Jarett's lighthearted company, despite having come here for a serious discussion. And as much as I was dreading that discussion, it was such a relief to have someone to talk to besides Morley about the mechanics of timeblinking.

Once we'd taken the first few bites of our sandwiches and there was little chance of being disturbed, Jarett said, "So. What's the plan?"

I wiped the side of my mouth with a napkin. Jarett was right. The onion jam was kickass. "You mean a plan that doesn't involve ripping the talisman right off Lizzy's neck?"

"Ha, yes. Thankfully you had the presence of mind not to do that last night. The *ears* would have had a field day."

I glanced around me, realizing I hadn't been paying attention to whether or not I'd been followed here from Port Raven, not that I would even know how to spot a tail. I lowered my voice just to be safe. "I've been thinking about that. Why would the FBI plant bugs at Sam's house? He's not connected to *The 444 Five*, apart from his friendship with you, a fellow cop. Could it be that he wasn't trying to warn us about bugs at all? Maybe he just didn't want us to say too much in front of Lizzy?" I stopped short of telling him about my fleeting worry that Sam and Lizzy were somehow involved in Christopher's abduction. The idea seemed preposterous to me in the light of the day, though I still couldn't quite shake it completely.

Jarett shook his head. "I don't think it's that. If you recall, Lizzy left the room at least a dozen times. He could've told us then."

My shoulders slumped. "Wishful thinking on my part. Truth be told, I'm almost certain he's told Lizzy about time-blinking, anyway. She's a smart cookie. I find it hard to believe she would've bought his bullshit witness-protection story."

"I agree," Jarett said, taking a swig of his beer. "So, we're back to bugs."

"Maybe the FBI discovered it was Sam who disconnected the one at my place."

A gradual understanding swept across Jarett's face. "Damn. I'll bet you a million bucks that's what happened. And if that's the case, they may have even asked him to assist in their investigation. And by *asked*, I mean *ordered*."

"Oh no!" I blurted. A woman at the nearest table flashed me a concerned look then went back to her meal when I smiled reassuringly.

Jarett scratched his neatly trimmed beard. "Well, damn. His behavior makes sense now. He warned us about the ears, but to satisfy the Feds, he also had to make it look like he was trying to extract information from us."

"He didn't try very hard."

"He may have persisted if you hadn't had your anxiety attack. I'm sure he was expecting us to stay longer than we did."

"Oh, Jarett. He wouldn't tell the FBI about timeblinking, would he?"

"No way. His allegiance is to us. That's something I wouldn't have said a few months ago—after we accidentally pulled him five years into the future—but now I'm sure of it."

"What's changed?"

"Fishing." He chuckled. "Have you ever been?"

I shook my head.

"There's a lot of down time out there on the water. Lots of time to shoot the shit while you're waiting for a bite. It worked in our favor. With all that privacy at our disposal, we were free to discuss timeblinking openly. Particularly about how its power, in the wrong hands, could be extremely dangerous to mankind."

"I can't believe he's working with the FBI."

"He *might* be."

"But it's pretty likely."

"Yes. But I still think he'll keep timeblinking under his hat. The downfall of civilization is one thing. Looking like a raving lunatic in front of his peers is another."

"Seriously? He'd choose his reputation over saving the world?"

"We cops are a proud bunch."

"Okay. Good to know."

"Regardless, we need to get that talisman. Then at least you can figure out if it's the right one."

I took a small, half-hearted bite of my sandwich. "Any ideas?"

"Well, telling Lizzy the necklace belongs to you is out of the question."

"I'll say. Considering Sam might be working with the FBI." I gave him a playful look. "Maybe *you* could ask Lizzy where she got it? Tell her your mom collects dragonflies and you want to get her one. She would have no reason to lie about where she got it."

"Could work. I haven't told them I'm bunking with you yet, so they're expecting me to drop off a few of my things this weekend. I can ask her then."

"I can't wait that long."

"Maybe you won't have to. Lizzy did say to call her if you needed a friend. Why don't you ask her out for lunch tomorrow or Tuesday?"

"And say what? *Can I have my necklace back, please?*"

"You could start by asking her where she got it."

Just when I was beginning to realize how difficult this operation was going to be, an idea hit me. "Or I could accept her offer to go to yoga. If she's anything like me, she'll leave all her jewelry at home, and then you could break into their house when everyone's out and grab the talisman."

Jarett laughed. "Who do you think I am? James Bond?"

"You could definitely pass for a high-level British Secret Service agent."

He laughed again. "I'm flattered. But I wouldn't have to break in. Sam gave me a key in anticipation of my stay."

"Holy shit, Jarett! That's perfect!" I practically shouted. My heart hadn't felt this light since the night of my engagement.

"What if Lizzy doesn't leave the talisman at home? She hasn't taken it off the whole four months I've known her," Jarett said, bringing me back to Earth.

"Then I'll have to resort to Plan B."

"Which is?"

"Ripping it right off her neck."

"Now, now," Jarett warned, taking another bite of his sandwich.

"What, then?"

He washed his food down with some water. "Maybe you could ask Kendall to pose as a collector and offer to buy it from Lizzy. How much are you willing to pay to get it back?"

The muscles tightened in my neck. "I'd sell everything I own. Plus my left kidney."

"Even if it turns out *not* to be the right one?"

"It's the one. It has to be."

"Okay, we have a Plan B: Lizzy sells her necklace and gets a shiny new car out of the deal. Hopefully your sister is okay with pretending to be a jewelry collector."

"She knows how important that talisman is to me. Not because of its timeblinking powers, obviously, but because it was a gift from Morley. She'll be ecstatic that it's been found."

"We *think* it's been found."

"I wonder how Lizzy got her hands on it, anyway?" I said, ignoring Jarret's doubt. Then a realization hit me. "Oh my god. I wonder if Sam found it on the plane and then gave it to Lizzy, not knowing it was mine?"

He raised his brows. "Good theory."

It was a hell of a lot better than suspecting Sam and Lizzy had anything to do with Christopher's disappearance. "Fuck theories. That's what happened. There's no doubt in my mind."

"Don't get too excited. I'm warning you. If it's not the right one, you'll be in for a huge letdown. Why don't we try Operation Yoga first and see how it goes?"

He was right, of course. I couldn't get ahead of myself. "I hope it works. I'd rather not involve Kendall. What about you? Are you up for the challenge of breaking into the Douglas residence?"

"It's not breaking in if they gave me the key. Besides, if anyone from Sam's family—or, God forbid, the FBI—catches me poking around while you and Lizzy are twisting yourselves into pretzel shapes, I can just say I was dropping off some clothes early. As far as anyone knows, I'm still planning on staying with them."

"Perfect," I said. "I'll call Lizzy tonight. Apparently, she goes to yoga every day at noon, so I don't imagine it'll be too hard for her to arrange a guest pass."

"And noon works great for my schedule. I've got overnight shifts all week and have Tuesday and Sunday off."

"I hope you can sneak in and out of the house without anyone knowing you were there."

"Me too. That way, when Lizzy discovers the talisman missing, she'll have no one to blame but herself for losing it."

"Either that, or she'll assume one of the kids took it."

Jarett winced. "Damn. I hope no one catches heat for this. They're good kids."

"We can't worry about that. I can always get a replica made, which you could plant for Lizzy to find later. She would think she'd just misplaced it. Everyone wins."

"Unless we discover it's not actually your talisman. Then I can just put it back where I found it."

"I can't even entertain that thought right now, Jarett. I just can't."

Chapter Ten

Agent Jimmy Lopez

L opez flipped his small notepad shut and tucked it into his breast pocket when Jenkins entered the boardroom. "Oh good. You're here. I wanted to talk to you before Detective Douglas showed up."

Jenkins took a seat next to Lopez and opened his laptop. "What's up, sir?"

The senior agent took a cautious glance around the room, grateful for the privacy. "It's about your time-travel theory."

"My what?"

"Your speculation about what happened to the woman and the Brixton boy. It's best if you don't mention it to the detective. We need him on our side, not thinking we've lost our marbles."

Jenkins smiled sheepishly. "Oh, *that*. I was rattled, sir. I wasn't really being serious. Besides, I'm pretty sure it was a trick of the fieldscope."

"Oh, right. How'd the testing go out at the lake?"

"Exactly as I imagined it would. When I rapidly changed my

eye position on the eyepiece, the subject I was watching seemed to vanish. I replicated the effect several times and have come to the conclusion that I just hadn't been using the equipment properly."

"Fantastic news. It still doesn't explain where the Brixton kid went or why his disappearance hasn't been report—"

There was a light rap, and the boardroom door swung open. Lopez and Jenkins rose to their feet as Detective Douglas entered the room.

"Afternoon, gentlemen," Sam said, pulling out a chair.

Lopez undid his suit jacket and smoothed a hand over his tie. "Afternoon, Detective. Thanks for meeting with us on such short notice."

Once everyone was seated, Sam said, "I'm surprised you called me in. I already told Agent Jenkins here that I have nothing to report."

"Yes, I know the dinner party was a bust. It's like your guests knew we were listening." Lopez, said, giving Sam a sideways look. "You didn't warn them, right?"

"What do you think? Of course not. Syd had a meltdown just as I was about to start questioning them."

"A meltdown?"

"Meltdown, panic attack, mental breakdown, whatever. I don't know what happened. Everything was going great. She and my wife, Lizzy, were hitting it off and talking about getting together again, then something happened that triggered her, and she went totally quiet. They took off soon after that. Lizzy figures she was just missing her little boy."

Agent Jenkins looked up from his computer. "It can't be easy for Ms. Brixton. Even a regular child abduction would be hard to handle. This one's kinda bizarre."

"To say the least," Sam said. "I spoke with Jarett yesterday morning. He said Syd was feeling better but embarrassed about the whole thing. She thought she'd ruined everyone's night."

"Did he say anything about what might have set her off?" Jenkins asked.

"No. I wish I had more to tell you."

Lopez narrowed his eyes at Sam. "Are you sure about that?"

Sam cocked his head defensively. "Say again?"

"Are you sure you don't have more to tell us?"

"I don't. How about you? It sure feels like you've got a bullet in the chamber you can't wait to fire."

Lopez paused for several seconds before nodding to Jenkins who punched a few buttons on his laptop. He slid it in front of Sam. The room fell silent while Sam clicked through a series of grainy photographs taken from outside his house. He didn't show an ounce of emotion.

When Sam finally looked up, Lopez raised his brows at him. "Any idea what your buddy Jarett was doing at your house today?"

"He has a key."

"Right. You mentioned he'll be living with you temporarily. Is he staying in your bedroom with you and Lizzy?"

Sam glared at Lopez, not giving him the benefit of an answer.

"Considering that's where he spent the bulk of his time during his visit today, and all."

"I don't know what he was doing in there."

"Looks like he was searching for something, doesn't it?"

Sam opened his mouth as if to speak but closed it again quickly.

"Can you at least wager a guess? What do you think he was looking for? Money? Diamonds?"

"Maybe. Or gold," Sam said, pushing the laptop back to Jenkins. "I do keep several bars in my underwear drawer."

Lopez chuckled. "Don't we all."

"Honestly, I don't know what the hell he was up to."

"Don't worry, I believe you. It's not like he'd tell you he was rifling through your private things. And your wife's."

Sam's nostrils flared, probably involuntarily, Lopez thought.

"Aren't you curious to find out what he was looking for?"

"Sure. But obviously I'll have to do it without him becoming suspicious. It could take some time."

"I can save you the trouble. We followed him after he left your place, and do you want to take a guess where he went?"

Sam shrugged. "Disneyland?"

"Close. First, he went to the gas station on Seventh and Main. Filled his tank. Then he stopped in at an independent jewelry shop for about fifteen minutes. Harrison's, if I remember correctly. Finally, he met up with our star subject, Ms. Brixton, at a coffee shop on Fourth Avenue. They're still there, in fact."

Jenkins tapped a few more keys and turned the computer back to Sam, where a second collection of photos flashed in front of his face. "These were taken moments ago. There's video, too, but I think the photos tell a pretty good story."

"Huh. The Bold & Bean. Best coffee in town. Have either of you *bean*?"

Lopez ignored Sam's joke. "No. But if you scroll through the sequence, you'll see our friendly Seattle police officer, Jarett Cooper, handing something to Ms. Brixton. Our guy couldn't zoom in far enough for a clear picture, but I think you'll agree it looks like a necklace. And look at the expression on their faces. They might as well be at *gad*-damn Disneyland."

"I'll give you that. They do look happy."

After a brief silence, Jenkins asked, "Does that necklace belong to Lizzy?"

Sam leaned forward and squinted at the screen. "Maybe? The photos are terrible."

Lopez let out an exasperated breath. "How about you ask Lizzy if she's missing a necklace when you get home today."

"What does it matter, anyway? Jarett must have his reasons."

"Interesting." Lopez said. "A guy who claims to be your friend pilfers one of your wife's necklaces and gives it to his girlfriend, and you're okay with that?"

"I'm not okay with it. I'd just like to give him the benefit of the doubt. Besides, what on God's green Earth does a damned necklace have to do with suspected terrorism?"

"I don't know, Sam. But Ms. Brixton and her jewelry-thief boyfriend are our two main persons of interest in this investigation, and it's pretty clear they're up to something. And you happen to be our best hope of finding out what that is."

Sam tilted his head back and sighed before bringing his attention back to Lopez. "Look, I want to figure this thing out as much as you do, but the terms are bullshit."

"Oh? We didn't set out to make your life so difficult, Detective Douglas."

"Don't patronize me. All I'm saying is that I'll never get anything out of the subjects with you guys constantly hovering around. It puts me on edge, and I think these two can sense it."

"All right, then. Give us your terms, and we'll see what we can do."

Chapter Eleven

"For the twentieth time, this is the one," I said to Jarett across the table at The Bold & Bean, bubbling with delight. I flipped the talisman over in my hand to show him the back. "See that nick at the top, just under the chain loop?"

Jarett plucked the talisman out of my hand and inspected it closely, saying nothing.

"That little imperfection has been there since the beginning. It proves it's mine."

"So," Jarett said, handing it back to me, leaning closer. "What are you going to do now?"

I'd been envisioning this moment since my little boy had been taken and was surprised Jarett even had to ask. I told him anyway. "I'm going back to 2014 to bring Christopher home."

Jarett looked left and right. The coffee shop wasn't very busy, but he kept his voice low anyway. "When do you propose to do this?"

I got up from my chair and tucked the talisman into my pocket, keeping my voice equally hush. "As soon as I confirm this is my talisman."

"Where are you going?"

"To the ladies' room, if you don't mind."

He put his hands up in the air. "You do you."

I was grateful for the single-occupant washrooms at the back of the restaurant where I could conduct my experiment in private. I just needed four minutes and forty-four seconds to do it.

After securing the door, I pulled the talisman out of my pocket and fastened the clasp at the back of my neck. The pendant was warm and solid, and as I admired it against my collarbone in the mirror, I knew at once it was mine. Not even a hint of doubt crossed my mind. I smiled at my reflection noticing something else: a transformed woman. A woman with hope.

Despite my certainty about the talisman, it wouldn't hurt to spend five minutes testing it out. After all, it had been more than four months since my last timeblink—the longest hiatus I'd taken since the beginning. The thought made me gasp. Could underuse impair its effect? What if it didn't work anymore? With dread filling my heart, I grasped the talisman and recited my destination.

Several minutes later, I scooted back into my seat across from Jarett.

"Cute bracelet," he said, nodding at my wrist.

"Oh, right!" I studied the stretchy, candy-adorned band with the fascination of the child it was originally meant for. "You caught me, Officer."

"Caught you? Doing what?"

Resuming our earlier hushed tones, I fessed up to my successful test drive to October 10, 1998, the day of my eleventh birthday party—and of course, Isla's. I'd needed a cheerful memory to counter all the doom and gloom lately.

"It was mind-blowing to see all my old friends gathered in

our living room with my blissful, happy family." I sighed. "Everything changed after that. Isla was abducted less than a year later, and the rest of us fell apart, one by one."

He reached across the table and lifted my chin. "Hey. What happened to cheerful memories?"

"Sorry, got lost for a minute."

"So, the candy bracelet. A souvenir?"

I lifted my arm and bit into one of the sugary beads. "God, this is awful."

"Well, it *is* more than two decades old. Good thing you didn't pilfer a banana instead. I can only imagine what a twenty-six-year-old banana would look like."

I laughed. "Food retains its original age on a return time-blink. Kind of like Sam did."

"He'd be crushed to know you compared him to a banana."

"Would he, though? You two share the exact same sense of humor. Twisted." I laughed. "But we're getting off topic. The good news is that this is my talisman, and it still works."

"So, when are you going to rescue Christopher?"

"Right fucking now."

"Now?" he said, scanning his surroundings. "Here?"

"Of course not. I'm going to Sandalwood Lake. To the fallen tree where Christopher was taken, so that when we come back, he won't be too freaked out."

He shook his head vigorously. "Nope."

"Nope? What does that mean?"

"You've never heard it before? It means *no*, but less formal."

"Jarett!" I whisper-shouted. "Do you mean nope I can't do it now? Or not at Sandalwood?"

"I mean..." he paused to take a breath, "that you can't do it *at all*. Not until we talk to Sam and see what he knows about the FBI."

"Are you kidding me?" More whisper-shouting. "No!"

Jarett grabbed my hands and pulled them down, the candy bracelet clunking noisily on the wooden surface. "Syd. If you don't want the world knowing about this power, we have to be a hundred and ten percent sure the FBI isn't watching us anymore."

I slumped back in my chair, laying my hand protectively over the talisman. "Fuckety fuck."

"Either that or we divert them."

"Oh, sure. That'll be easy."

"If they're truly following our every move," he paused to glance over his shoulder, "maybe I could lead them on a goose chase and you could, you know, do your thing at the lake."

I gave him a pleading look but was too afraid to speak. What if the FBI were listening to everything we were saying right this minute?

"How's your chai tea?" I asked him.

He winked. "It's delicious. You were right. I've been deprived my whole life."

"If you love it so much, why is your cup still full?"

"I'm savoring it."

"Cold chai is nasty."

"I'll take your word for it," he said, leaning close again. "I'll talk to Sam. In the meantime, don't do anything crazy."

"I won't."

I meant it. As desperate as I was to get Christopher back, it would be all for naught if the wrong people got their hands on the power and triggered the downfall of humanity, which had always been Morley's biggest worry. And I certainly didn't want to be the cause of it.

Chapter Twelve

It was sunny and warm the next day at the condo when one of Sam's two surveillance sweepers came in from the patio and locked the giant glass door behind him. He dropped three tiny electronic devices into the plastic baggie Sam held up and went to join his teammate in the den, the final room in their search.

"Wow, these guys were thorough," Sam said, admiring the hardware in the bag.

"They seem to know exactly where to look."

"I meant the Feds. Three bugs outside? Overkill, if you ask me."

"Does this mean we can speak freely now?"

"As soon as my guys give us the all-clear."

"Okay, good. Were you able to find out about the rest of the gang's surveillance?"

"Yes. I meant to tell you earlier. Their houses were never bugged. They *were* being watched, but Lopez packed that up ages ago to focus solely on the ringleader."

"Me?" I asked, astounded. "Why would he assume I was the mastermind behind this whole thing?"

"Members of *The 444 Five* inevitably show up at one of

your two properties. Sounds like Lopez convinced his higher-ups they were wasting resources and manpower. They agreed to let him focus on you—and by association, Jarett. But his place isn't bugged. It never was."

"So no more eyes on Rose and Lainie?"

"Nope."

"What about Kendall and Isla? Surely the Feds were watching them—by association."

"The only time they were being watched was when you met up with one of them, be it at their houses or a park or what have you."

"Can you be sure, though? What if the FBI is lying to you?"

"It's policy not to mislead, colleagues especially."

I could feel the tension melting out of my neck and shoulders. "Sam, I could kiss you right now."

"I aim to please."

I glanced at the clock in the kitchen. "Jarett should be here soon. It's his day off, but he had to sign the lease at his new apartment first." I scrunched up my nose. "I take it he told you he'll be staying here instead of your place?"

Sam's hand flew up to his mouth. "What? No!" he teased. "I'm verklempt."

"Ha, you seem it."

"Yeah, as much as I love the guy, our house is a busy place. He would've lost his mind there. I'm glad he'll be staying here and keeping you...*company*."

"Excuse me? What do you mean by that?"

He raised his hands. "Hey, I just call 'em as I see 'em."

As I opened my mouth to object, the sweepers trudged into the room carrying duffle bags full of equipment. They added the fruits of their search to the baggie, a small collection of futuristic-looking doodads.

"Shit," I croaked, feeling extremely violated. My mind

shot back to Friday, the day I arrived here and blubbered like a baby for hours. "The fuckers."

The younger of the two technicians said, "You don't have to worry about them listening—or watching—this apartment anymore, ma'am. We found all the cameras and listening devices. There were none in the bedrooms or bathrooms."

"That was good of them."

"Even the Feds have their scruples," Sam joked.

"So you're absolutely sure they're all gone now?"

Sam answered for them. "These guys are the best in the state. And remember, *I* brought them in. Not the Feds."

Once they were gone, Sam and I made ourselves comfortable on the couch. "Does this mean what I think it means?" I asked.

"Unfortunately, no. The investigation isn't over. It just means I was able to buy us some privacy. Temporarily."

"No, no. I meant…does it mean the FBI really roped you into helping with the investigation?"

Sam's eyebrows went up. I couldn't tell if he was shocked or impressed that I knew.

"That's what I thought," I said. "But I can't take credit for figuring it out. It was all Jarett. After you warned us on Saturday night, his wheels started turning."

"The bastards got me when I deep-sixed that bug at the lake. Oh, and I'm sorry to say that not only did they have ears on the place, but they also had video surveillance set up at your neighbor's cabin across the lake."

"What? Which neighbors?"

"The Duncans, I believe."

"Bob and Mildred are in on this?"

"Don't be upset with them. They had no idea. The Feds posed as filmmakers shooting a documentary, and the Duncans were only too happy to accept a boatload of cash and stay in the city for the season."

"Fucking FBI. How did you explain your connection to me?"

"Through Jarett. They think he and I became acquainted at the golf club and he introduced me to the rest of you. Fortunately, they haven't been able to connect my five-year disappearance to *The 444 Five*. At least, that's what they're telling me."

I smiled, thankful for his loyalty to our group. "Will your sweepers be doing their magic at the lake, too?"

"Apparently the Feds already took care of that. They packed up their operation out there a few days ago, but I'd still be careful about saying too much if I were you."

"I will. Do you think it's safe to bring Christopher back here? To the condo?"

"Bring him back? Does that mean you've regained your timeblinking ability?" he said with genuine surprise.

"Yes. I'm just waiting for an opportunity to use it when no one's watching."

"If it's within the next three days, then yes, it's safe to bring your little guy here."

"That's the best news I've heard in months."

I twirled Morley's ring around on my thumb. "The truth is, I'm worried I may not be able to bring Christopher back at all. He's on Collette's return timeblink to the past, much like you're on my return timeblink to the future." I snorted bitterly. "I have no idea how Collette is even doing any of this. She died in 2015 and shouldn't be able to timeblink beyond her own lifetime."

"Clearly she figured out a way."

I squeezed my lips together then let out a long breath. "Which is why I'm so worried. Either Christopher is fourteen years old now, living God knows where, or he…" I couldn't say it out loud. Christopher simply could *not* be dead.

"You need to stay positive, Syd."

"I know. But it's hard."

"Is there any hope that Collette will do the right thing and just return Christopher to you?"

I sighed, knowing the near impossibility of that ever happening. "I think she's got a bone to pick with me...for having a baby with her husband."

"Didn't she die before you and Morley got together?"

"Yes, but remember, she's got timeblinking skills I never thought were possible. She probably came forward in time, found out about me and Morley, and then made it her personal mission to hurt me. Fuck. I'll bet she's told Christopher I don't love him anymore, too."

"I urge you not to dwell on it, Syd. It'll just make you crazy."

He was right. My energy would be better spent on getting my son home. Not speculating about terrible things.

He took a drink of water and leaned back on the couch. "Listen. I hate to bring this up right now, but I have a question for you. Remember, you can be candid now."

"Of course."

"Any idea why Jarett would've let himself into my house when no one was home?"

My heart leapt, and I stuffed my hand into the pocket of my hoodie, finding the talisman right where I'd left it. As I opened my mouth to suggest Jarett must've been dropping off some clothes for his upcoming stay, Sam cut me off.

"...and why he helped himself to one of Lizzy's necklaces?"

I tried to look surprised. "He did?"

"Come on, Syd. I've gone to great lengths here, and I'm probably putting my job in jeopardy in the bargain. How about the truth?"

Shit.

He went on. "The only reason the bugs have gone bye-bye is because I've cut a deal with the FBI. Your privacy in exchange for full disclosure about our conversations."

"So, what's the difference, then? Bugs versus you reporting our every word? It doesn't exactly compel me to speak freely."

"The difference is that you have your privacy back. You watched my team remove the bugs, and you have my word that no one's listening. But…"

"But you've gotta give the FBI *something*."

He nodded. "They're the ones who informed me Jarett was rooting through my house. So, why did he take the necklace?"

"It's embarrassing," I said, realizing even the tiniest detail would keep him happy.

"Embarrassing for who?"

I rolled my eyes. "For me. I'm embarrassed because I asked Jarett to steal the necklace. It's just that, well, it looks exactly like one I used to have. One that Morley gave me."

"Is that so?"

"Yes. When I saw Lizzy wearing it, I kind of lost my senses. That's why I flipped out at dinner the other night." I could've confessed right there—told him I believed it *was* my talisman, but I wanted to fish a little more.

"Hmm," he said, eyeing me curiously.

"Hmm, what?"

"When was the last time you saw it? The necklace you lost?"

My heartbeat quickened. If he was about to admit he'd found it on the plane, it would solve a shitload of problems.

"Well, I know I had it on the flight because I distinctly remember it getting stuck on my chin while I was trying to help free Lainie—when you were holding her by the ankle. But I have no idea if I was wearing it when we jumped out of the plane. The only thing I know for sure is that it was gone when Lainie and I dragged ourselves out of the pond later."

He licked his lips tentatively. "Okay, then. It's probably yours."

"Pardon me?" I could barely contain my glee.

"The necklace is probably the one you lost. I found it in my shirt when Jarett and I were on our way to find you guys in the cornfield."

"Sam! For real?"

He nodded. "Now I'm the embarrassed one. I wanted to believe it was a sign when it ended up in my clothes. It was exactly the kind of bauble Lizzy would love, and I couldn't wait to give it to her. Of course, that was before you hit me with the news that I'd never be able to see her again. I held onto it anyway. To keep Lizzy close. I vowed to find a way to give it to her someday, but as you know, I didn't have to wait long."

"Oh, Sam."

He waved his hand dismissively. "It's good to know it didn't belong to one of the deceased passengers because I had been wondering about that."

I drew the talisman out of my pocket and clutched it to my heart. If I'd only told him months ago that I'd lost a dragonfly necklace during the chaos of the crash, he might've put two and two together and simply returned it to me. He still didn't know about its power. Just that it meant a lot to me.

He smiled wistfully. "Lizzy was pissed when she discovered it missing yesterday, but she'll get over it."

"Sounds like you're going to let me keep it."

"Of course. It's obviously yours."

I leaned over and hugged him. "Thank you, Sam. So much." When I sat back, I gave him a worried look. "Does Lizzy know Jarett took it?"

"God, no. She thinks it was her own carelessness. She thought she might have lost it during her run yesterday morning. Of course, she couldn't find it when she retraced her steps."

"Jarett and I discussed getting a replica made so she wouldn't miss it. We could still do that. You could plant the copy somewhere for her to find."

"Hell no. That's way too much trouble. Lizzy will forget about it soon enough. Just don't wear it around her."

This couldn't have worked out better. "I can't wait to tell Jarett."

"I can't wait to tell him what a pathetic thief he makes."

I giggled. "At least now you have an explanation for the FBI."

"Which is what? Oh, yes. That he wanted to impress his girlfriend by stealing a necklace from his buddy's wife."

"You mean you're not going to tell them you found it on Flight 444 after you accidentally time traveled five years into the future?" I teased.

"Never. Our agreement to keep the world safe still stands."

I laughed. "I hate to break it to you, but the world is not safe."

He ignored my remark. "I can assure you I will never provide the FBI—or anyone—with information about time-blinking. Although, the Feds do know something weird is going on. Our friendly fake bird documentarians saw Collette appear out of nowhere and then disappear just as mysteriously with Christopher."

I groaned. "What do they think happened?"

"They have no idea, but given my friendship with you, they're pressuring me to find out. It's a damn shame. They were just about to pack up their investigation, too."

I could've screamed. "All this time we've kept it under wraps, then Collette comes along and blows it all apart. What next?"

"Don't panic. Only eight people know about timeblinking. Plus little Eli, but fortunately he's a nonverbal toddler."

I counted on my fingers and held up the ninth one. "What about Lizzy?"

He pursed his lips. It was all the confirmation I needed.

"Damn it, Sam. I knew it."

76

"I had to tell her. For obvious reasons. Besides, you never told me *not* to tell her."

"There was a reason for that. I'd foolishly assumed you were going to be invisible to her forever."

"You're going to have to trust me. And Lizzy."

"Did you tell her the *whole* story?"

He gave me a sheepish look.

"Well, you might as well come clean about the necklace to her now—tell her you found it on the plane and didn't realize it was mine."

Before he could respond, our attention turned to the soft beeps from the keypad at my door. I'd given Jarett the code yesterday. It had been a big step.

Sam and I stood as our friend let himself in and hung a bulky black garment bag on a hook next to the door—his uniform, no doubt. Then he turned to us and spread his arms wide with a big, shit-eating grin plastered across his face. "Hi, honey, I'm home!" he sang, completely for Sam's benefit.

I shook my head. "Good grief."

We waited for him to join us in the living room. "Hey, Jare," Sam said. "Thanks for inviting me over to the new pad. You've done well for yourself."

Jarett wrapped his arm around my shoulder and gave me a couple of rough squeezes. "Thanks. Me and the little lady here are pretty proud of it."

"Would you two be serious?" I said, wiggling out of Jarett's grasp. "We have work to do."

"Sorry." Jarett scooted over to the armchair across from Sam and sat down. "I forget my head sometimes."

While Jarett settled into his chair, Sam gave him the news about the bug-free apartment, his involvement with the FBI, and the fact that he'd been shown pictures of Jarett rifling through his wife's underwear like a *"damn pervert"*.

Without missing a beat, Jarett said, "That hot pink bra, though, Sammy! *Bow chicka wow wow.*"

"Taking notes for what to buy Syd, were you?" Sam shot back.

"You two are incorrigible." I pulled the talisman from my pocket and held it up for Jarett to see. "Look what Sam found on the plane."

His playful expression disappeared. "So, he knows——"

"Yes. He knows this is the necklace that Morley gave me right before he died." I leveled a warning look at Jarett that said *shut up about its timeblinking properties.*

Sam eyed me solemnly. "Actually, I wasn't aware Morley gave it to you under such dire circumstances. I'm sorry, Syd. Now I know why it was so important to you."

"What's most important to me right now is getting Christopher back. Sam, how long will our privacy last?"

"Five days, tops. Three if I don't produce any useful information in the next twenty-four hours."

Jarett piped up. "So, what...they're just going to waltz in here after five days and reinstall the bugs?"

"No," Sam said. "No more bugs in this apartment, or anywhere, but there'll still be people monitoring your movements."

"All right. We have three days to find Christopher and bring him home."

"We?" Sam asked.

"I'm assuming your offer to help is still on the table?"

"You bet."

"Okay. I'll be going on a few trips to other timelines, and it would be helpful if you could make damned sure we're not being watched."

"Sure thing. Is that it?"

"That's it."

"Easiest surveillance job ever. The Feds will think I'm watching you, not them." He tilted his head toward Jarett. "What's lover-boy's job?"

"For God's sake, where have you gotten the idea there's something going on between us?" I asked.

He gave me a crooked smile. "I'm not blind, deaf, or dead."

"Hey, buddy. Syd and I are just friends," Jarett said, not too convincingly.

"Yeah okay. Whatever you say."

"Guys! Enough. Jarett will be joining me on at least one timeblink. I'd rather go solo, but I have a feeling Christopher's abductor is going to throw me some curveballs that I won't be able to dodge."

"I can't wait," Jarett said through clenched teeth.

My heart swelled. It wasn't an army, but what it lacked in numbers, it made up for in skill: one cop running surveillance, another acting as my bodyguard. And then there was the third and most menacing member of the group: the fair-haired mother whose child had been ripped away from her without warning. Collette was going to be sorry she'd crossed me.

Chapter Thirteen

SEPTEMBER 10, 2024, 2:09 P.M.

W hen Jarett closed the door behind Sam twenty minutes later, he was smiling from ear to ear. "Well, that was awesome. Sam's all in."

"What a relief. Thanks for not spilling the beans about the talisman's power. It's best if Sam doesn't know—or anyone for that matter."

"Oh, I agree." Jarett clapped his hands together. "So, when do we go get your boy?"

I grabbed my phone from the coffee table and flopped down on the couch. "Soon. But first, I've got to see Morley."

"By yourself?" he said, sinking into the chair across from me.

"Yes. I need to find out the exact dates he and Collette fostered Christopher…or rather, *Tristan*."

"Don't you need my help?"

"Not for this. Besides, Morley hasn't even met you in the timeline I'll be visiting."

"So, introduce me."

I winced. "No way."

"That was pretty definitive."

"No need to put Morley through *that* torture twice."

"Oh, the jealous type, is he?"

I shook my head and focused on my phone. "Bingo," I said, looking up. "June fifteenth is open."

"Open?"

"Remember how I told you I had to keep a diary of all my visits with Morley?"

"Sure. To avoid running into yourself in another timeline."

"Bingo," I said again. "And I've spent so much time with him in 2019 that it's pretty slim pickings now."

"Why can't you just go back to 2018 or whenever?"

"Morley didn't learn about the talisman's power until January 2019."

"Why does that matter?"

"Think about it."

He rolled his eyes when he realized the obvious. "Because he wasn't aware of timeblinking before then. I know: bingo."

"That being said, I did timeblink to 2018 once. I was feeling mischievous one day and thought I would try watching Morley without him knowing."

Jarett leaned forward without speaking.

"He was so predictable. He liked to walk to The Bold & Bean on Saturday mornings, so I followed him there. But it was a stupid mistake. About two weeks later, when he was at The Merryport for his monthly martini, he asked me why I didn't join him for coffee instead of sneaking around spying on him. He was being cute about it. The guy doesn't have a mean bone in his body. But of course, I had no idea what he was talking about because that was 2018 me—not the 2021 version that had recklessly dropped in to stalk him."

"Oh no."

"Oh yeah. Eventually, I convinced him it hadn't been me. But at the time, I wondered if he'd actually seen *Isla*—who hadn't been found yet, remember."

"Holy shit. You must have freaked out."

I shook my head. "Do you know how many false Isla sightings I'd had by then? How many times I'd cried wolf to the police? I couldn't pester them for the hundredth time."

"Why not? You thought Morley had seen your missing sister. That's huge."

"Says the cop who didn't have to deal with my relentless phone calls."

"I'm trying to wrap my head around this. In 2021, surely you must've remembered that stalking incident from 2018. Yet you still went."

"I couldn't help myself. Timeblinking is weird that way. It's exactly what happened to Morley the night he died outside my pub. He knew it was going to happen, yet nothing could stop him from walking through those doors and into the path of a speeding truck."

"You make it sound like he had a death wish."

"No, no. What I'm saying is, any rational person—having been to the future and witnessed his own death—would've simply left through the back door. Right? It's like if you had information that a bomb was going to explode at a Mariners game, you'd stay home."

"Or try to prevent it."

"You know what I'm saying though, right? Maybe Morley left the pub that night not fully convinced he was about to die —even though he'd been to the future and watched it happen."

"Why would he think otherwise?"

"I don't know. My brain hurts. That's a question for another day."

Jarett raised his eyebrows at me. "So, what are you waiting for?"

"Nothing," I said, jumping to my feet.

Jarett got up equally as fast and stuffed his hands into the pockets of his jeans. He looked like a kid waiting for a three-scoop ice-cream cone. I headed down the hall.

"Where are you going?"

"Stay there until I get back."

"Stage fright?" Jarett mocked.

"Yes. I'll be back in five."

In my bedroom, I listened at the door to make sure Jarett hadn't followed then hurried over to my full-length mirror. Good, I wouldn't have to change. My leggings and sleeveless tunic were perfect for a trip to June 2019, and my favorite black flats were still at the end of the bed where I'd kicked them off earlier.

Once I'd gathered my hair into a loose bun and shrugged into my favorite blue cardigan, I took the talisman between my fingers, eagerly anticipating my reunion with Morley. For him, it would only be a few short minutes or hours since he'd last seen me, but for me, it had been four long months. I gripped the talisman tighter and recited my destination.

A moment later, I materialized with just a slight wobble in the shadowy, deserted parking lot at Chapman Falls. The split-second journey would always make my breath catch, like a near misstep on the stairs or a plunge into a cold lake. In the blink of an eye, you're someplace else—in a completely different time—none the worse for the wear.

I smoothed back my hair and started the hike up the hill to the cabin, my heart as light as a cloud. In a few short minutes, I would be reunited with my soulmate, and soon after that, with Christopher.

A solitary streetlight flickered as I passed under it and crossed the road, my pace quickening with every step. I'd missed so much about Morley. His laugh. His witty humor. His unassuming hotness. His warm breath in my ear as he whispered *"I love you."* And the thing I'd missed the most these last four months: our bodies moving together as one, cele-brating our love.

The very thought of it made me break into a run, and by the time I reached the cabin a few minutes later, I was out of breath. Morley greeted me in the front hall with a quick peck on the cheek and a strong, warm hug. I resisted the urge to jump him right then and there.

"You've been here so often it's almost as if we live togeth-er," he said as we made our way to the living room.

"I wish."

"Date?" he asked, picking up a journal from the coffee table to record our visit.

"September 10, 2024."

Morley's eyes lit up. "Christopher will be four soon. How is the little guy?"

I didn't want to get into that right away. If at all. "Still cute as a button. Talking up a storm."

"Aha. Takes after his mom. What can I get you to drink?"

I followed him into the kitchen. "I can get my own drink. Since we're living together and all."

"Fair enough. How about you whip up a chocolate cake while you're at it?"

I laughed. "You know I hate baking."

"Poor Christopher. I hope you at least make him oatmeal cookies."

"Oatmeal? What kind of monster do you think I am? Chocolate chip all the way, baby."

"Seems I would have been the bad cop in the family."

"Don't talk to me about cops," I said, savoring my freedom from the FBI…and perhaps from Jarett, too.

I poured myself a glass of sparkling water, and when I turned around, Morley took my glass and set it on the counter. He wrapped his arms around my waist and pulled me close. "Hi, love." He leaned down and kissed my neck, right where it always drove me nuts.

When we parted, I said, "Well, that was a much better greeting than the one I got at the door. God, I've missed you."

"Me too. And the funny thing is, we just had the craziest sex on the bearskin rug two hours ago."

I blushed when I remembered that day. It had been an afternoon of pure carnal joy. Oh, to be blushing this far into our relationship! "Seriously, that was today?"

"None other."

With the memory of it flooding back to me, I began feverishly unbuttoning his pants. I'd waited long enough. But he seized my hands and brought them to his lips, kissing them tenderly. "Let me catch my breath first."

"Are you kidding? Do you realize it's been four months for me? Four freaking months!"

He reached behind me and collected my glass then motioned for me to follow him into the living room. "Then you must tell me what you've been up to. Sounds like it might be interesting."

I trudged along behind him like a dejected teenager. "You're cruel, Dr. Scott."

He kept walking, letting out his best evil-scientist laugh.

How much was I going to tell him about what had been going on in my life? Everything? Nothing? Bits and pieces? I should have figured that out before I got all hot and bothered.

When we were seated on the couch together, I folded my arms across my chest.

Morley gave me a self-satisfied grin. "You're adorable when you're angry."

"I'm not angry," I said. "I'm horny as hell. And you're enjoying every minute of it."

"My dear, I do not enjoy your discomfort. You just have to remember that I've had an exhausting day." He winked and took a sip of the wine he'd been enjoying when I arrived. "Come on. You say it's been four months? That's definitely a record between visits. What's been keeping you busy?"

"Family, mostly."

He shrugged questioningly and waited for me to elaborate.

"Give me a minute, will you? My mind is still on the bearskin rug."

"You know what? I think you're stalling. What's this thing about the police you mentioned?"

I glanced at the ceiling and let out a slow breath. "A lot has happened since I last visited, which was the week leading up to your accident."

When I looked back at him, his face was bright. "You'll be here for an entire week before I get smucked by the truck?"

"Must you?"

"If you mean: *must I be so cavalier about my upcoming demise?* Yes. Better to joke about it than to spiral into perpetual misery."

Damn, he was brave. "Anyway, *yes*. I'll be here for the five days preceding your accident."

He smiled mischievously.

"Don't get too excited. We aren't going to spend our days rolling around on the floor together."

"That's a shame."

"You can say that again."

"You've always said you never wanted to visit me right before my accident. What changed your mind?"

"All I can tell you is that something big happened that forced me to timeblink without warning. I didn't have time to think about it, and I—"

"You knew the week before my death would be wide open."

I nodded.

"Well, I'm pleased to know I won't be spending my last week alone."

"Ha, quite the contrary."

He looked at me sideways. "Now you've really got me wondering."

I pressed my lips together. It was my turn to tease.

"So what's happening in September of 2024?" he asked.

"What, like, celebrity scandals? Environmental disasters? The Dow Jones?"

"I'd rather hear about your little corner of the world. And Christopher's."

The hopeful look he gave me just about broke my heart, but it solidified my decision not to tell him about Collette's cruelty. He didn't need to know she'd stolen our little boy right out from under me and that today's visit had everything to do with getting him back.

"Christopher is growing like a weed. He's fascinated with rocks. And poop."

Morley laughed. "The poop thing is normal. Especially for boys."

"Was your foster child obsessed with it, too?"

Morley cocked his head. "I don't recall telling you I had a foster child."

That's right. Morley didn't tell me about "Tristan" until the week of September ninth, which was still three months away. I shrugged it off. "Not yet. But you will."

"Ah, timeblinking. A surprise around every corner."

"His name was Tristan, right? Your foster child?"

Morley gave me a strained smile. "Yes. Amazing little guy. So sweet and well-adjusted. The first few days were rough, of course, but once he shook off the shock of being separated from his biological mother, he was as happy as a clam."

No shit. He was living with his biological father.

"Oh, that's such a relief."

"How do you think I felt? You never know how a child is going to react to a whole new environment. But Tristan *slayed it*, as the kids say. His resilience was remarkable, considering his history."

Yes, his history. Despite the fact it had all been a big ruse for Morley's benefit, it was hard not to take it personally. In addition to stealing an innocent child, Collette had painted his mother as a hopeless heroin addict.

"You mentioned his mother had drug problems," I said.

"Yes, as many foster kids' parents do."

"Well, at least his mom turned herself around. I don't imagine that happens very often."

"It doesn't. All too often the drugs win out. But in Tristan's case, the system worked the way it was supposed to. His mom cleaned up her act, and Tristan left us eight months later."

"Do foster kids usually stay that long?"

"Sometimes it's only a few days, but it can be months. We were lucky to have Tristan as long as we did."

"Did you get updates afterwards?"

He flashed me a sad smile. "Yes, Collette spoke with the agency several times. They assured her Tristan's mother had made a complete turnaround and that the boy was thriving under her care. To be honest, I had rather hoped for the opposite. Collette too. We'd both been on board for adoption if it ever came to that."

"Tristan must've really left an impression on you."

Morley nodded vacantly, as if his mind was on another planet. When he noticed me staring, he shook his head vigorously as if trying to chase away whatever thoughts he'd been lost in. "I'm sorry. That was insensitive of me."

"What, admitting to bonding with a little boy who needed your help?"

"No, I mean all this chatter about my late wife."

I reached over and rubbed his knee. "I'm glad you're opening up to me."

He picked up my hand and kissed the back of it. "I've always sensed you didn't want to hear about my life before you."

He wasn't wrong about that, and it made me sad for him. For us.

"Anyway," he said, "Thanks to the mother's miraculous

about-face, Tristan was going to be just fine. And that was that. I said goodbye to him one morning, and when I got home from work, he was gone."

"You and Collette didn't take him back together?" I pressed, feeling a little guilty when I already knew the reason why.

"No. Collette insisted on looking after the whole process, right from the start."

I huffed. *Of course she had.*

Mistaking my annoyance for confusion, Morley went on to explain. "She was on a leave of absence at the time, and I was extremely busy at my practice, so it was by good fortune that she could take care of the details. And there were plenty. She filled out all the forms, attended orientation meetings, and picked Tristan up after we passed the police checks and psychological assessments."

"That was good of her," I said, barely masking my contempt. "So, you never met Tristan in person before he came to live with you?"

"It wasn't necessary. I trusted Collette's judgement."

"The agency didn't need to meet both of you?"

He winked at me. "The perks of being a respected pedia-trician in the community."

"You're the real deal, aren't you?"

He fluttered his eyelashes at me. "Well, you did tell me they renamed a whole wing at St. Barts's after me."

I forced a laugh. This was all good information, but I had yet to ask the question that brought me here. "When did Christopher come to live with you?"

"You mean Tristan."

I flushed. "Yes, Tristan. Slip of the tongue."

"Easy mistake," he said, winking again. He clasped his hands in his lap and looked up at the ceiling. "Let's see... When did Tristan arrive? Oh, of course. It was February four-teenth, 2014."

"Valentine's Day."

"The date is embedded in my mind. It's the day Collette had a particularly bad bout with her mystery illness—one that she'd battled on and off for several years."

"Mystery illness?"

"She was stubbornly private about it. Refused to tell me anything. Wouldn't let me help. It was hard knowing she wanted to face it alone, but I had to respect her wishes."

"Did she ever let you in on it?"

"No," he said sighing. "She must've felt it was her burden to bear. All I knew was that the episodes would come on without warning and take about a week to clear up. The Valentine's Day spell just about did her in. And in fact, one last bout of that strange malady finally took her a year later."

"I'm sorry, Morley."

He smiled ruefully. "It was hard to watch her suffer like that. But you know, she always downplayed the severity of it. Didn't want me to worry. Of course, I did."

"So, no clues about what it was, then?"

"No. As I said, she was extremely private about her health matters. But now that I've experienced the power of time-blinking, I've been wondering lately if it had something to do with that."

"Oh? You've always said you didn't think she knew about the talisman's power."

"In the last few years of her life, she lost a lot of weight and was exceedingly fragile and weak. It happened gradually, so I didn't notice it right away, but in retrospect, I can't help but think she was aging at an accelerated rate before my eyes. Lines up, doesn't it?"

I wanted to confirm his suspicions right then and there—that I was certain Collette knew how to timeblink—but it would surely derail our conversation, and I'd be forced to leave without the information I'd come for.

"I'm sorry you had to go through all that, sweetie. That must have been so hard, not knowing what was going on."

He nodded. "That's an understatement. And it was certainly no way to welcome Tristan into our household. Gosh, she was so sick. I wanted to send Tristan back to the agency, but Collette begged me to keep him with us, insisting it would help take her mind off her illness. And wouldn't you know it? She'd been right. Tristan was a delight, and Collette's condition stabilized nicely."

"A happy ending."

"I suppose. Tristan went back to his mother eight months to the day later. October fourteenth."

"Another very specific date." And super helpful intel for me.

A shadow passed over his face. "It was my mother's birthday. I remember thinking how much she would have loved Tristan if she'd still been alive. And how sad she would have been when he left."

"Oh, Morley. You really did love the little guy."

I watched his Adam's apple move as he swallowed. "Apparently the universe was looking out for us. Collette died less than a year later. If we'd gone the adoption route, I would've had a young child to raise on my own. Not to mention he would have been orphaned at nine years old."

I slipped my arms around his torso and hugged tight. He snuggled into my embrace like a child seeking comfort after a fall. Neither of us spoke.

Our stillness gave me time to imagine him as a father. He obviously loved children, and they certainly loved him. Would he really have been the bad cop, insisting on oatmeal cookies instead of chocolate chip? Water instead of soda?

A tear slid down my cheek. I would never find out.

"October fourteenth was indeed a terrible day," he said, pulling out of my embrace. "And not just because Tristan left us. Collette was assaulted at Lighthouse Park that same day."

My eyes went wide. "She really had the worst luck."

"It would seem so. I didn't find out until a colleague told me she was in the ER. By the time I got down there, she'd already been released. Fortunately, it was just a minor concussion, and she just needed rest. Her assailant was never found."

"Why would someone attack her?"

"No idea. Just some random whacko, by her account."

Whether she was my nemesis or not, the information was troubling.

"That's awful. I'm glad she wasn't hurt too badly."

Morley rubbed his hands together wearily. "I'm tired, love. Think I'll hit the hay. Join me?"

We both stood up together, and surprising myself, I said, "Not tonight."

He looked as surprised as I felt. "Well, that was a quick change of heart. Twenty minutes ago, you were trying to rip my clothes off."

I shifted from foot to foot.

"It's fine, love," he said. "Another time."

"It's not that I don't want to stay."

He tucked some loose hair behind my ear. "It's okay, I'm dead tired anyway thanks to that workout on the bearskin earlier. Go on, go give that little boy of ours a big hug."

I threw my arms around him and laid my head on his chest. "You would have been an amazing dad."

"I know." He chuckled, a mirthful sound that lifted my spirits. Good. I could leave knowing Morley was in a peaceful frame of mind.

If only I could say the same about me.

Chapter Fourteen

After two hours of much-needed solitude after my timeblink, I emerged from my bedroom and padded into the living room. Jarett was standing on the deck, leaning against the waist-high flower planter that doubled as a railing, seemingly lost in thought as the condensation from the cold beer in his hand dripped off the bottle and onto his sneakers. I admonished myself for thinking about how sexy he looked against the backdrop of flaming red geraniums I'd planted in the spring. How could I even think about someone that way when my child was missing?

Jarett's face lit up when he saw me.

"Well?" he asked expectantly. "How'd it go?"

I gave him a full rundown of my visit with Morley—at least as it pertained to Christopher's whereabouts—then joined him at the planter where I watched a sailboat maneuver into a berth in the harbor.

Jarett turned around to watch the activity in the harbor with me and took a swig of his beer. "Did you tell him that Tristan was actually Christopher?"

"Are you kidding? It would've crushed him to find out what Collette had done."

"Or he would've been thrilled to learn he'd spent eight months with his biological son."

"What he doesn't know can't hurt him."

"Maybe he already suspected that Tristan was Christopher."

"Nope."

"What makes you so sure?"

"Well, he never brought it up when I took Christopher to see him. Surely, he would have said, 'You know, Christopher bears an uncanny resemblance to the little boy I once fostered'."

"You're probably right. I just find it hard to believe he didn't make the connection."

Noticing a few spent blooms in the planter, I fetched my pruning shears from the cabinet next to the grill. "Remember, Morley only saw Christopher as a baby when I took him on those timeblinks. *Tristan* was almost four when Collette abducted him. God, I'm talking about Christopher in the past tense. He's with them *now* in 2014. This is so messed up."

I grabbed an orange utility bucket and began deadheading geraniums in earnest.

"So, that's it? You guys just talked about Tristan's fostering experience the whole time you were there?"

I laughed. "The whole thirty-two minutes? Yeah. It was all the information I needed. Besides, Morley was exhausted." I could feel my cheeks getting hot and turned away from Jarett before he noticed.

"Now for the hard part."

"Shit!" I cried, shaking my fingers vigorously. I'd nicked myself with the pruning shears.

"Let me see," Jarett said, holding out his hand. I gave him mine.

After inspecting the cut, he applied some gentle pressure and held my hand above my head. "Come on. In the house. The cut's pretty deep, but I don't think it'll need stitches."

In the bathroom, he cleaned the wound with some soap and water then got me to hold a tissue around it while he fished a small bandage and some antibiotic cream out of the drawer.

"Thank you," I said, watching him expertly dress my cut. "Looks like you've done this before."

"It's part of the job," he said, smiling but still focused on my finger. From this angle, his eyelashes looked longer than ever. Kendall was right. She was always telling me Officer Jarett Cooper was hot as fuck.

When he looked up to get my approval on his handiwork, I put both my hands on the back of his head and pulled his face toward mine. I kissed him. Hard. He didn't resist.

Before I could even think about it, we were tearing each other's clothes off with abandon, right there in the bathroom. When I was down to my bra and panties and he was in his boxers, he lifted me up onto the quartz countertop. I was mad with desire and let him do what he wanted.

He slipped one strap off my shoulder and buried his face in my neck, right under my ear. I was vaguely aware of his beard tickling my skin as his gentle kisses traced a path to my collarbone, then between my breasts. He undid the clasp on my bra and let it fall to the floor. Now his tongue licked and teased me until I could barely form a coherent thought.

I called out in ecstasy. He wrapped his hands around my waist to pull me off the counter. We kissed like it was our last day on Earth. Hungrily. Without a care.

His hand slipped inside my panties. I cried out again. God, I didn't want to explode. Not here. Not yet.

Now he was lowering himself to his knees, slipping my panties down as he went. I dared to open my eyes. To see if it was all real.

"Fuck!" I yelled.

Jarett looked up at me, surprised. It hadn't been the response he was expecting. It hadn't been mine either, but I hadn't been able to help it. I'd spotted Christopher's tub-toy basket where I kept it on a shelf, and an inner voice screamed at me for being a terrible mother. To make matters worse, an image of Morley's disappointed face popped into my mind. *Fuckety fuck.*

Jarett must've thought it was just my odd way of expressing pleasure, because he returned to his pursuits, gently nuzzling his face between my legs.

I groaned, but not with pleasure. The longer Jarett explored me, the more agitated I got.

"Stop," I said, backing away and pulling up my panties. "Please stop."

"What?" He rose to his feet breathlessly, raking his fingers through his short, dark curls.

I grabbed a bath towel from the shelf and wrapped it tightly around my torso. "I can't do this."

For a moment I wondered if I'd lost my mind, denying him, but my resolve only strengthened as images of Christopher and Morley persisted in my thoughts. I bent down to gather up my clothes then made for the door.

He grabbed my bicep—not forcefully. It was an innocuous gesture that in words might have translated to *please don't run away.*

"Where are you going?"

When I turned to face him, it took all my willpower not to drag him to my bedroom and finish what we'd started, guilt be damned.

"Syd," he said. "What's this about?"

"What kind of mother does this when her child is missing?"

He rubbed my arm. "A mother who's trying to take her mind off things for a little while. It's natural. Not disrespectful."

"I should be looking for Christopher. And not cheating on Morley."

"Ah, *there* it is."

"There *what* is?"

He pulled his jeans on and guided me down to the tile ledge surrounding the tub, then sat next to me. "Whatever happens between us? It's not cheating on Morley."

"How so? I've been in a committed relationship with him for five years. He's the father of my child."

"Syd." He took my hand, rubbing the back of it with his thumb. "I hate to break it to you, but Morley died five years ago."

"You don't know what it's like," I said, reclaiming my hand, willing myself not to cry.

"You're right, I don't. And I can't even imagine it."

I locked eyes with him. "I can go see him whenever I want. We even talked about that today. How I practically live there."

"It's not real."

"Fuck that."

"It's *not*, Syd."

"Christopher was conceived on a timeblink. Don't tell me that's not real."

"You know what I mean. It's not healthy."

I got up and drifted over to the vanity where I slipped into my bra, clumsy fingers fumbling with the clasps. Jarett came up behind me. "May I?"

I nodded, still on the verge of tears, trying to ignore the jolt of electricity that surged through my body when his warm, supple hands worked at my back.

Once we were both dressed, I said, "I know it's not ideal. But we've made it work."

"You want to know how I see it?"

"You have already. You think I'm foolish."

"Not foolish. Blinded by love, maybe, but not foolish. No, the real problem is Morley. He's holding you hostage."

My head snapped up and I glared at him.

"See, you know it's true."

"What a load of crap. Morley's not the bad guy here. When he handed the timeblinking power over to me, back when we didn't know how it might affect my health or my future or even world events, he begged me not to come visit him anymore. But I couldn't stay away. I'd found my soulmate. Don't tell me you wouldn't do the same thing in that situation."

He pondered this for a moment. "You're right. But if someone came along in the meantime—a living, breathing person who didn't exist only in my past…"

He touched his finger to my jaw, turning my head to meet his eyes. "Someone who obviously loved me—"

Woah. That came out of left field.

I shifted my focus to my hands where I was twisting Morley's ring in circles around my thumb. Jarett placed his hands on mine to still them. "Syd. Tell me what you're thinking."

I tore myself away from him. "I'm thinking I'm a shitty mom. Christopher needs me."

"Let me help you," I heard him say as I hurried down the hall, scolding myself for hoping he would follow me to the bedroom; but when he kept his distance, I was relieved, not disappointed. There was a lot to unpack with Jarett, but not before I brought my little boy home.

Chapter Fifteen

With the sun dropping behind the McLaren Lofts across the street and my bedroom falling into shadow, I lay on my bed, legs draped over the side, my eyes fixed on the ceiling.

Everything was so complicated. Christopher. Morley. Jarett. Me. The most important thing was getting my son back. But now that the time had finally come to embark on his rescue, I found myself hesitant, doubting it was even possible.

There was a faint rap at my door.

"What?" The bite in my voice was sharper than I'd intended.

Jarett had left me alone for a whole fifteen minutes, which was longer than I'd expected. "Can I come in?"

I let out a tired breath.

"Yes, come in."

I heard Jarett enter the room tentatively. He flicked on the bedside lamp then sat down beside me. "I thought you'd gone to 2014 without me."

"I still might."

"You don't need my help?"

99

I sat up, shoulder to shoulder with Jarett. "I will. When I eventually go."

"Why are you procrastinating?"

"I'm scared."

"Of what?"

I gave Morley's ring a couple of twists. "Morley told me Christopher, or Tristan, was simply gone one day when he got home from work."

"Isn't that good news? Doesn't it mean you were successful in bringing him back to 2024?"

I shook my head grimly. "No. That's why I'm so worried. What if Collette hid him somewhere or took him to a different timeline altogether just so I would never be able to find him? Or what if she harmed him? Or…worse?"

"Don't think like that," Jarett said, grasping my hands. The numbing effect of the antibiotic cream had worn off, but the pain in my finger paled in comparison to the ache in my heart.

"How can I not? We have no idea what happened. It's Isla, two-point-oh."

He gave me a questioning look.

"When Morley gave me the talisman—and the power to find out what had become of Isla—I was terrified to learn the truth. I didn't want to know if she'd been tortured or raped. Or killed."

"Come on, Syd. Even if Collette was capable of harming Christopher, there's no way Morley would let it happen."

"Collette took matters out of his control when she insisted on looking after the whole 'fostering' sham herself. How can he possibly protect Christopher when Collette's pulling all the strings?"

I pulled my hands out of Jarett's grip when he couldn't give me an answer.

"So, let me help," he said, getting up. He offered me his hand.

I was out of excuses. The talisman was in its rightful place, I knew the dates of Christopher's abduction, and apparently, I had my ride-or-die at my side.

Jarett pulled me up and gave me a quick, friendly hug. "Come on, let's go get your little man."

As I settled my tattered old *Port Raven Fire Station #3* ballcap on my head, Jarett gave me a curious look.

"I'm surprised you've held onto that."

"What, the ballcap? Yeah, Kendall always says the same thing. But I don't keep it for the nostalgia. I keep it as a reminder."

"Of what?"

I tugged the brim down over my eyes a little. "To be vigilant. It's the only memento I have left of that time. It's my personal reminder not to trust people at face value because I used to do that a lot, and I only got burned."

Jarett's face grew somber. "I hope you don't think that about me. I would never hurt you."

I flashed him a quick smile. "We've only known each other for four months. I'm pretty sure you're one of the good guys, but don't be offended if it takes me a while to make the final call."

He winked playfully. "I'm not offended at all. You'll come to your senses one of these days."

"Okay, then. Let's get on with this."

To kick things off, I outlined my extremely rough plan, reminding Jarett of the most important nuance of timeblink travel: anything we wanted to bring along had to be touching our skin. For instance, I told him that his shiny new Vans would make it to the other side as long as he got rid of the socks. He wanted to bring his phone, but I pointed out that it wouldn't work there anyway. Once he understood the basics, I got him to put on his reading glasses. I didn't want Christopher recognizing us and blowing our cover.

I made sure Jarett was looking directly at me when I spoke next. "I'm pretty sure you already have a good idea how this all works," I said, retrieving the talisman from inside my shirt and zipping up my thin down jacket.

"I think I've got the basics, yeah."

"And I'm sure I don't have to say it, but I will anyway. Promise me you won't tell another living soul about it."

"You have my word." He crossed his heart.

"Even my family isn't privy to this information. You're the only person that knows apart from me and Morley—and Collette, of course. Don't make me regret it."

"You won't. Your trust is important to me."

"All right. You're clear about what we're doing?" I asked, donning a pair of oversized sunglasses.

"Timeblinking to some bushes at Lighthouse Park just before sunrise, then waiting until the Wooden Spoon Diner opens at six so we can monitor Collette's movements at the condo." He looked around as if realizing we were standing in that condo right now then padded over to the floor-to-ceiling window. He let out a barely audible gasp. "Shit, that's a long way down."

I'd forgotten about his fear of heights, which he'd bravely pushed aside when he rescued my half-sister from falling eighteen floors to a certain death from this very building then went on to jump out of a plane with his good buddy Sam strapped to his chest. It seemed we were both facing our biggest fears lately.

"I don't see The Wooden Spoon down there," he said.

"That's because it's a Shoe Emporium now."

"Of course it is. This city has more shoe stores than fire hydrants."

He joined me in front of the floor-length mirror as I pulled my ponytail through the gap in my ballcap and did a quick once-over of our transformation. It would do. Jarett's simple, black-rimmed glasses gave him a scholarly vibe that made him look even hotter, if that was possible. He could have been an eyewear model—or an underwear model, I thought, my mind wandering back to our encounter in the bathroom. As for me, the only time I ever wore sunglasses and baseball caps was at a game or when I ran, so I was reasonably sure Christopher wouldn't recognize me if he spotted us.

"Come on," I said, pulling Jarett behind my dressing screen in the corner.

"Why here?"

"Sam might be convinced no one is watching, but I'm not," I said.

"Aren't you being a little paranoid? The tallest building in the area is the McLaren Lofts, and none of those windows have a direct view of this apartment."

"I'm not paranoid. You just aren't suspicious enough, which is odd for a cop."

"Oh, we're going there, are we? Ask anyone at the station. Suspicion is my superpower."

I took his hand and pulled him to a squat then grasped the talisman in my fingers. "Ready to experience *my* superpower?"

"As I'll ever be."

"All right. We'll end up behind a hedge, but it's only three feet tall, so stay crouched down until we confirm we're alone."

"Okay, boss. Let's do this."

As I raised the talisman between us, guilt washed through my entire body. Morley had strictly forbidden me from teaching others about timeblinking. But...surely he would forgive me for enlisting Jarett's help to save our little boy?

I couldn't torture myself with doubt any longer. It was time to go. "Lighthouse Park, washroom exterior, south wall, five thirty a.m., October 14, 2014."

Half a second later, all hell broke loose.

I heard Jarett cry out in pain, shattering the early morning silence in the park.

"Shh!" I whisper-shouted, even though I felt like screaming myself. Hundreds of tiny prickles assaulted my face, my hands, and the entire length of my legs from some unknown source that I couldn't see. It was too dark. I didn't want to move. The pain was too intense.

Beside me, I heard Jarett letting out stifled grunts as he thrashed about, snapping branches so loudly it could have been heard from space. When the racket finally ceased, his voice came to me in a whisper (like it mattered now). "What is this?"

"I don't know. Give me a minute," I said through chattering teeth. The damp ocean wind had gone straight to my bones.

Still crouched, I slid one of my hands behind me to inspect the cold, hard surface at my back. Relief washed through me. It was the cinderblock wall of the washroom facility. We'd made it to the right destination, but it was anyone's guess as to what happened to the immaculately groomed boxwood hedge surrounding the building.

In the darkness, I felt Jarett's warm hand seize mine. He helped me up while tiny barbs slashed at my skin. When I finally made it to my feet, I was dizzy with pain and had to take several calming breaths. I'd never experienced a more harrowing timeblink, and that was saying a lot considering my first one had deposited me in a hundred-foot waterfall and another one had me zapping off a crashing plane.

As my eyes adjusted to the early morning light, I realized my mistake. We'd landed in a cluster of climbing rose bushes planted next to the building—bushes that had obviously been there in 2014 but not 2019, the usual year of my timeblinks.

"Roses," I whispered. "A fucking rose bush! I can't believe this."

Once we'd extracted ourselves from our thorny hell, we

stood facing each other, illuminated by the small, caged light hanging above the washroom doors. Jarett winced when he saw me. "Holy crap, your face."

My hands flew up to my cheeks. "Is it bad?"

"You look like a plane crash survivor."

"I *am* a plane crash survivor."

He chuckled and reached up to inspect the areas of his own face not covered by his beard. "How about me?"

"Just a tiny scratch above your eyebrow. Were we even in the same bush?"

"Ah, the benefits of facial hair. Sexy *and* protective."

"Come on. We gotta go."

Jarett glanced back at the rose bush as we walked. "You seriously couldn't think of a more welcoming place to land?"

"Yeah, but it wouldn't have been as exciting."

"I could've done without that kind of excitement. Give me a drug addict or someone having bush sex any day."

"Bush sex?"

"You've never heard of people doing the nasty in bushes before? Were you never a teenager?"

"Even a teenager wouldn't do it in *that* bush."

"Not a sober one. You'd be surprised at what goes on after dark. *Policework: humanity at its finest.*"

I laughed. "I've never run into any shady characters at this park. Not once."

"How many times have you timeblinked here?"

"I don't know, twenty, thirty? I'd have to check my calendar."

"Thirty? And you've never seen one druggie or whacko? Those are amazing odds."

"Not really. Port Raven is pretty sleepy. You might get bored working here."

"I doubt it. Every city has its dark underbelly, even a small one like PR. You've been lucky."

I laughed. "Oh, yeah, I ooze luck."

When we arrived across the street from Morley and Collette's condo a few minutes later, I removed my sunglasses and peered up at the window where I knew Christopher would be sleeping. I closed my eyes. As much as I hoped he missed me, it was more important that he was happy and safe. There was no doubt in my mind that Morley would make sure of that, but Collette was a wildcard.

An icy gust slithered down the back of my neck, making me shiver. "This is so surreal," I said. "My little boy is right there, and I can't do a damned thing about it."

"Not yet, but we'll figure it out. We just need to be patient."

"We'll go over the plan at the restaurant."

"I've been thinking about that. You're assuming they'll leave the building on foot. What if they don't? What if Collette only takes him out in her car?"

"Look around, Jarett. One of the reasons I finally warmed up to condo living was the proximity to literally everything. Grocery stores, parks, movie theaters, work. Christopher and I walk everywhere. In fact, my car battery has died three times from neglect."

"Really? Your car is so new."

"That's exactly why it kept happening. They call it *parasitic draw*. It's from all the fancy computer stuff running in the background. The second time it happened, I called the dealership, and they suggested I take the car for a spin once a week to keep the battery charged."

"Good to know since I'll probably be walking to work from your place."

"Anyway, I can almost guarantee Collette and Christopher will venture out on foot at some point. And I'll bet we won't have to wait long, either."

"So, what...we just walk up to them and grab Christopher?" Jarett said, zipping up his jacket, obviously feeling the cold as much as I was.

"Unfortunately, that's not how timeblinking works. Take Sam, for example. He's on my return timeblink right now, and even if he did want to go back to his natural timeline in 2019, I would have no clue how to get him there."

"Maybe it's different for Christopher because he's gone to the past instead."

A jogger whizzed by us as we ducked into the diner's alcove to get out of the wind. I cupped my hands to the window in the door. The cuckoo clock on the back wall showed eleven minutes to six.

"That's why this whole thing is so tricky," I said, turning back to Jarett, bouncing up and down to keep warm. "Nothing's certain. We're figuring things out as we go."

When Jarett didn't offer any more reassurances, I continued. "According to Morley, *Tristan* went back to his mother today, October fourteenth; but I keep wondering: is it because I figured out how to take him back with me? Or did I convince Collette to return him?" I shuddered. "Or is my little boy about to end up somewhere else entirely?"

Jarett rubbed my arm. "Don't torture yourself. We'll get him back."

The neon OPEN sign flickered to life in the diner's window and a heavy-set gentleman in a rumpled brown business suit came to the door and unlocked it. "Come in. You look frozen, the pair-a-ya."

"Thank you," I said, following him inside. He offered us a booth near the back of the diner, but we asked to sit in the window instead.

"Suit yerself. You might have to wait a few minutes until my servers get here. They usually show up at the crack-a-six." He grabbed some menus from the counter and brought them over, cringing when he saw my face in the light. "Dang, what happened? Get into a fight with a coupla feral cats?

My hand shot up to my cheek. I'm not sure how I'd managed to forget about our run-in with the rose bush and the resulting sting. "Long story."

The man shook his head. "Cats are cunts if y'ask me. Coffee?"

Jarett snickered. "A man after my own heart. I also happen to hate cats and love coffee. My friend will have peppermint tea if you have some on hand."

"Ya kiddin'? This is Port Raven. Herbal tea and incense capital of the damn free world."

"I thought that honor belonged to Portland," Jarett said as the man walked away muttering something about craft breweries and stinking hippies.

"Wow," Jarett said, lifting his eyebrows briefly. "Interesting fella."

"Don't piss him off. We might be here a while."

If *a while* meant two hours, then the timing was bang on. At eight o'clock, I seized Jarett's hand across the table. "There they are."

He sprang to his feet and snatched his jacket off the back of the chair. "I'm on it." He hustled out the door without another word.

I hurriedly counted out some bills from the stash in my bra (cash only on timeblinks) and tossed them onto the table, keeping an eye on Christopher and his captor across the street. I couldn't have hated anyone more in that moment. Collette was beautiful and elegant and stylishly dressed in a long, fuzzy taupe sweater that was cinched at the waist with a matching tie. On her feet were some comfortable-looking black Chelsea boots, much like the ones I favored in the fall and winter.

An unexpected wave of jealousy hit me just then. Not

anger. Not dread. *Jealousy*. It was like seeing your ex with another woman for the first time, and it was all I could do not to run out there and punch her in the face.

During our two-hour stakeout at The Wooden Spoon, Jarett and I reviewed the plan several times, allowing for every possible outcome. The one thing we were in complete agreement about was that Jarett would approach Collette alone. We couldn't predict if Christopher would recognize me, despite my disguise, and I didn't want to risk causing a scene in public, possibly attracting the attention of the police or a good Samaritan jumping in to help a little boy in distress. Never mind that even in 2014, the world was full of nosy people going around recording literally everything on their cell phones. No, we didn't need any of those complications.

I shrugged into my jacket and scooted over to the door to wait for Jarett's signal. Behind me, the café had filled to capacity with chattering, happy diners. I envied them. None of them shared my problems.

In my peripheral vision, I saw our server—a scrawny middle-aged woman with crooked teeth who'd probably been working at the place since it opened in the late eighties— collect my cash from the table. She paused to watch me for a few moments, as though trying to place where she'd seen me before.

"Shit," I murmured, refusing to acknowledge her stare, but a few seconds later, there was a tap on my shoulder. I reluctantly turned around.

"Sorry to bother you," the woman started. Great. Here it came. "But aren't you Syd Bixby?"

"No," I said, truthfully, taking full advantage of her mistake.

People would always think the Brixton Twin Abduction was their business, and here in October 2014, the fifteenth anniversary had just passed, spurring a fresh burst of speculative news stories looking for answers. The reporters wouldn't find them, of course. I wouldn't discover Isla in that basement for another five years. My heart tightened at the thought. It would be so easy to go there right now and unlock that door, but—as Morley had proved over and over again when he'd tried to prevent his own death—there was no point. He'd never found a way to influence future events during a time-blink or to change past ones, either.

"Oh, sorry. My mistake," the woman said, looking dubious, nonetheless.

"It's okay, I get it all the time, which is flattering, to be honest. Isn't Syd Bixby like, twenty-six or something?" I pointed to my thirty-six-year-old face, hoping she could see past all the scratches. "Clearly not me."

She nodded, still not quite convinced it seemed, but chose not to harass me further. She wished me a good day and went about her duties.

By the time I looked back to the street, I couldn't see my little entourage anywhere, and I practically ripped the door off its hinges to get outside. Once there, I put on my sunglasses, adjusted my ballcap, and scanned the area in the direction of Collette's likely route. Every nerve in my body was zinging.

To my relief, I spotted Jarett almost immediately as he hopped onto the sidewalk across the street, maybe fifteen or twenty paces behind Collette and Christopher. I remained in the shadows, using the rising sun's angle to help shield me from Collette's view.

That meant I was free to watch them at my leisure. Free to watch Collette virtually dragging my son along the sidewalk, her long, lean limbs no match for Christopher's pudgy little baby legs. I could tell he was doing his darndest to keep up, his wispy blond curls bouncing with each step.

Without warning, Collette stopped, dropped Christopher's hand, and crouched down in front of him. Jarett made a quick yet composed ninety-degree turn, pretending to peer into a shop window. I did the same. By a stroke of luck, there was a massive gold-rimmed mirror in the home accessory shop I'd stopped at, giving me a perfect view of everything going on across the street. Collette seemed oblivious to her surroundings, focusing solely on Christopher's face as she removed one of her earbuds to talk to him. Earbuds! The woman didn't even have the decency to leave her damned music off. Christopher was that far down her priority list.

As she spoke, I saw Christopher's bottom lip quiver. Damn her! Did she just scold my little boy for walking too slowly?

Christopher nodded shyly before Collette whisked him off the sidewalk, spread his legs around her hip, and continued on her way.

My blood was pumping so hard I could almost feel its path through my heart. Jarett's presence gave me little peace of mind. I knew he would intervene if Collette got any rougher, but I prayed it wouldn't come to that.

Jarett fell into step behind them, perhaps half a block back, with a young professional couple keeping pace in between. If Christopher happened to notice Jarett, I wouldn't expect him to recognize him. He was only three. Actually, that was no longer true. Eight months had passed in this timeline for Christopher, making him four years old now. Anger gripped my soul. I'd missed his birthday. But that wasn't the biggest consequence of his little adventure to 2014. Chronologically, he would be eight months older when he got back to 2024, which also meant he probably should've started kindergarten this week rather than next year. Fuckety fuck.

But I was getting ahead of myself. *Way* ahead. In order for any of that to matter, Christopher would first have to get back to 2024.

Jarett glanced across the street making the slightest eye contact with me before turning his attention back to Collette. Good. He knew I was nearby, ready to pounce when necessary.

Earlier, when Collette and Christopher had emerged from the condo and turned south, the decision had narrowed their likely destination down to a few places instead of dozens. And now that they'd turned left onto Fraser Street, they could only be headed to one place: Lighthouse Park. It couldn't have been a better spot for our soft ambush. There would be far fewer witnesses to contend with in the park compared to the bustling city. Witnesses who would no doubt see two women having it out before one of them disappeared with a hot guy and a screaming toddler right in front of their eyes. Again, I stopped my fantasy short. I was getting ahead of myself.

As we kept our targets in sight, I wondered why Collette would want to take Christopher to the park so early in the morning, but then I remembered Sweet Briar Daycare. It was an exclusive childcare center backing onto the park with sweeping views of the rose garden and Alice Bay beyond. It wouldn't surprise me if Collette had been dumping my baby there while Morley was at work, allowing her to enjoy her sabbatical unencumbered.

On most weekdays at this hour, the park was mostly deserted, but today there was a smattering of cyclists, runners, and dog walkers about. Granted, the extra activity helped mask our presence, but it would do Jarett no favors when it came to go-time. He was supposed to approach Collette for a friendly chat when there were the fewest witnesses around to account for whatever might happen, which, at the moment, could be anything.

This made me think back to Morley's unsettling information that Collette had been assaulted at this park the day Christopher went home. Was Jarett about to come to blows with this woman? God, I hoped not. At least not in front of my baby boy.

I stayed on the opposite side of Fraser Street to keep an eye on Jarett's movements behind Collette, who, as I'd predicted, entered the rose garden, a shortcut to the daycare.

If we were going to act on this plan, it would have to be quick, before Collette dropped Christopher off.

I was so focused on what was happening across the street that I only vaguely noticed the two joggers beating a path toward me.

"Syd? Is that you?" one of them said, slowing as they approached. I recognized them instantly. It was Candace and Jenny, whose husbands had once worked with my psycho-pathic child-abducting ex at the fire station. How the hell she even recognized me past my disguise and scratched-to-shit older face was beyond me. But then again, I *was* wearing a PRFD ballcap. Not too many of those in circulation.

I put my head down, feeling mildly disconcerted about seeing Jenny at all; I'd heard she'd been involved in a horrific hit-and-run that had put her into a coma that—as far as I knew—she'd never come out of.

"Who are you talking to?" Candace said to Jenny.

Oh, shit. Candace couldn't see me.

I pretended not to hear Jenny and darted into the street without even looking for cars. Fortunately, there were none, but unfortunately, as I mounted the sidewalk on the other side of the street, I could hear Jenny saying, "What do you mean you don't see her? It's Syd Brixton. She's right there!"

"Fuck," I muttered under my breath. The mission was going off the rails.

Jarett must have been laser-focused on Collette because he didn't even hear me coming up behind him. And he obviously didn't register the presence of the two nattering women across the street, one of them calling my name intermittently, trying in vain to get my attention. When Jarett was no more than fifteen steps behind Collette and preparing to confront her, I seized his arm. He whirled around and opened his mouth to protest but stopped when he saw the panic in my eyes. He shrugged questioningly but didn't have to wait long for an explanation. And it didn't come from me.

"Syd!" Jenny yelled. Jarett's head snapped in her direction. Jenny was dashing across the street, leaving a very puzzled Candace on the other side. "It's me! Jen—"

Before she had the chance to finish her sentence, the pickup truck was on her. Literally. The young driver—whose attention had been on his phone—hadn't even seen her run into the street, and by the time he'd stomped on his brakes and came to a screeching halt, Jenny was lying motionless in the street ten feet in front of him.

Everything happened at lightning speed after that: Candace screaming hysterically. The blood-spattered truck speeding away from the scene. Two dog walkers running to Jenny's aid on the road. Jarett making a move to do the same. Me grabbing his arm, ordering him to stay put.

"We gotta get out of here."

As we darted for cover behind a giant lilac bush, my ballcap flew off behind me, and when I whirled around to retrieve it, Christopher's head shot up from its perch on Collette's shoulder. He'd spotted me. I put my finger to my lips, imploring him not to call out, and he seemed to consider this for the briefest moment before erupting into a fit of screaming that could wake the dead. I fought every instinct not to run over there and take him into my arms and tell him I loved him. To tell him that I hadn't abandoned him and that I would never stop trying to bring him home. But that would be reckless given our current situation. We had to go *now*.

Collette seemed to be completely oblivious to the string of disasters going on beyond the buffer of her earbuds. The woman was a machine. Even my wriggling, squealing little boy didn't faze her. She simply switched him over to her other hip and maintained a steady pace toward the daycare.

"Fuck her!" I spat, fighting Jarett, who'd taken hold of my forearms and was trying to calm me down.

"Shh, shh. It's okay," he soothed as he drew me into his chest and held me tight, prompting me to burst into tears.

I cried even harder when I spotted Jenny lying in a crumpled, bleeding heap on the road. Her accident had been all my fault. She was in a coma *to the present day* because of me.

Trembling and desperate to get back to 2024, I reached for the talisman only to discover it buried beneath my shirt, under my jacket. *For fuck's sake.* We had to disappear before anyone whipped out a phone to record the chaos, which, at least for the time being, didn't seem to be an issue. Most of the bystanders were either tending to Jenny or snapping photos of the fleeing truck.

Finally, my fingers found my zipper. I yanked it down and ripped open my shirt, sending buttons flying through the air in every direction. Jarett's face was tight with concern, but he didn't know the talisman was necessary for a return timeblink.

After what seemed like an eternity instead of milliseconds, I located the talisman, snatched it out of my shirt, and grabbed Jarett's hand.

"Return!"

"Jesus!" Jarett blurted as we zapped into my bedroom half a second later, both of us buzzing with energy. Jarett bent over and put his hands on his knees to catch his breath, even though he hadn't exerted himself.

I tramped out from behind the screen, flinging my hat and sunglasses onto the dresser. "Well, that was a disaster," I said, too wired to sit down.

Jarett emerged from the screen, wriggling out of his jacket. "Definitely not what *I* expected."

"Fuck, Jarett! Jenny was run over by a truck because of me."

"That wasn't your fault."

"No? Who was she chasing?"

He grimaced. "Did she eventually die?"

"I don't know. I cut ties with that fucked-up group in 2019, but last I heard she was still hanging on. You want to hear something crazy?"

"Sure. I haven't had enough crazy today."

"A couple of days after that accident, the cops came to my house asking questions about my relationship with Jenny."

"Nothing unusual about that."

"No, but get this. They were looking for two witnesses—a man and a woman in their late thirties, the woman with some pretty nasty scratches on her face. Clearly, that was us."

"Aha, and here we are, all safe and sound in 2024."

I nodded. "I remember slapping one of the cops' hands away when she got all touchy-feely with my face. Now I know what was going on."

"She was looking for the scratches."

"And of course, there were none on my twenty-seven-year-old face."

"That *is* crazy. But what led them to you if you were nowhere near the scene?"

"Candace's statement, I'm guessing. She probably mentioned how Jenny kept insisting she saw *Syd Brixton*. Not too many people with that name in town."

"Or the country, for that matter."

I sighed. "Damn, why did she have to run after me?"

"Don't beat yourself up about it. What's done is done. Let's focus on the positive things right now, okay? We know Christopher is safe."

My stomach dropped. "Safe, maybe, but he looked absolutely miserable. Did you see how that woman was treating him?"

He shook his head. "I get the feeling we saw different things."

"Seriously? She was totally manhandling him."

"Sorry, but it didn't seem like she was mistreating him at

all. Is it possible you're looking for a reason to be angry with her and you're blowing things a little out of proportion?"

"I'm not blowing things out of proportion, Jarett. She kidnapped my son. Are you saying I'm not allowed to be concerned about his wellbeing?"

"That's not what I'm saying at all. Look, I've seen my share of mistreated kids over the years. It comes with the job. What I observed wasn't abuse. Stern treatment, maybe. But not abuse."

His calm words gave me pause. Perhaps I *had* read more into the situation than was warranted. I sighed. "Fine. I'll drop it, then."

"You're obviously on high alert, and the smallest things can seem huge. That's why I'm here. To be an objective voice. Your sounding board."

I smiled, thankful for his support. "You're right, I should be focusing on the great news that my baby is still alive, and that we know where he is. The question is…how do we get him back?"

"Why don't you ask Collette?"

"I thought we were finished with crazy talk." I pulled off my jacket and lowered myself wearily to the edge of the bed.

Jarett sat down next to me. "If there's anything I've learned from all my years on the force, it's that the biggest problems arise when people make assumptions. You're assuming she's this evil witch, but maybe she has her reasons."

"*Reasons?*" I cried. "What reason would someone have for stealing another person's child?"

"I'm not saying it's right, but it's happened, and you can't do anything about it now. Why not simply ask her why she's taken your son? Once you know that, you can build a strategy, because right now, you don't have one."

"Is that what it seems like to you?"

"Yep."

I frowned and folded my arms. "Okay, smarty pants, what if Collette refuses to tell me why she took him?"

"You're really good at that."

"What?"

"Asking *what if.*"

"Sue me. I prefer to look for sharks before diving into the water."

"That's fine, but don't forget there are angelfish in there, too."

"Ugh. Why do you have to be so rational? It's irritating," I laughed, despite my sour mood.

He patted my knee. "I wouldn't be a very good cop if I didn't consider all sides of the story."

"Collette is no angelfish."

"Just do me a favor and think about it, okay?"

"Fine."

"In the meantime, you should probably tend to your scratches, before they scar."

I got up to inspect my face in the mirror. "Shit. I can't go back until these are gone."

"That's okay. It'll give us time to work on our plan."

"You again, with the logic."

"Aren't you glad you made me your partner?"

Over my shoulder in the mirror, I saw Jarett take off his glasses and hang them on his shirt, completely unaware I was watching him. As much as I hated to admit it, with or without glasses, the guy was smoking hot. I shook my head. Morley had teased me about this once—me hooking up with Jarett. In fact, thinking back, he'd practically insisted on it.

As if sensing the thread of my thoughts, Jarett looked up, caught my eye, and smiled.

I returned the gesture, and as I tucked a few loose strands of hair behind my ear, Jarett's phone buzzed on the dresser, breaking the spell. He all but leapt off the bed.

"I bet that's my new boss. He's got a ton of paperwork for me to do before next week."

Giving him some privacy, I hurried out of the bedroom, and as I leaned against the kitchen counter guzzling a glass of water a few minutes later, I could feel a shift inside my heart. Not a big one, but enough to make me wonder if perhaps Morley had been right. Perhaps it *was* time to consider my options in the love department. I let out a long, heavy sigh.

"Sounds serious," Jarett said, rounding the corner. I hadn't heard him coming.

"Oh? Was it your boss?"

"I was referring to your sigh. Sounds serious. You okay?"

"Sure. Yeah."

"Guess I'll have to take your word for it."

"I'm fine. Just angry. And frustrated."

He reached out and stroked my forearm, an innocent gesture that sent a burst of electricity through my body just the same.

"Hey," he said, getting me to look up at him. "I need to know if you're going to be okay, because I have to go out for a bit."

"At this hour?"

Jarett pulled his phone out of his back pocket. "It's five o'clock."

"God, it feels like midnight."

"Doesn't it? I'm beat."

"That happens sometimes after a physically or mentally challenging timeblink. Morley coined it *blink-lag*. I've gotten used to it."

"I'll never get used to it—and I don't mean the fatigue. I mean the freedom we have to visit the past whenever we like."

"And the future, too. Perhaps when Collette so willingly hands over my son, she'll explain how she's been able to timeblink beyond her own lifetime. Not that I would want to do that myself."

"Really? You wouldn't want to go to, say, 3024, and see how the world is chugging along?"

I pushed myself off the counter. "I don't want to know what *tomorrow* brings, let alone a thousand years from now. Besides, what if the world has self-destructed by then?"

"Aha, there you go with your *what ifs* again."

"Whatever. I gotta go clean up these scratches. What time will you be home? I mean, *back?*"

Jarett gave me a mischievous smile, relishing my slip-up. "No later than eight, honeybunch."

I shook my head. "You just don't stop, do you?"

Chapter Sixteen

After Jarett had left, I couldn't sit still, so I'd changed into my sweats, whipped my hair into a French braid, and went for an invigorating run along the seawall. When I got back an hour later, I was relieved to find the condo still empty. Without stopping to shower or change, I threw on my green hoodie and drove over to Kendall's place for some big-sisterly commiseration.

As I kicked off my shoes in Kendall's front hall, Jinx ambled in on his rickety old legs to greet me. He followed me into the kitchen where I found Kendall editing photos on her laptop.

"Jinx looks happy," I said. "Thanks for looking after the old guy through all this."

"Of course," she said, without looking up from her screen. "The boys adore him—in fact, they keep asking for a labradoodle of their ow—holy shit, Syd! What happened to your face?"

I laughed, grazing my fingers over my cheek, having forgotten how terrible I looked. "I was hoping it wasn't that noticeable."

"Maybe not to a blind person."

"Don't hold back on my account," I said.

"Seriously, though. Did you provoke a cat or something?"

The cat thing again. "I got into a fight with a rose bush."

"Ouch. It looks brutal."

I looked over each shoulder as I shrugged out of my hoodie. "Are the boys still at soccer practice?"

"Yep. I swear extracurricular activities were invented by a frazzled mom. They'll be gone another hour, maybe more if I'm lucky. My angel of a husband is taking them for burgers afterwards."

She slammed her laptop shut, picked up her half-full glass of white wine, and padded into the living room in bare feet. "I'm done," she said, settling onto her favorite spot at the far end of the couch where she had the best view of Alice Bay. Today the whole room was filled with a vibrant orange glow from the dipping sun, which calmed me instantly. I helped myself to a glass of water and joined Kendall on the opposite end of the couch, hugging my legs to my chest. Jinx padded in after me and cautiously lowered himself to the floor where he let out a contented grunt.

"I still can't believe *roses* did that to your face." Kendall said. "How? When?"

"Ha, you're full of questions, aren't you? The *when* part might surprise you: 2014. At Lighthouse Park."

Her face lit up. "Oh my god! You can timeblink again?"

I nodded. "I was right. It was Collette who took Christopher."

"Where is he?" She peered around me as if I'd left him waiting in the front hall.

"I didn't say I brought him back with me. He's still in 2014."

"Uh-oh."

"That's why I'm here." I licked my lips and focused on the dazzling sunset reflecting off Alice Bay. Earlier, as I'd cleaned the blood from my face and applied a bandage to a deep scratch along my jaw, I'd had a disturbing revelation. It was why I hadn't been able to just sit at home by myself, waiting for Jarett to come back. It was why I needed my sister's support.

"What's going on?" she said.

"I don't think Christopher will be coming home." I inhaled deeply. "Ever."

She sat up straighter and opened her mouth to say something, but what could she say? No words could ever soothe the pain in my heart.

"He's on Collette's return timeblink. Just like Sam is on mine," I said.

The worry lines in Kendall's forehead made her look ten years older. "That means nothing," she said. "Sam hasn't even tried going back to his natural time, so how would you know it's not possible?"

"Think about it. Collette took him, so obviously, Collette needs to bring him back. I've been so focused on finding Christopher that I didn't even think about the logistics of getting him home. And now that I have, I'm sure about one thing: it's out of my control."

Kendall made a huffing sound like my concerns weren't valid.

"We were *this* close to him, Kenny," I said, thrusting my thumb and forefinger in the air. "This fucking close. But then everything spiraled out of control, and we had to get out of there."

"We?"

"Me and Jarett."

Her eyebrows went up. She was hurt, perhaps, that I hadn't taken her with me instead.

"He's a cop." I was too tired to elaborate further. "Honestly though, I'm a little relieved we had to cut our mission short, given what I just told you."

Kendall shook her head slowly, not ready to embrace the

defeat I'd already accepted. "Are you going to go back and try?"

"What? Bringing Christopher home? I honestly don't know. Even if I somehow succeeded, I'd run the risk that Christopher might not be able to see any of us when we got here. Or worse, what if Christopher got stuck somewhere in between? I'm terrified to do *anything*."

"So now what?"

My shoulders sagged. "No idea."

"What about Sam? Couldn't you do a test run with him first?"

"No. It's totally different."

"How?"

"Sam's on my return timeblink...to his future. Christopher has been taken to the past."

"Why would it be any different?"

On the surface, using Sam as my guinea pig wasn't a terrible idea, but my hope quickly faded. "He'd never go for it. He's happy now. His marriage is great. The kids are fine. He got to skip the whole freaking pandemic. Why would he voluntarily go back to 2019 and throw that all away?"

"I bet he'd be willing to give it a shot. For Christopher's sake."

"I don't know, Kenny."

"Well, don't rule it out. You don't seem to have a lot of options."

"Fine, I'll think about it. But only as a last resort. I need to talk to Collette first."

Kendall's eyes went wide. "Wait, you two are friends now?"

"What? No! She *stole my son!*"

"Don't bite my head off. I'm just curious why you're meeting with Collette."

"I don't know. I'm a glutton for punishment."

"Maybe you could ask her why she took Christopher."

I groaned. "Are you and Jarett in cahoots? Who *cares* why she took him?"

"Because maybe you could talk her off the ledge. Convince her to return Christopher, no strings attached."

"Are you sure you haven't teamed up with Jarett?"

She shook her head. "How are things going with him, anyway? He seems pretty smitten with you."

My cheeks went pink. Kendall noticed, even though the whole room was now bathed in the same color. "Ooh, do I detect some hanky-panky going on?"

"Whatever. Who even says 'hanky-panky' anymore? What are you, eighty?"

"No, no, no. You're not getting out of this so easily. Come on, girl, what's up? Jarett's dick, I hope."

"None of your business," I said, rising to my feet to get a refill of water. "More wine?"

"Nah, I'm good. I want to be sober for this conversation!"

"I told you—"

"Yeah, yeah. None of my business. But guess what? You don't have to say a thing. You've always been an open book when it comes to the men in your life, even when you're trying desperately to keep things to yourself."

As I watched the water streaming into my glass, my mind went back to Coop—a.k.a. Viktor—the vile, child-abducting asshole that had almost killed me and my sisters the night I'd discovered Isla in his secret house. Kendall was right. I'd been head over heels, too mesmerized by his phony love, fake kindness, and drop-dead gorgeous exterior to see the monster he was inside. Kendall had always sensed something off about him. She'd even tried to steer me away from him several times before he'd moved in with me.

"I wish you'd met Morley," I said, returning to the living room.

"Don't change the subject."

"I'm not. It has to do with Jarett."

Her head cocked the way it does when one of her boys was trying to fib his way out of trouble.

"For real," I sighed. "Jarett insists Morley is holding me hostage."

"Is he?"

"No. Not on purpose. What does it matter, anyway? It's my choice to be with him. He's never forced me to do anything. In fact, when he spent that week helping me and my friends get back to 2024, he pretty much begged me to get on with my life."

"As in, finding someone else?"

I nodded. "He even suggested Jarett—as a joke, mind you, but it did come up."

"So, what's stopping you?"

"I'm not ready. I won't be until this Christopher thing is resolved, at least."

"I get that. You're a family, despite its bizarre makeup."

Neither of us spoke for a few moments. A table lamp next to Kendall clicked to life as the last sliver of sun dropped out of sight.

"What do you think?" I said, clearing my throat. "About Jarett?"

"It doesn't matter what I think."

"Oh, I beg to differ."

She gave me a curious look.

"Don't act dumb. You have the craziest ability to smell a skunk before anyone else."

"You mean Viktor? Sweetie, that was as obvious as the nose on his face."

"So, how could I have been so blind to it?"

"It's amazing what a person will ignore when they've set their sights on the object of their desires. I see it all the time in my business. And it's not always the groom that's the bad apple. It works both ways."

"Thank goodness I never walked down the aisle with my bad apple."

"No kidding," she said. "So, back to Jarett. It doesn't matter what I think about him. What do *you* think?"

I shrugged. "He's good-looking, I guess."

"Well, obviously. But do you see yourself with him?"

"Maybe? I don't know. We've only known each other a few months."

"A pretty intense few months. The dude's been coming to Port Raven weekly since you met. And now he's moving here."

"Because of *Sam*. The two of them are attached at the hip."

"I got news for you: it has nothing to do with Sam. When was the last time Jarett came to hang out with Sam that he didn't make plans with you afterwards?"

"We almost had sex."

Her eyebrows raised. "*Almost?*"

"Fortunately, Christopher and Morley stopped me. Well, not literally. The guilt got to me, and I stopped that train before it left the station."

"That's a damned shame."

With weariness settling in my bones, I closed my eyes, reliving that moment of possibility. This time, the *what ifs* would've made even Jarett blush. What if I'd heeded Morley's advice to move on with my life? What would it have been like to surrender myself to Jarett and shut the world out with him for—

Kendall's voice broke the silence, anchoring me to the present. "Good grief, Syd. Don't wait too long or that ship's going to sail."

Just then, my phone burst to life with the first few bars of Jarett's text-tone music from the coffee table. "Speak of the devil," I said, snatching it up.

"*For Your Eyes Only?*" Kendall chuckled. I'd added it months ago, after watching an old Bond film with Pierce Brosnan playing the lead role. Kendall always insisted Jarett looked like Carlos Sainz Jr., the F1 racecar driver, but the moment I saw the Bond movie, I knew she'd been wrong. He was the spitting image of a young Pierce Brosnan, and of course, I had to make his text-tone the greatest Bond song of all time.

"That was fast," I said, ignoring Kendall's teasing. "He's home already."

"Ahh! I forgot he was living with you now."

"*Staying* with me. I've got him set up in the spare bedroom."

Kendall flashed me a look; one that said, "*Let's see how long that lasts.*"

When I didn't get up, she said, "What the hell are you waiting for? Go finish what you started!"

"I'm not in the mood."

"Surely you can rustle up some libido from your dusty loins. You've been single for nearly five years."

That stung. "I have *not* been single."

"Right. How could I forget about your boyfriend in the black hole?"

"He's my fiancé if you don't mind. And he's the father of my son. You'd do the same if Brett died and you had a way to visit him anytime you liked." I unfolded my legs and jumped to my feet. "As a matter of fact, that's what I'm going to do right now."

"Oh my god, Syd. Forget Morley. You have Officer Dreamboat waiting for you at home. Don't blow it!"

I grabbed my hoodie off the chair in the kitchen. "Don't tell me what to do."

"For God's sake, even Isla's dating now."

She followed me as I tramped into the front hall and slipped into my shoes. Jinx plodded up behind me where I offered him a quick scratch under his chin. His old, sad eyes tore right through my soul.

"Don't be angry," Kendall said. "I'm just saying that maybe Jarett's right. Maybe Morley *is* holding you hostage, even if it's unintentional."

I opened the door. "I'm not angry. I'm exhausted. And you know what? None of this bullshit matters when Christopher is still out there, and I don't know how to get him home."

Kendall rubbed my arm reassuringly then pulled me in for a hug. "You'll find a way. If there's anything I know about my little sister is that she's pretty good a smashing through brick walls with her bare fists."

I pulled back. "Thanks for the chat. Say hi to the boys for me."

She sighed deeply. "I will. And don't dismiss the Sam option. I'm sure he'd be happy to help get your baby home."

I nodded but had no intention of asking Sam to be my lab rat. I'd already marooned him in one foreign timeline. There was no way I was going to drag him into another.

Fifteen minutes later, I pulled into a parking spot at the seawall where I'd gone for my run earlier and rolled my window down partway. I closed my eyes and listened to the surf lapping against a low, wind-beaten concrete wall separating the road from the sea. This was my happy place. It helped me think.

I was in no state to face Jarett; the mere thought of going back to the condo and seeing him there made me anxious. I considered dropping in on Isla and Finn, but I was in no mood to go over the latest developments in my quest to get Christopher back or to make idle chit-chat with an inquisitive ten-year-old.

I settled on the next best thing: some "me-time" on the beach. It was dark already, but I had never been worried for my safety on the seawall path at night. Bright streetlights and well-tended heritage homes lined the entire stretch, and there was always someone peering out a window at the ocean and its ever-changing canvas.

As I walked south, my sister's words persisted in my head. I hadn't been serious about slipping to the past to see Morley, because as much as it saddened me, I was starting to see the logic in Kendall's—and Jarett's—observations. I was losing myself to a ghost from the past at the expense of building a life in the present.

Still, I'd told them time and time again that this arrangement between Morley and me couldn't last forever. They knew it came with an expiry date. Why couldn't they just let me ride it out?

An elderly couple trundled by and said hello as they passed. I imagined them arriving home a few minutes later, hanging their coats by the door, and shuffling into a living room filled with a lifetime's collection of photographs and keepsakes. They'd revel in all the beautiful memories of a life well lived, or perhaps share quiet tears about people they missed.

I couldn't envision a similar future for me just then. Not with my life in its current state of flux.

I passed only three other people—a young couple walking a rambunctious Dachshund puppy and a middle-aged man who smiled but made sure not to hold my gaze any longer than necessary after a quick hello—before coming to the break in the low wall I'd been watching for. As I ducked through the gap, I took a quick scan of my surroundings. I was alone, save for the man I'd passed who was settling onto a bench a safe distance down the path. Satisfied no one was going to bother me, I descended the wooden stairs to the small cove where I brushed some sand off a log and sat down. I'd been there often enough to know that this section of the beach was on high ground, and I wouldn't have to worry about the tide flowing in and soaking my shoes.

As the waves tumbled restlessly over stones at the shore, they made soft, rushing noises that sounded like whispers. If only those whispers could provide the answers to my problems —the biggest one, of course, being the question of what to do about Collette.

"Fuck this," I said out loud, not worried about anyone hearing me. I was clearly alone. It was the second Tuesday of the new school year and already the city seemed hunkered down, immersed in its post-summer groove. Thus, there was little danger of anyone bothering me. It was just me and the whispering waves.

It gave me a chance to review all the balls I was currently juggling.

One: Christopher was alive and seemingly healthy.

Two: Collette didn't appear to be aware that Jarett and I had been following her.

Three: I couldn't go back to 2014 until the scratches on my face healed.

Four: I categorically could not go home and jump into bed with Jarett.

This left me with one obvious course of action: to seek refuge in Morley's world.

Long enough to say goodbye to the love of my life for good.

A certainty surged into my heart as I keyed in the entry code at the cabin a few minutes later. This was for the best. Morley had been hounding me to get on with my life ever since I'd started timeblinking, so it wouldn't come as a shock that I was finally acting on his counsel.

Stepping inside, I felt my nerve dwindling. "Don't chicken out now," I whispered, padding up the stairs.

There was one thing I knew for sure: I wouldn't dare tell

Morley what Collette had been up to or that I might lose Christopher. No. Morley had so little time left as it was; news like that would make his last days miserable. I would have to be content with losing myself in his arms one last time, tucked away in our little hideaway where life wasn't so complicated.

It was eleven-twenty on June fifteenth, the same night I'd last come. That timeblink had in fact only been about an hour ago in Morley's timeline, so for all intents and purposes, we were picking up exactly where we'd left off after my abrupt exit earlier.

It was safe to assume Morley would be dozing heavily since he'd mentioned how beat he'd been after our romp on the bearskin rug, but I made sure to be quiet anyway, so as not to disturb him. I don't know why. By this point in our time-blinking journey, Morley hardly ever stirred when I slipped into bed late at night. To him, it was as though I'd merely gotten up to go to the bathroom, whereas for me, days, weeks, or even months could have elapsed in the meantime. He was lucky in that respect. My constant presence meant he wouldn't spend his final days alone.

After a quick shower, I tossed my sweats on the armchair and pulled a silk nightie from the dresser. It was one of the few articles of clothing that stayed rooted in this timeline—unlike my daytime clothing, which often wound up in different realms. At first, my misplaced wardrobe had been an annoyance, but after a while, I'd come to accept it as a charming little quirk of timeblinking. I'd even started buying duplicates of my favorite pieces so I could access them in both timelines.

When I approached the bed, Morley was facing away from the window, as was his habit on such bright, moonlit nights. He had one hand tucked under his cheek and his legs bent into a loose fetal position. His breaths came in small, fragmented bursts suggesting a lighter stage of sleep, but he didn't so much as twitch when I tucked in behind him. With my cheek pressed between his shoulder blades, I felt my throat tighten, remembering what I'd come to do.

A thought popped into my mind about how utterly bizarre my visits must be for Morley. Whereas he remained perpetually forty-nine years old and looked the same to me every time, I would always come to him at different ages, perhaps with a different hairstyle, a little more weight around my middle, or with sun-kissed skin in the morning that might be ghostly pale when I returned later the same day. No matter how many years passed in my timeline, none of the changes seemed to faze him. His flattering words and gentle caresses reassured me I was still as beautiful to him at thirty-six as I'd been at thirty-two, and every age in between.

I took a deep breath, ready to wake him, undeterred by the late hour. Delaying things any longer would make me crazy. But Morley made a crude snorting sound that roused him out of sleep, beating me to the punch. He rolled over and swept his fingers along my cheek.

"There you are, love. I've missed you," he said, partly in jest, before asking me what date I'd come from.

"Same date, a few hours later. Just picking up where we left off."

"Aha. So you're here to coax me back down to the bearskin rug."

"Not exactly." It was tempting, though. One last hurrah before we parted ways wouldn't hurt, would it? I clamped my eyes shut, silently screaming *No!* inside my head. It was too late for that. My mind was made up.

"Come on. I know you're hopeless to resist my charms," he teased, slipping my nightie strap off my shoulder. I put it back immediately.

"Don't do this, Morley. Please."

"Don't do what, love? I thought you were raring to go."

"Yes, but…"

When I couldn't bring myself to go on, he tilted my chin up to look me in the eye. "Is everything okay?"

Well, that was it.

A barking sob exploded from my depths, startling Morley. He bolted upright, knowing I reserved tears only for the worst events. And there were plenty of those lately.

"Has something happened to Christopher?"

I wailed even harder. They were just a few simple words, but they packed a wallop.

Morley guided my head into his lap. Much to my relief, I found he was wearing his pajama bottoms, making my meltdown less awkward for both of us.

He handed me some tissues from the bedside table and rubbed my back while I sopped up my tears, and when I had no more left, he remained quiet. His dread was palpable. He expected the worst, no doubt. It wouldn't be fair to continue keeping him in the dark now.

He propped a pillow against the headboard for me to lean on and helped me sit up. Once he'd flicked on the lamp, brought me a glass of water, and made sure I was comfortable, he sat down next to me.

"Everything's a mess," I finally said, before spilling my guts about the whole wretched state of my life in 2024: that Collette had kidnapped our son, that I'd gone back to 2014 to retrieve him, and that over time I'd come to believe a rescue wouldn't be possible. Then I confessed my feelings for a cop named Jarett. He took that part amazingly well—which hurt, honestly—though he was clearly devastated by the news of Collette's betrayal. That hurt, too, but for different reasons.

"I wish it wasn't true."

He lowered his gaze to his lap. "It can't be," he said. "She just wouldn't do that."

His denial stung. It felt like he was accusing me of fabricating the whole thing.

"Well, she did. We spotted her with Christopher in 2014."

His head snapped up. "We?"

Shit. I hadn't meant to tell him that part.

I inhaled deeply. "I couldn't do it alone. Jarett's been such a huge help with this whole fiasco, first with getting the talisman back and—"

"Getting it *back*?" Morley exclaimed, pushing himself up off the bed, thrusting his hands to his hips. "Where did it go?"

"I...I—"

"And what happened to keeping timeblinking between you and me?"

Two timeblinks in one day must have made my brain fuzzy. I was gushing information like lava spews from Vesuvius, with similar devastating results.

"Don't be angry. Just...hear me out."

I'd never seen him so agitated. He went over to the armchair and shifted my running clothes to one side so he could sit down. Apparently he felt the need to put some distance between us.

"I'm listening."

"First of all, how I lost the talisman isn't important. Just know that it was gone, and Jarett helped me get it back. It's why I didn't come here for four months. I *couldn't*."

He pressed his lips together and let me finish.

"Now that I have the power back, my sole focus is on bringing our son home. Whatever it takes. And if it means enlisting outside help, you can't be upset about that."

The tense set of his shoulders softened. "So, why did you come back? You already got the information you needed earlier today."

I scooted over to the edge of the bed, drawing the blanket from the end of the bed over my shoulders.

"When I lost the talisman," I began, "I was devastated. It meant I would never see you again. We would never go paddling on the lake or enjoy romantic dinners together or have crazy sex on the bearskin rug." He smiled wistfully at that. "And I wouldn't be able to bring you updates on Christopher anymore."

"That's life, love. We lose people we care about. And we move on."

I glanced down at the chunky ring encircling my thumb without drawing attention to it. I hadn't yet given it to Morley in this timeline, and it took all my might not to recite its inscription to him now. *To live in hearts we leave behind is not to die.*

"Deep down, I know that. But with the power of time-blinking at my fingertips, it's impossible to walk away. Believe me, Morley. I've tried."

He shook his head knowingly.

"Naturally, when the talisman went missing, I went into shock. I might as well have lost a limb." I paused, choosing my next words carefully. "On the other hand, its absence would've forced me to get on with my life. And it had, to a point. I'd pretty much come to terms with the fact that the talisman, and you, were lost to me forever. Then, *wham*, Christopher disappeared, and I was back to square one. Worse, because our innocent little boy had been dragged into Collette's jealous hissy fit."

Morley flinched at those words, and I regretted saying them. Collette's motives were still somewhat of a question mark.

He sighed. "So, your search for the talisman resumed."

"Yes, but I wasn't even looking for it when it showed up."

He gave me a puzzled look.

"About two weeks after Christopher's abduction, it literally appeared out of the blue. As did a whole world of opportunity. It meant that I would be able to find Christopher *and* be reunited with you."

He got up and joined me on the bed, sliding his arm around my waist. "I apologize for lashing out. I should have waited to hear the whole story."

I leaned into him. "It's okay. You couldn't have known

what I was going through. I just didn't want to burden you with all this bullshit in your last days. Especially since there's nothing you can do about it."

"You think not? I still have the ability to timeblink. I could go back to 2014."

I twisted away from him, allowing myself to become excited about the idea before recognizing its major flaw. "What's the point if Collette can't see you?"

"Ah, but invisibility could be an advantage. I could follow her, maybe prevent her from taking Christopher in the first place."

"We both know that's not possible."

"Until now, we believed timeblinking beyond one's own lifetime wasn't possible. Collette has certainly blown that theory out of the water."

I gasped. "Oh my god, Morley. If we find out how she does it, maybe you could live with me and Christopher in the future and—"

He put his finger to my lips. "Syd. You know that's not going to work."

As usual, he was right. Damn it, anyway. Why was I still trying to keep the flame alive when I'd come here to snuff it out?

"I don't know what's wrong with me."

"You've been through a lot. It's natural to be scattered."

"Scattered? More like completely unhinged."

We sat in quiet reflection for a few moments, allowing my nerves to settle. I curled into him again, resting my head on his chest.

"Oh, Morley. I wanted so much to believe our story wasn't over."

"Me too, love." He gave me a quick kiss on my temple. "Me too."

"I guess it's really coming to an end, isn't it?"

He chuckled. "I never thought I'd hear you say that."

"Maybe I'm just growing tired of it all. We've been at it for five years now. Well, at least I have."

"You've done a spectacular job of making this long-distance relationship work so well—for so long—and for that I'm grateful. Most people wouldn't have had the patience."

"I'm just stubborn as hell. You must know that by now."

"*Tenacious.* Not stubborn. It's one of your sexiest traits."

When I didn't answer, he cupped my cheek and tilted my face up to meet his eyes. "Maybe it's time you got on with your life in 2024. Once you bring Christopher home—"

"*If* I bring Christopher home."

"*When* you bring our little boy home, I implore of you: leave me in your past. By all means, tell Christopher what an amazing, talented, handsome father he had," he said facetiously, "but try to keep our love in your heart. Not in your head."

It was good advice. Advice I hoped to be able to stick to. "I'll try."

"It's all you can do, love. Besides, don't you have Jared to think about now?"

My tummy did a backflip. "Jarett."

"Jarett, then." He paused to bite his bottom lip. "Is he a good guy?"

"Sure. I guess."

"Wow, sounds like a real Cinderella story."

I patted his leg and nodded to the clock on his nightstand.

"Aha. Just like that, the clock strikes midnight on our fairytale."

Chapter Seventeen

SEPTEMBER 11, 2024, 6:45 A.M.

Agent Jimmy Lopez

"I appreciate your continued assistance," Lopez said, joining Sam on the same seaside bench he'd occupied the night before. Beyond the low concrete barrier separating them from the rocky beach, the water was calm, glistening in the first rays of morning sunshine. "There's been a development in the Flight 444 case since we last met."

Sam took a sip from his insulated mug, his face turning solemn. "I'm guessing it's a doozie, given the early hour. And the fact that we're not meeting at the station."

Lopez caught a whiff of coffee on Sam's breath, feeling annoyed that he'd had to give up the juice last year. "A doozie indeed. I tailed your friend Syd here last night. She parked just over there and went down to that small cove." Lopez pointed to the gap in the barrier about fifty feet down the path. "She was dressed in black leggings and a lime-green hoodie, and her hair was pulled into a braid at the back. I think they call it a French braid. And she had a bunch of nasty-looking scratches on her face."

Sam leaned forward—intrigued, Lopez thought—but he didn't speak.

Lopez trained his eyes on a seagull picking at some garbage down the path. "It's amazing, the weird things you learn in the course of this job if you're patient."

"Weird as in a thirty-six-year-old woman dressed in a neon green hoodie? Or weird as in you know the type of braid she had in her hair?"

"Not even close," Lopez said. "Weird that when she re-emerged not fifteen minutes later, the scratches on her face were gone."

"Woah. That *is* a huge development."

"Cut the sarcasm. You didn't let me finish. I also noticed she was wearing a completely different outfit, and her hair was loose. Curly."

Sam took another pull of his coffee. "So?"

"So…the hoodie was gonzo, and she was wearing a long-sleeved black blouse instead. And ripped jeans instead of black tights."

"Couldn't she have changed while she was down at the beach?"

"That's what I told myself at first. I mean, what else could have happened? Then I remembered Abby's hair."

"Abby?"

"My daughter. When she was a little gaffer, she always had her hair in braids. My wife insisted on it 'cause Abby hated getting her hair brushed, and she especially hated getting the tangles combed out. The braids kept her hair tangle-free."

"I don't see the connection."

"When Abby let her hair loose after a day in braids, it was invariably kinky. Not curly like Syd's was. There's a difference."

"True. I have a daughter too. I still don't see why any of that matters."

"Come on, Sam. You're a detective, and a damn good one, from what I hear. This is elementary observational stuff. It doesn't make sense that Syd was sporting a headful of salon-perfect curls—not a hair out of place—when only a few minutes earlier, it had been tightly bound at the back of her head."

Sam shrugged indifferently. "So? Maybe she braided it right before you saw her, and it didn't have time to get kinky."

Now satiated, the garbage-eating seagull took three running steps and launched itself into the air. Both men watched it dive toward the water and soar along the surface.

"Why are you trying to sweep the facts under the rug, Sam?"

"That's not it at all. I'm simply keeping my mind open. I've been burned too many times when I've made assumptions."

"Facts aren't assumptions. I know what I saw."

"What you *think* you saw."

"What does that mean?"

"You do realize Syd Brixton has an identical twin, right?"

Lopez opened then shut his mouth without answering.

"Aha. Are you sure it was Syd that came up from the beach and not Isla?"

"As a matter of fact, yes. I went down there after she left, and the place was deserted. Not another soul in sight."

"Did you check the whole beach?"

"Sure did. It's a small cove, only accessible by that one sct of stairs. Go on, take a look."

"Not necessary. I grew up here."

"Anyway, the tide was in last night, cutting the cove off from the rest of the shoreline. That means one of the twins would've had to take a frigid late-night swim—in her clothes, no less—to get to the other beach."

"What are you getting at, Jimmy? So what if Syd changed her clothes or if she and her sister were pranking you."

Lopez smiled at a fit-looking gray-haired couple in matching jogging suits as they strode by. He spoke again when they were a healthy distance down the path. "Well, Sam. The green hoodie is what really got me spooked."

"You were spooked by a sweater? That *is* odd. I usually get spooked by snakes. And lawyers. Though they're kind of the same thing, aren't they?"

Lopez ignored Sam's joke. "What got my attention was that she wasn't carrying the hoodie when she came up from the beach. Again, it wasn't there when I went down to check."

"And this is relevant because…?"

"Don't play coy with me. You know exactly what's going on, and yet you continue to dance around the truth."

"Exactly what truths do you think I'm dancing around?"

"It's not so much what you're hiding—because I'm pretty sure that list is long—but more that you're hell-bent on leading me away from obvious clues. Like this beach incident. A skilled detective—which I know you are—wouldn't be arguing with me about these facts."

"Sounds like you've got trust issues, Jimmy. Remember, *you* recruited *me* for this investigation. I didn't weasel my way in."

Lopez looked at Sam thoughtfully, remembering the real reason he'd recruited him. It mostly had to do with the old adage about keeping your friends close and your enemies closer.

Sam shook his head irritably. "Give me the facts so far. I'll tell you if I think they're relevant to your investigation."

"I've told you everything. *The 444 Five* boarded a plane in Chicago on April 11, 2024. That same aircraft crashed fifty-one minutes later in farmland on the Iowa-Minnesota border. Around the same time, your friend Syd called 911 to report that she and four other people from the flight had woken up, disoriented and unscathed, in a cornfield near Waverly, Iowa, without a clue as to how they'd arrived there. Now we have last night's green hoodie incident where not only did Ms. Brixton undergo a complete makeover in less than fifteen minutes, but her previously scratched face had also completely healed."

"So, what do you think this all points to?"

"Something that could change the world as we know it."

"Well, now I'm intrigued. Do tell."

Lopez raised his hand to his mouth and began chewing at his thumbnail, thinking out his next words carefully. When he lowered his hand, he caught Sam's gaze and held it.

"This is classified, Sam. I'm trusting you to keep it to yourself."

"Of course."

Lopez looked left and right. "It was something Jenkins said during our stakeout at Sandalwood Lake. It got me rethinking the whole situation with Ms. Brixton and her crew."

"And?"

Lopez shook his head impatiently. "Look, I believe *The 444 Five* are onto something huge. Something that could end wars and famine and disease."

"For chrissake, Lopez, spill it already."

The agent inhaled deeply through his nose. "I believe *The 444 Five* have some kind of supernatural powers. A lot of the evidence we've gathered points to the possibility that they may even be time travelers."

Sam's head snapped back in surprise before his expression softened into wry amusement. "Hah! Good one."

"I'm serious. And I haven't even told you the main reason I believe this."

Sam took a worried glance over his shoulder. "Have you shared this theory with anyone else?"

"Only you, so far."

"Good. Because crazy talk like that will get you early retirement."

The agent grunted irritably. "I've got less than a year left anyway, so that's the least of my concerns. I'm just asking you to think about it. How else would they have gotten off that plane intact?"

"I'm working on it, my friend. You just gotta give me time."

"Time," Lopez grumbled. "I'm telling you. Syd and her little entourage have found a way to defy the established constraints of time. Mark my words."

Sam wrapped his bottom lip over his top one, apparently considering the possibility. "I mean, it's not a terrible theory. But again, I would caution you about throwing it out there before you have proof."

"Why do you think I called this off-the-record meeting?"

Sam drained his cup and set it on the ground in front of him. "You need my help."

"Yes. You're in the best position to do it, considering your affiliation with the group."

"All right, lay it on me."

"First of all, don't worry." He patted the left side of his chest. "The only place I've recorded this theory is in my good old-fashioned notepad. I'll submit a full report eventually, but not until I get the conclusive proof I need to make a water-tight case. And I'm close. Too damned close to risk being slapped with mental health leave now."

Sam nodded in acknowledgement.

"Secondly, as I mentioned, the only reason I'm involving you is because of your connection to the group. In fact, if I didn't know better, I'd swear you were in bed with them on this."

"You mean the superpower thing?"

Lopez rolled his eyes. "Yes, the superpower thing. You still haven't formally reported young Christopher's disappearance. A disappearance I my colleague witnessed with his own eyes. Agent Jenkins insists he was there one minute, then poof!"

Lopez burst his fingers in the air like fireworks. "He was gone."

Sam's eyes narrowed. "I thought you said you saw a woman take him into the forest."

"Ah yes, that's the major development I mentioned, and it's the reason I'm leaning toward the time travel theory. But before I tell you about it, I need a little something from you."

"Let me guess: the real reason I haven't filed a report on the missing boy."

"You got it," Lopez said, pulling a crumpled handkerchief out of his pocket and giving his nose a thunderous blow. "I must be allergic to seaweed. Or fresh air. I don't get much of either in DC."

"Regarding Christopher—"

"Save your breath if you're about to say you're just trying to protect Ms. Brixton's privacy. I already know that's a steaming load of bull crap."

The detective's silence told Lopez everything he needed to know.

Lopez patted Sam's shoulder amicably. "So, my friend. How about it?"

Chapter Eighteen

SEPTEMBER 11, 2024, 6:47 A.M.

W hen I walked into my cheery, light-filled kitchen the next morning, Jarett was sitting at the island drinking coffee, staring at his computer screen. As I approached, a pleasurable tingle sped up my spine when I noticed his navy-blue cotton robe hanging open, giving me a glimpse of his smooth, tanned chest beneath. He snapped his laptop shut when he saw me.

"G'morning, Sunshine," he said. "I didn't hear you come home last night. What time did you get in?"

"Eleven. I was at Kendall's."

It wasn't exactly a lie. I *had* been at Kendall's. But I didn't want to tell him about my timeblink to see Morley or that I'd driven out to the cabin for a couple of hours afterward to avoid returning home.

While there, I'd also gone on a three-day timeblink to allow the worst of my scratches to heal. I'd chosen to spend the time alone at the cabin in April 2024, when I knew my family and I had been in Buffalo for my father's funeral. It had been nothing short of restorative. With the off-season solitude working in my favor, I'd gone for runs every day, read Stephen King's latest novel, *Holly*, and had even gone so far as to give the cabin a top-to-bottom scrub—which solved the mystery as to why I'd found the cabin squeaky clean after the Flight 444 fiasco.

"Impressive. You obviously have more practice dealing with blink-lag than me. I was dead tired after my meeting. Crawled into bed at eight-thirty and didn't move until half an hour ago."

I grabbed a glass and filled it with water at the fridge door, keeping a side eye on Jarett. I found myself feeling slightly giddy about this setup. It had been a long time since I'd woken up to a handsome first responder drinking coffee in my kitchen—I couldn't help but remind myself that this particular kitchen had once been Morley's, though I quickly pushed the thought out of my head.

"Good to see you getting out and about. Did you have a nice visit with your sis?"

"Yes. I told her about being able to timeblink again. She was so excited. I also got my Jinxy fix."

"How is the poor old thing?"

"Good," I said. "Jinx seems happy, too."

We both laughed. It was pleasant, this arrangement. I caught myself wondering if Morley would have approved.

"Hey!" Jarett exclaimed. "Your scratches are gone."

My hand flew up to my cheek. "Yes. I went on a timeblink to speed up the healing process."

"How long did it take?"

"Three days," I said, turning to the fridge to pull out some frozen fruit. "Can I make you a smoothie?"

"I'm good."

"Are you sure? Word has it I make the best smoothies in town." I grabbed a bag of blueberries.

"I'll take a rain check, thanks."

"Your loss. Ooh! Strawberries. I thought I was out."

"Did you see Morley?" he said to my back.

I stopped rummaging through the freezer. His question had been innocent enough. Why did it irk me so much?

"Did you have a nice time?" he continued.

I spun around, tossing the bags of fruit onto the counter with more force than I'd intended. "Do you have a problem with me visiting my son's father?"

"Not at all. I just wondered how it all went. Did you tell him about the situation with Christopher and Collette?"

Arms folded, I held his stare. "Yes. He didn't take it well. Couldn't believe his beautiful bride had done such a thing."

I deliberately chose not to mention that I'd only spent a couple of hours with Morley and that I'd pulled the plug on our relationship. If Jarett was fishing for details to feed his suspicions, I was happy to leave his hook empty. Let him stew.

Bending down, I pulled the blender out of the cupboard and set it on the counter. "Seems to me you're a teensy bit jealous."

"Of what? A dead man?"

That stung, but I refused to rise to the bait. I went to the fridge for some yogurt and bagged spinach and brought them back to the blender where I layered them in with the frozen berries and a glug of water. I could feel Jarett's eyes on me as I focused on the thick, brownish-purple liquid whirling between us. When the whine of the machine stopped, Jarett cleared his throat. "Okay, I'll admit to feeling a little threatened by your smart, handsome fellow in another time realm."

His candor tugged at my heart. If my split with Morley hadn't been so fresh, I may have offered Jarett an olive branch and confessed about the breakup. But I opted to keep him at arm's length for now.

He went on. "The whole reason I'm here right now is to support you through all of this. Nothing more. Honestly." He folded his arms and rested them on the counter. "Though I gotta admit, when you kissed me in the bathroom, I thought you wanted to take things up a notch."

I bit my bottom lip. "I'm sorry I misled you. Things are really fucked up right now. I don't know what the hell I'm doing."

"Exactly. I should've been more aware of that."

"It's not your fault."

"But it is. I should've pumped the brakes immediately—for both our sakes. Maybe then I wouldn't have been feeling quite so prickly about you ditching me to be with Morley." He flashed me a wry smile and reached his hand across the island. "Friends?"

Oh, how I wanted to tell him I'd spent less than two hours with Morley—and on a platonic level to boot. But my senses prevailed. A little distance would give my fragile heart some time to recover.

I took his hand. "Friends."

He caressed my fingers tenderly with his thumb for a few moments before letting go and leaning back. "I'm glad we had this talk."

"Me too."

"So. Now that your face is healed, is a trip to 2014 in order?"

"It sure is." I poured out two smoothies, sliding one glass toward Jarett and holding the other up. "Just as soon as I finish this."

"I still have to shower."

I took three healthy gulps of my smoothie. "I'm going by myself."

"What? I thought you needed me."

"I did, and you were a great help on our last blink. But now that I know where Collette is, I don't have to drag you into it. Sounds like it's going to get messy."

"Messy? How?"

"Morley told me someone attacked Collette at Lighthouse Park the day 'Tristan' went home. I'd rather not take the chance that it was you."

"Collette didn't get a look at her assailant?"

"Not according to Morley. Apparently, she couldn't even say for sure if her attacker was male or female. They got away clean."

"Then what does it matter if I tag along?"

I sighed. "As much as I appreciate what you've done for me—what you continue to do for me—I'd rather confront the bitch myself."

"Which is why you need backup. Emotions can cloud your judgment in situations like this."

I slugged back the rest of my drink and wiped my mouth with the back of my hand. "I appreciate your concern, Jarett. But let me have this."

He shook his head. "Oh, you can be stubborn."

"*Tenacious*," I corrected. "Look, I'll come and grab you if things start going off the rails."

"Promise?"

"Scout's honor." I raised my hand. "Now drink your smoothie before it gets warm and disgusting."

I landed in the cover of a lilac bush near the scene of Jenny's accident, but ten minutes later. Paramedics were already tending to Jenny in the street, and several police officers were busy interviewing bystanders. Collette was nowhere in sight, but I imagined she was inside the daycare dropping Christopher off and would be exiting any minute.

Keeping hidden behind the wall of lilacs, I inched my way toward the daycare and positioned myself so I had the best possible view of the front doors, praying I hadn't missed Collette. I would wait five or ten minutes before resorting to Plan B: visiting her at the condo. It wasn't a bad idea now that I knew Christopher wasn't there and Morley had surely gone to work. Collette and I could have a civil discussion in private, with no violence necessary.

Keeping my eyes glued on the daycare, I shivered in the chilly October morning. I'd been so eager to get back that didn't even think to change out of my thin yoga pants, baby tee, and flip-flops before I left.

Moments stretched into an eternity before Collette finally broke through the doors into the icy wind. She stopped to cinch the tie of her long, fuzzy sweater tighter around her waist, then set off in the direction from which she'd come. I glanced down at my exposed, unmanicured toes and felt instantly foolish. It hardly mattered. My comfort was the least pressing issue right now.

When Collette entered the far end of the rose garden maze, I knew I had to stop her before she drew us too close to Jenny's accident. I dashed across the field, my chest tight with dread. When I paused to catch my breath under a flower-covered arch at the entrance, a bittersweet memory flooded through me: I'd come here with Isla and our boys earlier in the season when the garden was a riot of color and intoxicating scent. Christopher, with his unfiltered observations of the world, had pointed to a bright red Crimson Glory rose and said, "Auntie Kenny's lips!"

Under normal circumstances, I might've stopped to admire all the late-blooming varieties, which were in surprising abundance today, but I wasn't here to smell the roses. It was all business.

We reached the center of the maze together where a weathered bronze sundial stood as a silent witness to our standoff. I'd anticipated this moment for weeks, and now that it was here—now that *she* was right in front of me—I could barely contain my rage.

But I reigned it in, remembering the assault that had sent her straight to the emergency room, because as implausible as it seemed, I had to face the distinct possibility that I had been the one to attack her.

As worry churned in my stomach, two tiny blue dragon-flies fluttered up between us and twirled around each other momentarily before darting out of sight. My eyes locked with Collette's as the buzz of retreating wings faded and a passing cloud dulled the cheery garden around us.

And in the thick silence that followed, I feared this might turn out to be the darkest day of my life.

Chapter Nineteen

SEPTEMBER 11, 2024, 6:50 A.M.

Agent Jimmy Lopez

S am drew in a long, deliberate breath of the salty air, maintaining his attention on a band of pink clouds on the horizon. When he turned to Lopez, his expression was serious. "All right. You win. It's obvious we need to start working on this thing as a team."

"Weren't we already?"

"I haven't been totally up front with you about the Christopher situation."

"No shit."

Lopez watched a middle-aged couple amble by, their laughter punctuating the quiet morning. The lighthearted sound made him long for his wife, Darlene, back in DC. By now, Darlene would be heading out the door to her part-time gig at the garden center down the street, having taken Buster, their old, decrepit bulldog out for a last-minute pee. God, he hoped Buster would still be there to greet him when this was all over.

Sam waited until the happy couple was out of earshot before addressing Lopez again. "Syd has this ex-boyfriend who's been getting increasingly unstable. Uttering threats, driving by her properties. Telling her he's going to sue her for custody now that she's under investigation for terrorism. You know, all the typical intimidation tactics. The jerk's not even Christopher's father."

"I wasn't aware she had an ex...other than the asshole who abducted her sister. What was his name? Viktor?"

"No, not Viktor. He's in prison. This is someone else."

"She doesn't have much success in the love department."

"Not at all. It's terrible what she's going through with this loser."

"Sounds like something your team might be able to help her with."

"I tried to talk her into making a formal complaint—getting a restraining order, the whole nine yards. But she was adamant, no cops. Well, except for me. And Jarett, of course."

Lopez licked his lips and waited for Sam to continue digging his hole.

"She doesn't trust the process. She's been burned by the system before and wanted to handle things off the books. To be honest, I can't really blame her."

"*To be honest?* Damnit, this is bullshit, and you know it."

"It's not. She just wanted to put the kid in hiding for a little while...a month, tops, and see if she couldn't persuade this dick to lay off."

"I don't know. It's still not sitting right with me."

"Look, I told her I was going to take it to the next level if things didn't simmer down. She wasn't happy about it, but she agreed. Just give her some time."

"So you lied to me. About why she hadn't reported the boy missing."

"No, I didn't. I said she didn't want to end up in the lime-light again. It would take one reporter on a slow news day to blow this up."

Lopez scratched his chin, wishing the detective would just

come the fuck clean, but it seemed that wasn't going to happen today. He decided not to point out the obvious: that if what Sam was saying was true, then why hadn't the FBI noticed this stalker jerk hanging around? No, it was just more evidence of Sam's duplicity and that he was doing his best to cover up the Brixton kid's disappearance.

"Remember," Sam continued, "Syd's life has been a circus sideshow more than once—first when her twin went missing, and again with the plane crash. As her friend, I only wanted to help her avoid another public spectacle. That's it."

Lopez noticed the detective's face was completely unreadable. He wasn't surprised. The man had likely undergone the same emotional intelligence training as he had and knew all the tricks.

"You're killing me here, Sam. But I've got a shit ton of work to do today, and I still haven't told you about this big break I've stumbled across."

Sam wasted no time embracing the change in topic. "Lay it on me."

"It's regarding the woman who disappeared with the Brixton kid in a puff of smoke. The thing is, we haven't been able to confirm her identity."

"Go ahead. I know you're dying to ask me if I know who she is."

"Not necessary." Lopez bent forward, resting his elbows on his knees. He felt a joint pop in his lower back. It was a good pop. "As I was saying. This woman. She didn't initially come up on facial recognition. That is, until we handed the photos off to our tech team in DC. It took a few days, but we finally got a match."

Sam groaned. "You literally just said you couldn't ID her. Which is it?"

Lopez leaned back, clasped his hands, and flipped them upward, stretching them toward the sky. His back cracked pleasurably again. After he settled his hands back down in his lap, he said, "She was ID'd as Dr. Collette Scott, a physicist at the University of Washington working out of at a satellite lab in Port Raven."

When Sam didn't respond, Lopez filled the silence. "But do you want to know the bizarre thing about that?"

"You're going to tell me anyway."

"My guess is you already know, but I'll say it anyway. Dr. Scott died in 2015."

Sam's face registered no alarm. Again, this didn't surprise Lopez.

"Well, your guys obviously got the ID wrong," Sam said, his eyes following two tattooed young men whizzing by on e-boards.

Lopez laughed humorlessly. "My thoughts exactly when I saw the report. But that was before the green hoodie incident. Before I started piecing it all together. I went back to my field notes from that day at the lake."

He pulled out his phone and found what he was looking for immediately. "August 24, 3:37 p.m. My exact words: *I observed a woman with shoulder-length brown or black hair appear mysteriously, seemingly out of the blue, on the lakeside path. Having no reasonable explanation for her abrupt appearance, I had to assume I'd been momentarily distracted and just hadn't seen her arrive.* Between you and me, Sam, I didn't really believe that, but I had a deadline and needed to finish the report. And then...just a minute," he said, focusing on his small screen, "Ah, here it is, and I quote: *Less than a minute later, I had junior agent Tom Jenkins take over the fieldscope to survey the woman's movements and to describe his observations. It was a teaching moment that I didn't expect to amount to much, but about thirty seconds in, Jenkins uncharacteristically uttered an expletive and reeled back from his fieldscope, terrified. He shouted, 'They're gone!' and went absolutely white. Worried he might faint, I had him sit down and*—look, the rest doesn't matter, but you get the gist. That woman was Dr. Collette Scott—a gad-damn time-traveling quantum physicist!"

Sam was unmoved, but Lopez couldn't hide his euphoria. This discovery had the potential to rocket his career into the stratosphere. "You think I'm about to be walked out the Bureau's shiny glass doors? Think again, Sam. Decades—hell, *centuries*—from now, I'll be known as the guy who cracked time travel wide open!"

Lopez leapt to his feet and swept his hand through the air. "Agent Jimmy Lopez. Father of the phenomenon that the whole world thought was impossible. Well, Sam, it's not. Time travel is a reality!"

Sam patted the bench. "Jimmy. Buddy. Sit down."

Lopez whirled around, eyes wild. "Ah, damnit, look at you. You're still denying it."

"I'm just saying we need to take a breath. Think this through."

Lopez lowered his voice as a young woman jogged past them. "Hell, no. I'm going to the director today. Before some junior fuckin' yahoo beats me to it."

"You haven't shared your theory with anyone but me, right?"

"No, but—"

"—that's all it is right now. A theory. You have no proof."

"The Bureau has tentatively identified Dr. Scott as the woman in that photo. But like you, they're putting it down to a false positive since she's been dead for almost a decade. Once I let them in on my findings, they'll have to accept the truth."

"Won't they need more evidence than that?"

"For chrissakes, how much more proof do they need?"

"Lots, I would say. You'll be presenting a pretty mind-blowing concept to a group of people with no scientific background. Don't you think you should wait until you have a rock-solid case?"

Lopez shook his head. "It won't be long before they figure it out for themselves. I mean, it's so damned obvious! Maybe they already have and are just sitting on it. Which would suck for me."

Sam picked up his empty mug and rose to meet Lopez face to face. "Look, I gotta get going. Can we meet again later?"

"Sure thing. I'll walk you to your car."

When they reached the vehicle, Sam made an enticing proposition. "What if I could get my hands on some solid proof?"

Lopez's eyes lit up. "Ahh, see? I knew you were involved."

"No, no. I'm not *involved*. But I *have* become very close with this group. If what you're suggesting is even partially true, you're right—it'll be the biggest discovery since fire. Let me help you prove it's real."

Sam pulled his door open and slid into the driver's seat, the leather creaking under his weight. He fired up the vehicle and lowered his window, allowing Lopez to shut the door for him.

Seizing the moment, Lopez dropped a tiny electronic listening device behind Sam's seat, commending himself silently. Maybe he'd finally learn what happened to the Brixton boy...or get some final intel to support his time-travel theory. "Don't get any crazy ideas about scooping me on this, friend."

"You don't have to worry about that. If this turns out to be legit, I want nothing to do with it. Can you just hold off a bit longer? Two days?"

Lopez shook his head as he backed away from the SUV. "Twenty-four hours. That's it. Then I'm hauling all their time-traveling asses in."

Chapter Twenty

The arrival of the clouds over the rose garden had turned the cool fall day even cooler, especially for someone dressed in flip-flops and lightweight sweats. I fought a shiver, refusing to show my discomfort to Collette.

She looked me up and down as if to say, *Really? This scruffy thing is the woman Morley had a baby with?* I wished she wasn't so elegant. So smart. So patently evil. Her slight frame and sharp facial structure made me think of Cruella de Vil, but beautiful, not frightening.

"Take a guess why I'm here," I said.

Collette removed her earbuds and dropped them into her sweater pocket. "I don't know. To admire the flowers?" Her voice was husky, catching me off guard. It didn't match her graceful charm. "Or maybe to steal my husband," she said, wincing slightly as if she hadn't meant to reveal her jealousy.

"Woah, that's rich," I said, and then, because I felt some stupid obligation to explain my relationship with Morley, I added, "You do realize that all happened years after you died, right?"

"Never mind. You have bigger problems to worry about."

"Yeah, like Christopher. Were you honestly so outraged

about Morley and me having a baby that you had to steal him from me? How fucked up is that?"

Collette cleared her throat noisily, making me wonder if she was a smoker. "If only the issue were that trivial."

I bristled. "Okay, then what?"

"Would it surprise you to know that you brought this on yourself?" She waved her slender fingers in the air. "All of it."

I crossed my arms and stayed quiet. She *would* say that, wouldn't she? Especially now that I'd caught her.

"But what's done is done. And you're the only one who can fix it."

"*You* have to fix it," I said.

"I wish I could, but I'm limited in what I can do at this point."

"Apparently not as limited as me. You can timeblink past your own lifetime."

She snickered under her breath—probably because of my use of the word *timeblink*.

"I don't have time for this. Hand over my son or—"

"Or what?" she croaked. "What are you going to do? Flag down the cops? Kill me?"

I didn't know how to answer her, though murder did cross my mind.

"Can't you see how wrong this is?" I shouted. "How cruel?"

"Why don't you ask me a constructive question? Like why I took Christopher in the first place?"

"For fuck's sake, I don't care why! Just hand him over."

Her naturally long eyelashes fluttered. "I can't."

"That's bullshit."

"It's not. And I'm pretty sure you already know that."

I bounced impatiently on the balls of my feet, trying not to scream.

"It all started with your decision to save yourself—and your friends—from that doomed plane."

I was surprised that she knew about Flight 444. What other knowledge was she sitting on?

"Well, actually," she sighed, "if we want to get down to brass tacks, it started with Morley's discovery of temporal displacement—what you call 'timeblinking'— in early 2019. Everything would've been fine if he'd left it at that. He would have died eight months later like he was supposed to, and the knowledge of the power would have died with him. But no, he *had* to mess around and bring you in on it." She glanced at the sky. "What was he thinking?"

"He wanted me to find my missing sister."

"How chivalrous. Wouldn't he be crushed to learn it was all for naught? That you found your sister without the power of tempor—*timeblinking.*"

My anger was giving way to irritation. "That's not true. I used it to follow my psycho-ex to his secret house, which led me to discover Isla and Finn."

"No offense, but this just goes to prove how little you know about the phenomenon. Your sister was going to escape anyway, with or without the talisman. Don't you remember? Finn was already out when you found him. And Isla was on her way. Destiny is like a weed that way. Stubbornly resilient."

She was the stubborn weed.

"Whatever. This is about Christopher."

"Let's put it this way," she said, ignoring me. "Say you go back in time and try to prevent a key historical event, like the JFK assassination. You'll find that every time you attempt to change anything, the universe will reject your efforts to make sure that the event still happens in some way or another."

I thought back to Morley trying to prevent his own death. And my failed attempts to get a stranger to intervene the day I witnessed Viktor's father pushing Isla toward his dank basement. "Yeah, so?"

"It's called the 'Novikov self-consistency principle'," Collette said, waving a fly away from her face. "It suggests that if you were to change the past, you'd create a paradox in direct violation of the laws of physics. So, the universe must course-correct the timeline to remain stable."

"I didn't come here for a science lesson."

Collette let out an impatient breath. "Anyway, as I mentioned, you have a job to do."

"Yes. Collect my son."

"You're not listening. This thing is bigger than Christopher. It's bigger than anything you could even begin to imagine." Worry lines gathered between her eyes. "It's about humanity itself."

"What are you talking about?"

"In simple terms: you screwed up the world, Syd. And now you have to save it."

I shook my head incredulously. "Do you think I'm stupid?"

"Actually, no. Just extremely careless."

"Oh, I agree. I never should've let Christopher out of my sight."

When she laughed huskily under her breath, I had to muster all my strength not to shove her into a rosebush.

"On the contrary," she said. "This was Christopher's fate all along."

She locked her eyes on mine, and I was arrested by their beauty. Rich, golden amber sprinkled with copper and chartreuse flecks—like a kaleidoscope—and the longer I peered into them, the more untethered to the earth I felt. Was she the original time traveler? Visiting from centuries ago, or millennia?

Remembering my purpose, I thrust my finger toward the daycare. "We're going into that building, and you're going to return Christopher to 2024."

"As I've already told you, I can't."

"Fuck that," I barked, stepping closer until we stood toe to toe. I'd been imagining this moment for weeks and was trembling with rage. "Don't tell me you can't undo this."

When Collette gave me a disinterested shrug, something deep inside me splintered, razor-sharp. I wound up and smashed her jaw with my fist. I'd been powerless to stop myself.

So it *had* been me all along.

As she stumbled back, those mysterious, neon eyes grew wide and fearful, sparking a disturbing thought within me—a thought I hadn't cared to entertain before now: she was telling the truth. About everything. Which meant that Christopher was beyond retrieval. That it may have been my fault. And the craziest prospect of all…that the world's destiny might indeed rest upon my shoulders. The last idea wasn't exactly farfetched in light of the FBI's relentless pursuit of my activities and the growing number of people who were privy to the secret of timeblinking.

But it was too late to retract the blow now.

Either Collette hadn't anticipated my sudden act of violence, or she'd given herself over to it much like Morley had surrendered to the truck. She teetered backward, grappling for a lifeline only she could see. When her head whacked against the sundial on the way down, the sound reminded me of a sack of cement dropped from a great height, and I was so horrified I couldn't even scream.

My reaction after that will probably weigh on me forever. I didn't bend down to find out if she was okay. I didn't think to shout for the paramedics tending to Jenny for help. I merely took a couple of wobbly steps backward and ran…straight into the arms of a police officer.

Chapter Twenty-One

OCTOBER 14, 2014, 12:34 P.M.

My name is Syd Brixton, and this is my confession. I'm here from ten years in the future with the sole purpose of rescuing my three-year-old son from his abductor, Collette Scott, a quantum physicist up at the university. Apparently, she's hell-bent on punishing me for my future relationship with her husband. I really must hand it to her, she achieved her goal beyond a shadow of a doubt. I do regret hitting her and causing her to fall. But my only intent was to retrieve my son from this woman who'd stolen him away and return him to 2024 where he belongs.

I grabbed the pink eraser that Detective Townsend had kindly provided twenty minutes earlier and feverishly rubbed out the penciled words. If I started blabbering on about time travel now, I might never get out of here.

I started over.

My name is Syd Brixton, and this is the first time I've ever truly wanted to kill someone.

I sat back and reread the words on the lined steno pad. I'd never written truer words, but I erased those as well.

I slumped down on the beat-up chair, sliding my hands along its cool metal sides wondering if any *actual* murderers had ever sat here. Of course, they had. And now my butt would be added to the chair's long list of shady occupants.

164

Earlier, I'd asked for a pencil and paper, telling my captors I wanted to write out my account of what had happened at the park, and they'd eagerly agreed. A written confession? Gold to law enforcement. Oh, they pretended to be all cool about it, but there'd been a sizzle in the air when I'd asked them for the writing implements, and the sizzle had only increased when Townsend appeared ten minutes later with a pen, paper, a steaming cup of coffee and a packet of cookies. Was I warm enough? Did I need anything else? I'd told him I was fine but that I didn't drink coffee. He brought me tea with honey.

Now I sat sipping lukewarm Earl Grey from a paper cup, and staring at a blank page, occasionally looking up to search for moving shapes behind the mirrored glass next to the door. I pictured my friend Sam back there, but it was currently 2014, and he hadn't been transferred from the Landon Department yet. It was fortunate. He might have recognized me in 2019 when I'd slammed the trunk lid on his head and then subsequently landed him smack-dab in the middle of 2024.

By further good fortune, no one at the Port Raven Police Department seemed to recognize me as a Brixton twin, but then again, I was a decade older than I should be. For once, the fine lines between my eyebrows and the puffy circles under my eyes were an advantage.

I heard an electronic click at the interrogation room door. A moment later, Detective Townsend trudged back in, his previous energy replaced by a disgruntled air as he secured the door. He stalked over to the table, set a metal travel mug down, then flumped down across from me on a molded plastic chair.

"I see you're going great guns there," he said, eyeing the blank page in front of me, perhaps trying to decipher the ghostly remnants of what I'd scribbled and erased.

I shrugged. "I've lost my muse."

"This isn't a joke, Ms. Doe. You're on the hook for assault. Possibly something more serious if your victim doesn't pull through."

Mild panic rose in my belly, but I quickly dismissed it, comforted by the thought that Collette was never meant to die today. She'd even intimated it herself. Her date with destiny was next year when she succumbed to the cancer that was probably already eating away at her body.

Townsend's mug bumped the table and jarred me out of my thoughts. "I understand. You don't want to say anything incriminating, which is fine, but you haven't requested a lawyer, which is unusual. Or even a phone call. You plan on going this alone, do you?"

"It was an accident."

"So you've said...several times in the past four hours."

"You don't believe me."

"The witness—Officer Keane, who was in the area attending a hit and run—said you appeared to be out of control."

I huffed. "Out of control? Come on. It was one hit."

"That one hit caused your victim to bump her head pretty hard."

"I've told you over and over, I didn't mean for her to fall."

He went on. "Officer Keane also claimed you appeared to know the victim. Is that true?"

I suddenly regretted leaving Jarett behind. He wouldn't have let any of this happen. He'd have used his sensible, down-to-Earth negotiating tactics on Collette. Not a right uppercut.

"Ms. Doe?" Townsend said. "Did you hear me? Do you know your victim's identity?"

"You're referring to the wrong person as the victim. I'm the one who's been wronged. But you'll find that out eventually."

He gave me a tentative look. "If that's true, why are you being so vague?"

I lowered my eyes to the pad of paper on the table, imagining what would have happened if I'd left my original confession intact. My guess was that it would have put an end to Detective Townsend's incessant questions, but it would've sparked a whole crop of new ones. And unless I demonstrated timeblinking right in front of him, I'd have landed in a psychiatric hospital with absolutely no chance of saving Christopher.

Just as the detective opened his mouth to ask another question, the door buzzed again, and he got up to find out who was there. Through the small crack in the door, I could hear indistinct whispering which Townsend answered with surprised little grunting sounds. He thanked the person and turned around to face me, keeping the door propped open with his hand.

"Well, this is an interesting development."

"Interesting as in *good*?"

"I'm not sure. You have a visitor."

My eyes went to the mirrored glass where I assumed the visitor was waiting, but my attempt to see anyone was futile. I shifted uneasily in my seat.

"If you'll excuse me a minute," Townsend said, disappearing into the hall. The door banged shut.

I smiled, despite my unease. Who would be visiting me here? On a timeblink, nonetheless. Oh my god, what if it was Morley? I'd told him about Christopher's abduction. Maybe he timeblinked here to rescue both of us?

My heart did a major flip when the door popped open and Townsend shuffled into the room saying, "Come on in, Dr. Scott."

I jumped to my feet, sending the metal chair screeching across the floor. Morley *had* come for me!

"This is rather unprecedented, though. Are you sure you

want to do it?" Townsend said as he swung the door wider for my guest.

But it wasn't Morley who entered the room. It was Collette.

The *other* Dr. Scott.

When the detective excused himself and it was just me and my nemesis in the room, we both sank into our chairs at the same measured speed. For her, the careful movement was surely to avoid vertigo, given the bulky bandage slung around her head. For me, it was a matter of distrust. I didn't want to be at a disadvantage if she decided to strike back.

"Sorry about that," I said, nodding at her head. "But you've recovered well. The cops had you dancing on death's doorstep."

"I'm tough." That gravelly voice again. It was so incongruent with her refined image. If I closed my eyes, I would have pictured it coming from a 70-year-old chain-smoking bingo player.

"Good thing for me."

"Yes, you got lucky," she said, adjusting the bandage, wincing. "But you certainly needn't have resorted to violence."

"What did you expect? You stole m—"

She shot me a look that said *shut the fuck up*. I complied, remembering where we were.

"Do they know who you are?" she asked, tilting her head at the mirror.

I shook my head, too afraid at this point to speak out loud and say something wrong.

"Okay, let's keep it that way." She looked over her shoulder at the mirror and back at me again, lowering her voice, which was silly. They could hear everything. "I'm not pressing charges."

"Excuse me?"

"You heard me. I'm here to make sure they let you go."

My head jerked back involuntarily.

It didn't make sense. With me locked up, she was free to do whatever she wanted with Christopher without my interference. And then a frightening thought struck me. Once I was out of police custody, I was on my own.

"I'll take my chances in here, thanks."

Collette's face grew sober. "You're going to have to take a leap of faith. It's not what you think."

"You don't give a flying fuck what I think."

We were both silent for a few beats as we sized each other up. Despite her thin, almost gaunt facial structure and the thick bandage wrapped around her head, she possessed a striking beauty that went beyond the ordinary. Her hair, dark as midnight and falling with perfect, sleek symmetry to her shoulders, complemented her olive-toned skin. Her willowy form exuded an air of grace and privilege. Yet it was those otherworldly eyes that commanded my attention and drew me into a place across space and time.

"Where's your dragonfly?" she asked, breaking the spell.

My hand flew up to my neck before I remembered that the police had made me remove my jewelry and put it in a brown envelope when they brought me in.

"It's at the front desk."

Collette pushed back the sleeve of her crisp white linen blouse and glanced at her FitWatch. "We should leave."

"We?" I said, staying seated as she slowly got to her feet.

"Yes, *we*." She looked toward the faceless observers behind the mirror. "We're ready."

The door buzzed a final time. A defeated-looking Detective Townsend flung it open, standing aside to let us pass.

"Thanks for your help, detective. We've settled our dispute," Collette said, brushing past Townsend's big round belly before continuing down the hall. I admired her spunk.

Not to mention her sure-footed jaunt to the front desk, despite her head injury.

I scurried after her like an obedient dog, catching up to her at the reception desk where she asked for her purse and "Ms. Doe's belongings."

"Sign here, please," the clerk said, sliding a clipboard through an opening in the window.

Collette scribbled out an exaggerated, loopy signature and snapped her designer bag from the clerk's hand the moment it appeared in front of her. She headed to the exit without another word.

After I signed a separate form with an X, the clerk pushed a small envelope toward me. "Have a good day," he said, nodding toward Collette who was already outside. "Though it might be a challenge with that one around."

"You have no idea."

As I stalked after her, I couldn't help but wonder what the hell Morley saw in this arrogant, self-serving robot. Maybe she'd captivated him with her eyes. Or the sex was good. Either that or she'd used her obviously brilliant mind to trick him into marrying her.

Once I was outside in the bright but cool afternoon sun, I fished the talisman out of the envelope and slipped it around my neck, thankful that Collette was too preoccupied with her phone to notice. This was her talisman, after all, and without it, Christopher wouldn't have existed. I shuddered at the thought.

As Collette put the phone to her ear and ordered a taxi, I was struck with a sense of utter indecision about what to do next. Return to 2024? Follow her? Go to Christopher?

Done with her call, Collette tucked her phone inside her purse and stared straight ahead, as if she were trying to ignore an annoying car salesperson. As if this were any normal afternoon where she hadn't been assaulted by her husband's future fiancée, gotten sent to the hospital, and busted that same bothersome fiancée out of jail. She was lucky her head was wrapped in a bulky, blood-stained bandage, or I might have been tempted to give her smug little face another taste of my fist. But no, I reminded myself that I couldn't hurt her again. I needed her healthy enough to fix this mess. And to explain her absurd claim about me saving the world.

When a yellow taxi pulled up a few minutes later, I was even more unsure about what to do. Collette still hadn't said a word to me since the interrogation room, making it impossible to know what she expected of me. As I opened my mouth to ask her, she glanced over her shoulder with one arched eyebrow. "Coming?" she asked, before folding herself into the car.

What choice did I have but to follow? She was my only link to Christopher and the one person on this earth who could bring us back together.

I could hear Jarett's voice echoing reassuringly in my ears with each begrudging step toward the taxi: *There are angelfish in the sea, too.* I hoped he was right.

Chapter Twenty-Two

Collette unlocked the door to her condo—*my* condo in 2024—and allowed me to enter first.

I kicked off my flip-flops and took in the grand open space while Collette deposited her sweater and boots in the closet. "Wow," I said. "It's so...*clean.*"

I momentarily worried that she didn't know I'd inherited the whole kit and kaboodle from Morley when he'd died, but that would be ridiculous. Of *course* she knew.

"Clean? Hardly. Your little boy is a dirt machine." When I frowned, she said, "I mean that in an endearing way. All little boys are dirt machines. My cleaning lady was in this morning. That's why the place is spotless."

She motioned for me to follow her into the kitchen where she pulled out a stool at the island. "Have a seat. I'm making tea. Care for a cup?"

I nodded, though I wasn't in the mood for a tea party.

After filling the kettle with water and setting it on the stove, Collette turned around, catching a glimpse of herself in the mirror behind me and cringing. "Will you excuse me for a moment?"

I nodded.

She took a quick look at her FitWatch, dropped her arms to her sides, and shut her eyes. After three deep breaths, she vanished. No clutching her talisman, no uttering a destination. Nothing. She just disappeared. Clearly, there were some things about timeblinking I had yet to learn.

Her absence worked in my favor, though. It meant I could take advantage of the solitude to decide if I should get the hell out of there, perhaps to see Morley again and ask him for help. But in the end, imagining Christopher's face kept me glued to the spot. I wasn't leaving without him this time.

Just over four and a half minutes later, Collette popped back into the kitchen dressed in a completely different outfit and holding the bloodied bandage at her side. She casually tossed the bandage onto the counter then turned to pull a bone china teapot out of the cupboard. Not surprisingly, there was no sign of trauma where she'd bonked her skull. In fact, her hair was so smooth and perfect, I wondered if she'd just stepped out of a salon.

"That was interesting," I said.

"Liberating, more like. I've only done that in front of someone once in the twenty-five years I've had the power."

If that was a dig, I chose to ignore it. "What else don't I know about timeblinking?"

She tucked a strand of her sleek brunette hair behind her ear. "It would take a week to tell you."

"Come on, there can't be much more to learn."

"Would you say that to a concert pianist if you only knew how to play Chopsticks?" She scoffed.

"Okay then. For starters, how did you timeblink without even touching the talisman?"

"Temporocardiokinesthesia."

"Temporo-what?"

"Temporocardiokinesthesia. It's a term I coined for the mind-body-heart connection necessary for spontaneous time-blinking."

"And? How is it done?"

"By slowing the heart rate to less than sixty beats per minute and visualizing your destination, time, and date. I haven't had to hold the talisman in my fingers for over fifteen years."

"So why do you continue to wear it?"

"It's still necessary to facilitate the temporal displacement."

"I'll have to try it sometime."

"Be careful. The visualization method takes practice and can lead to some unpredictable results. But in my opinion, it's worth the risk. This method also gives you access to destinations you've never visited before."

"You're kidding."

"I rarely kid."

"How exactly does that work? Say I wanted to go to Stonehenge in 1990 even though I've never been there before."

"As long as you know what your destination looks like, from photos or seeing it on TV or what have you, all you have to do is visualize it, choose your date and time, and you're good to go. So, if you wanted to go to Stonehenge in 1990, your best bet would be to find some relevant news footage of it and watch it until you could form a strong mental image. It's a method I've used with great success."

I was fascinated despite my lingering annoyance. If what she was saying was true, it meant I could've avoided all those late-night trips to the parking lot at Chapman Falls and the bushes at Lighthouse Park.

"That would've come in handy over the last five years," I said. "Morley had been positive that it was impossible to timeblink to a place you hadn't physically been before, and that it was also impossible to go somewhere before your first contact with it. He said that he'd experimented with it with no luck."

"As I said, you and my husband only scratched the surface of the phenomenon."

I wished she would drop the *"my husband"* dig when Morley's name would suffice. "So, obviously you've been spying on us."

"Only when necessary."

"Was it necessary the night Morley and I got engaged at Dominique?" I said, relishing her immediate discomfort. "That *was* you, wasn't it?"

She dropped two teabags into the delicate teapot. "Look, we have lot to cover before I have to pick Tristan up."

"*Christopher.*"

Her nose scrunched up. "Sorry." She seemed sincere.

"What happens next? Do you really expect me to leave Christopher here and sail off into the sunset?"

"I wish it were that simple."

"Seriously?" I spat. "You think abandoning my child is *simple?*"

"That's not what I meant."

I took a long, deep breath—the kind they teach at yoga to induce a sense of calm. It didn't help. I was twisted as tight as a nylon rope.

"Why don't you have a seat in the living room, and I'll bring the tea when it's ready."

So you can poison it? I almost said. But she would be foolish to kill me now, what with this mission she apparently wanted me to complete. Plus, how would she explain my lifeless body to Morley when he got home?

Satisfied she was going to keep me alive, I jumped off my chair and headed for the couch. On my way, I stopped at the massive built-in bookshelf that, in my timeline, held cookbooks, coloring books, framed pictures of my family, battery-operated candles, a carved wooden elephant, several tropical plants in various stages of decline, and a shoebox containing Christopher's rock collection. Today, the entire floor-to-ceiling case was rammed with physics textbooks and medical journals. That's it. Not a candle, dead plant, or rock collection in sight.

As I was about to settle onto the couch, one of the book spines caught my eye, and I padded over to the shelf to my make sure my eyes hadn't been deceiving me. Tilting my head to get a better look, I was filled with a sort of stunned reverence when I confirmed that the author was indeed one Dr. Collette Scott, Ph.D. I pulled it out and ran my fingers over the embossed title, *Chrono-Currents: The Infinite Loop of Time.* The cover depicted a simple twisted band forming a continuous loop that seemed to defy logic, hinting at the depth of the book's contents.

As I flipped through the pages—knowing I wouldn't understand one word of it—a photograph slipped out and fluttered to the floor. Bending to pick it up, I saw a younger Collette standing in front of an imposing structure that I recognized from a documentary I'd watched not long ago: the Large Hadron Collider. The huge smile on Collette's face clearly indicated it had been a pinnacle moment for her.

"Find something interesting?" Collette's voice made me jump, and I hastily replaced the photograph inside the book before sliding it back into place on the shelf.

"Just browsing," I said. "I see you wrote a book."

"I did. It wasn't a best-seller," she joked, setting our tea on the coffee table before we both took our seats—me on a pristine off-white leather couch, and her on a comfy-looking suede armchair of the same color.

"All right. I'm listening," I said, eager to hear her out.

"Good. We haven't got much time."

"Before what?"

She drew a deep breath, searching, it seemed, for the gentlest words.

"Remember in the park—right before you punched me— when I mentioned the Novikov self-consistency principle?"

"Yes, but it was a bit over my head."

Collette chuckled sympathetically. "It is for most people. In broad terms, Novikov's principle asserts that there is only one timeline in which the past, present, and future are connected in a single unbreakable chain. It may sound paradoxical, but if you go back in time and try to change something, you can't because it's already happened."

I frowned. "So, what you're saying is Morley and I were right. We can't go back and change things because they're already set in stone."

"Pretty much," Collette replied. "It's a bit like re-watching a horror movie you've seen before. You can shout at the screen all you want, but the events won't change."

"Destiny."

"In all its glory."

"Is it really a three-year-old child's destiny to be whisked off to an alternate timeline by a complete stranger?"

"Four."

"Pardon me?"

Collette bit her bottom lip. "Christopher is four now."

I could have screamed. "You're heartless, you know that?"

"You won't be saying that at the end of this conversation."

"Try me."

"Before I was forced to take a sabbatical to look after Christopher—"

"You were *not* forced."

She glanced at the ceiling irritably. "Before going on sabbatical, I was on the verge of a significant breakthrough in my temporal displacement studies. Specifically, how to override the set-in-stone destiny of the universe that Novikov presented neatly wrapped up in a bow."

"You learned how to change the past?"

"Almost. I had all my ducks lined up and was ready to begin testing when you came along and derailed the whole operation. Well, that combined with the state of my health."

She didn't elaborate, and I wasn't about to pry.

"So you're saying that this discovery—or near discovery—would've allowed you to change the past...and make it stick?"

"Yes."

The implications were huge. With that kind of power, I could've prevented Isla's abduction from happening altogether and saved Morley's life. And those were just the possibilities that would impact *my* little corner of the world. Collette's discovery had much bigger implications for all humankind, like warning people about impending natural disasters, preventing terrorist attacks, or stopping a pandemic in its tracks.

"I have a lot more to tell you," Collette said. "But first I'd like to explain why I took Christopher..."

I folded my arms across my chest.

"...Since you still haven't asked me about it. And since you've mistakenly blamed it on my jealousy."

"You can't deny you're bitter about my relationship with Morley."

"No, I can't. I wouldn't be human if I didn't carry a little resentment toward my husband's mistress."

I let that slide. At least she was being honest.

"But that's not why I took Christopher."

"Why did you, then?"

"Because someone asked me to."

"Oh, really? Please enlighten me. Who the hell asked you to snatch an innocent toddler away from his mother?"

"Well, Syd, believe it or not," she said, pausing to pick up her cup of tea. "You did."

Chapter Twenty-Three

OCTOBER 14, 2014, 1:52 P.M.

My mouth fell open, but I quickly shut it, not ready to accept Collette's allegation.

"I know, it sounds preposterous," she said. "But it's true. You asked me to abduct Christopher."

"What?" Out of a million questions in my head, *that* was the one that had come out first.

Collette continued, cool as autumn rain. "A future version of yourself from September 2024 visited me back in January. You stormed into my secretary's office, frantic, demanding to see me. When she couldn't calm you down and had to bring security in to restrain you, you got even more agitated. That's when I heard the commotion and came out to see what was going on. Of course, I recognized you instantly."

My head felt like it was filling with water, yet my mouth was as dry as sandpaper. I had a vague awareness of thirst. In my hands was a cup of lukewarm tea; I had no recollection of how it got there or what I should do with it. Collette's voice swam to the surface.

"—security to let you go, and I invited you into my office and got the story out of you."

"Why would I do that?" I mumbled before draining my

teacup and clattering it down on the saucer. "Why would I come to *you?*"

"Because you knew I was the talisman's original owner and a quantum physicist, no less. You hoped I would be able to help you out of a sticky situation."

"What sticky situation?"

"Your detective buddy Sam warned you about an FBI agent who was closing in on your time travel ability and was about to blow the lid off the whole thing."

"Blow the lid off *what?* I've never told anyone how the talisman worked."

She pressed her lips together briefly. "That's not true. You told your friend Jarett."

I couldn't deny that, but it didn't add up. "If you're insinuating that he would betray me—that he would tell the *fucking FBI* about timeblinking—try again. He would never."

"Be that as it may, this Lopez fellow had been so convinced you held the key to time travel that he kidnapped Trist—*Christopher*—to extract the information from you. That's why you resorted to asking me for help."

"What the...? You're saying an FBI agent kidnaps Christopher in the future? That's insane. I hear the FBI can be pretty shady at times, but surely they draw the line at child abduction."

"Apparently not. You discovered that this agent—Jimmy Lopez—had gone rogue and had taken it upon himself to work the case outside of the bureau's knowledge."

Every nerve in my body felt tightly stretched. "So, where did he take Christopher?"

"Unfortunately, that's where things got really bad."

"They weren't bad enough already?"

"I'm afraid not." Collette leveled her ethereal eyes on me before delivering the worst news I'd ever heard. "Lopez sped away with Christopher in his vehicle with you and Sam chasing behind. When Lopez was forced to stop for a group of schoolchildren crossing the street, you seized the opportunity and jumped into his vehicle. This apparently incensed Lopez, and as soon as the road was clear, he took off again. He eventually lost control of the car."

"Oh no." I didn't want to hear the rest.

"I'm sorry, but Lopez crashed through the guardrail above Blackfin Cove with you and little Christopher in the car."

I moaned. "No, no, no."

"I'm so very sorry. Obviously, *you* survived…"

She mercifully ended her account there. I rose to my feet and shuffled over to the patio doors, stepping outside. I took a few shaky steps before my legs went lax and I melted to my knees. I ran my hand over the cool tiles, remembering Christopher lining up his dinosaurs and trying to feed them goldfish crackers in this very spot a few weeks ago.

"He was here," I sobbed. "Right here!"

Collette graciously kept her distance, allowing me to wallow in my grief. When my tears ran out, I trudged back to the couch where a box of tissues greeted me. I pulled out a few, bunching them in my hand as I flopped down onto the cushions.

"So he died?" I asked despondently.

"You never said. Apparently the vehicle exploded and—"

"Stop. Please. No more."

I excused myself to the bathroom where I vomited and splashed water in my face, only returning to the living room after several minutes.

"You're asking me to take you at your word," I said, desperate to disprove her story while at the same time knowing it was absolutely true. "Can you prove it?"

"I wish I could, but the very act of me removing Christopher from his classical timeline has altered everything. Even if I could return him to 2024 now, Novikov's principle would kick in, fulfilling his destiny to die in that crash, no matter how many different ways you tried to prevent it." She bit her bottom lip. "You'll just have to trust that he's safe here, in 2014."

The idea of Christopher's continued safety should have comforted me, but it didn't. Not in the least.

"Morley told me you returned Christopher to the foster care agency today. Obviously, that was a lie, so what really happened?"

"You and I talked extensively about that. We batted around every possible scenario including leaving Morley and I to raise him until our deaths in 2014 and 2019 respectively. However, since you didn't want Christopher to be orphaned at nine years old, you ultimately asked me to place him with a family of my choosing. People I could trust to raise Christopher as their own."

"This is fucking nuts."

"I wish it could be different. I really do."

"Even if everything you're saying is true, who would possibly agree to take in a random toddler without documentation?"

"Sorry, that's classified."

"Excuse me? Classified by who?"

"You," she said with genuine empathy. "You didn't want to be tempted to find him, so you asked me not to reveal his location. Ever."

"Even now?"

"Especially now. You said if you ever came to me asking where Christopher ended up, I should resist every urge to tell you."

This was all too much.

Collette flicked her hair over her shoulder. "As for why someone would be crazy enough to take in a random toddler with no paperwork—it wasn't easy."

I let out a snort. "No shit. I don't imagine you rang this family's doorbell and said, '*Hey, you seem like nice people. This stray kid needs a home. Whaddya say?*'"

"Not quite. I had to resort to apprising them of temporal displacement."

"What? You told other people about timeblinking? When you flat-out berated me for doing the same thing?"

"It was the only way to convince them Christopher was in real danger and that I wasn't just some crackpot dumping an abducted child on their doorstep. They didn't believe me, of course, even when I provided proof that I was a quantum scientist. That helped, but they needed more."

"Wait, I thought you said you knew them."

"I knew *of* them. Through a friend. Don't worry, I vetted them thoroughly."

"Well, that's a relief." It was hard to hold my sarcasm. "But it doesn't make sense. I can't see myself asking you to keep Christopher's location a secret."

"Remember, you were desperate to save his life. And you were convinced that knowing his whereabouts after I abducted him would further jeopardize his safety."

She was right. I'd obviously resorted to desperate measures to protect him. By any means.

Collette cleared her throat. "We did discuss another option: you remaining in this timeline with Christopher and starting over in a new town where no one knew you."

"And?" I asked, leaning so far forward I nearly fell off the couch.

"When I reminded you that the rest of your family and friends wouldn't be able to interact with you—not to mention the issue of temporal elasticity—you decided that placing Christopher with a new family was the only viable option."

My shoulders dropped. "I'll probably regret this, but what the hell is temporal elasticity?"

"Right. I explained it to you the day you came for help. Temporal elasticity dictates that we can only remain in a foreign timeline for two and a half weeks before the universe pulls us back to our natural place. You told me you'd never experienced the phenomenon yourself because you hadn't timeblinked for longer than a week at a time. Consider it a blessing. The first time it happened to me, I was unceremoniously shot back to my living room buck naked. My only saving grace was that I hadn't been at work when I'd left—where I only would've had a lab coat to cover me."

I found myself chuckling despite the seriousness of the situation. "So, you always return after two and a half weeks?"

Collette nodded.

"So, why is Christopher still here? And what about Sam? He never boomeranged back to 2019."

"Both of them are on secondary temporal shifts, or what you call *return timeblinks*. Lucky them, they're immune to the effects of elasticity. I'd experimented extensively on rats, and you unwittingly carried out the first human trial on Sam. We talked all about this when you came to ask me to abduct Christopher. That's how we knew it was a safe option."

My mind was spinning. "So, on a normal timeblink, it's two and a half weeks, and then it's back to your normal timeline whether you like it or not."

"To be more precise: 444 hours."

"Well, that figures."

"I've likened the phenomenon to the lifespan of a dragonfly, which tends to be around two weeks."

"Why doesn't that surprise me?"

"Granted, they can live up to six months or more, but as a person who strives to draw parallels in such things, I'm disinclined to believe the average is mere chance."

I leaned back against the buttery leather seat, feeling exhausted. I wish she would just tell me what I needed to do and let me go.

"Do you know why I became a physicist, Syd?"

I gave a tired shrug.

"I've had the power of timeblinking a long time. Since childhood, in fact." Collette placed her fingers tenderly on her talisman in the opening of her luxurious linen blouse. "My grandmother passed the talisman on to me after a mudslide swept over my family's house in Peru, killing my parents and four siblings. I was eight."

I shivered, but not because of the air conditioning rippling over my bare arms. Inexplicably, my heart went out to this woman who'd caused me so much pain and suffering. So much grief.

"I'd been at my grandparents' house at the time."

I swallowed. "That was lucky."

"I didn't feel lucky. My whole family was erased in an instant. On the day of their funeral, my grandmother gave me the talisman, telling me that dragonflies symbolized the fleeting nature of life and that one must live it to the fullest. I've never forgotten that, nor the odd feeling of invincibility that surged through me the moment she placed it around my neck."

Collette's eyes glazed over at the memory.

"It was then that I realized my purpose was to contribute to humanity, but it wasn't until I stumbled on the talisman's power around my fifteenth birthday that I had my epiphany about studying quantum physics. Fortunately, I had a natural aptitude for the subject."

"You mean your grandmother didn't tell you about the power?"

Collette shook her head. "I don't think she knew. She never uttered a word about it, and there were no clues amongst her things after she died. Believe, me I went through it all with a fine-toothed comb. Anyway, that's why I became a physicist. So I could study the talisman directly with one goal in mind: going back in time and preventing my family's tragic end."

"Did you ever try?"

She snickered under her breath. "Are you kidding? Hundreds of times. They always ended up dying."

"Always in the mudslide?"

"Yes. It nearly drove me mad. This seemingly extraordinary power was totally useless."

I could relate. I'd posed the exact question to Morley on my first timeblink. What good was the power if it couldn't save his life? Isn't that what anyone would use it for?

"Do you know where the talisman came from? Originally?"

"My great-great-grandfather worked as a foreman for a silver mining company on the North Coast of Peru. Apparently, he was exploring the area on his own one day and stumbled on a hidden cave not far from the mining site. The talisman was inside."

She gripped the pendant tighter. "He gave it to my great-great-grandmother but made her swear to keep it secret. He thought that if the mining company found out, they would take it from him."

"I wonder how long it had been in the cave."

"Based on the metalworking and the dragonfly iconography, I've come to believe it dates back to the Moche civilization, somewhere between 100 and 800 AD," Collette said, turning the piece over in her fingers. "The Moche saw dragonflies as symbols of life, renewal, and transformation. Fitting for an artifact that manipulates time, don't you think?"

I stared at the talisman in her grasp with new awe. "Your great-great-grandparents must've eventually told someone in your family about its origin."

"Yes. When my great-great-grandfather retired, he felt it was safe to let his family know, but he cautioned them to keep it under wraps. And so began a tradition of the necklace being passed down from mother to eldest daughter across the generations. For obvious reasons, I received it from my grandmother."

I reached for my own talisman but dropped my hand halfway when a hot wave of guilt surged through me like lava.

To think, I'd broken a family tradition that had spanned more than a century.

"It was your destiny," I said.

Collette's eyes darkened. "More like a curse, as it turns out. But I'm sure you know about that."

My heart skipped a beat at the thought of my little boy's fate.

"What about this breakthrough you mentioned? Can't you use it to save your family?" I asked, even though I was more curious about how it might be used to save Christopher. And Morley.

She rose from her chair and glided over to the floor-to-ceiling window. There, she fixed her attention on the harbor which was still bustling with tourists despite the lateness of the season.

"It *could* have helped at one time. But not now."

She drew in a stiff breath before turning around to face me. "This disease I'm dealing with has weakened me to the point that time travel has become incredibly dangerous to my health."

"Your cancer?"

"It's not cancer."

I gave her a searching look, wondering why Morley would lie to me about that.

"It's something worse: *relativistic time dilation disorder*. In lay terms, it would loosely translate to *time-traveler's disease*."

My mind whirled off in a hundred directions. *Time-traveler's disease?* I'd been timeblinking for five years now.

"About three years ago, I noticed small changes in my health. Fatigue. Poor appetite. I was losing weight unintentionally—not a lot, but enough that it worried me."

"Understandably."

"Of course, cancer was my first thought. I went in for testing, but all the markers for a serious disease came back negative."

"Thank goodness," I said. This woman may have been my nemesis at one point, but I wouldn't wish cancer on anyone, including my worst enemy.

She glided back to her chair and sat down. "The investigations revealed that my body was aging at a rapid rate. You and I understand this as normal aging as a result of spending days or weeks in other timelines and then returning to our present where only minutes have passed. The doctors were naturally fascinated and wanted to probe further, but of course, I declined."

"You seem healthy now."

"You wouldn't have said that eight months ago. The day I brought Christopher here, I developed severe jaundice and anemia. Chronic coughing for about a week. That's why I sound like a chain-smoking trucker. I suffered permanent damage from all the coughing and the vomiting that came with it."

"That's terrible."

She stuck out her bottom lip. "The consequence of traveling to the future beyond your own lifespan. Every time we do that, our cells have to stretch across an exaggerated span of time. And it gets worse the further into the future we go."

I gave her a hopelessly confused look, which was becoming a common occurrence in our conversations.

"All it means is that when we come back to our original time and our dilated cells snap back into normal time flow, this sudden collapse disrupts the cells' functions and leads to systemic upset."

"So, returning to our regular timeline messes with our cells?"

"Yes. They're forced to abruptly contract, and that cellular disruption manifests as jaundice, anemia and the other symptoms I mentioned."

"I'm so sorry."

She shrugged. "I'm a scientist. Do you really think I'd pass up any chance to go to the future?"

"What about the past? Have you experienced any weird health issues from that?"

"Regrettably, yes."

My breath hitched, getting stuck in my throat.

Collette noticed my distress and quickly explained. "Fortunately for you, it seems you've been limiting your trips to no further back than 2019."

"That's not true. I've been to 1997 and 1999."

"How many times?"

"Maybe five?"

"You have nothing to worry about. In my case, I'd been consistently traveling several decades back, hundreds of times over. I learned too late that the further I deviated from my natural timeline—and the more frequently I went—the more pronounced the effects became."

"You went on a timeblink earlier, though. When we were in the kitchen."

"Yes, but only to a week ago."

"Meaning?"

"Meaning the body barely notices the difference and doesn't have to struggle so hard to reconcile the missing time. Trips like that are all I can handle now."

"Oh, Collette. If I'd known about any of this, I wouldn't have asked you to—"

She raised her hand. "Stop. It was worth it. Your boy is safe now."

Putting my pride aside, I got up and went over to her, picking up one of her slender hands. It felt almost skeletal in my grasp. "Thank you so much." A tear rolled down my cheek. "I had no idea."

She gave me a quick smile as her phone pinged in the kitchen. "If you'll excuse me," she said, scrambling to her feet, disappearing around the corner. She still hadn't elaborated on this mysterious mission she'd alluded to at the rose garden.

A moment later, she came rushing into the living room, wrestling the bloodied bandage back onto her head.

"It's Morley. He's in the elevator. You need to go," she said, gathering our teacups onto a tray and running them into the kitchen.

I dashed to the front door where I'd left my flip-flops, panicking about our unfinished business. And on top of that, how could I leave before seeing Christopher one last time, if only from afar?

"What about that thing you wanted me to do?" I called out, sliding into my flip-flops.

She reappeared around the corner and hurried over to me.

"Meet me tonight at the back entrance to my lab." She shoved a business card into my hand. "Ten-thirty."

"But…Christopher—"

She shot a frantic look to the door where the telltale beeps from the electronic lock were sounding. "You have to go!" she whispered urgently.

As I reached reluctantly for the talisman, the front door swung open, shielding me from Morley's sight.

"Darling!" I heard him say, his voice filled with concern.

My eyes locked on Collette's. She gave the slightest nod toward the closet. Without hesitation, I tugged it open and dashed inside, pulling the door toward me without fully closing it, praying that Morley wouldn't need to hang up his coat.

My fingers curled around the talisman as I prepared to leave, but I stopped short when I heard their muffled voices beyond the door. Collette spoke first.

"Hi sweetie. I thought you had a late clinic today?"

"I cancelled it. Dr. Barron told me you were admitted after being attacked at the park. Are you okay?"

"I'm fine. It was nothing."

"Dr. Barron said you were concussed. Let me have a look."

"Goodness, no. Why all the fuss?" Collette asked, her voice fading as they made their way into the living room.

I could have left then, but curiosity kept me rooted to the spot. I cracked the door open a smidge to hear their conversation better.

"I'm fine," Collette said again. "There's barely a scratch. Now sit down, and I'll get you a cup of tea."

"I've had enough caffeine today. Come on, what happened? Who attacked you?"

I heard Collette sigh. "Morley. Please. Just drop it."

Silence.

More silence.

"Look, I'm sorry sweetie, but I'd rather not talk about it. Please respect that."

Another long silence.

And then, Morley's voice. "I'm only concerned because you have a tendency to downplay your troubles. May I remind you about the Valentine's Day episode?"

Of course. That's when Collette had fallen ill and almost died. The day 'Tristan' had arrived in their home. And now I knew why. It was because of me.

I clutched the talisman and whispered, "Return."

Chapter Twenty-Four

I n the next moment, I was nose to nose with Jarett in the middle of my kitchen. His eyes were wild with curiosity.

"Well?"

I couldn't talk to him about what I'd learned. My head was too full of worry and dread. He followed me into my bedroom.

"What's going on? You look like you've been to hell and back."

"I have."

I rifled through my laundry basket, sniff-testing a few garments and deciding they could pass for clean. I hadn't done laundry in weeks. "I'm taking a shower then going out."

"Where?"

He trailed behind me to the bathroom where I turned around in the doorway. "Jarett, I'm sorry, but I just can't talk about it right now. A lot has happened, and I just need some space."

His forehead creased with worry. "Of course. Take your time. I'm here when you need me."

"Thank you."

With the door closed, I pulled Collette's business card

from my bra and shivered. It had been real. Collette wanted to meet me at her lab in 2014 so she could tell me how to save the world.

Once I'd showered and had gotten dressed, I reviewed what had to be done next. First, a quick reconnaissance mission to the university to get a visual on where I was to meet Collette. I remembered having gone on a field trip to that campus as a child, but I had no idea where Collette's office was located. Best to be prepared.

When I emerged from the bathroom, I heard Jarett in the living room talking on his phone. Good. I put on a hoodie, grabbed my keys, and gave him a quick wave goodbye as I slipped out the front door. I would explain everything later, but I just wasn't prepared to discuss it yet.

While I waited for the elevator, my condo door cracked open, and Jarett poked his head out. "Hey, Sunshine. Where're you off to?"

"The university. I have to meet someone." It was technically true. He didn't have to know that my trip to the university and the meeting wouldn't be occurring at the same time.

"What time will you be back?"

"About an hour. Probably less."

"Okay. Need anything from me? I don't work till later, so just name it."

I flashed him a sheepish look. "How about laundry? I'll be turning my underwear inside out soon."

"Ha, gotcha. Anything else?"

The elevator doors slid open. "Just patience. I'll tell you everything as soon as I'm ready."

Having completed my surveillance trip at the university, my route back to the condo took me past Lighthouse Park and Sweet Briar Daycare where I'd last seen Christopher in 2014.

Driven by some masochistic impulse, I pulled into a parking spot, cut my engine, and watched a young mother pushing a stroller towards the doors. That did it for me. The tears came in a flood, and at that moment I was sure I would cry every day for the rest of my life. The guilt was crushing, settling over me like a weighted blanket.

It wasn't just the guilt of losing Christopher, I realized. It was the knowledge that Collette had not been the monster I'd made her out to be…that she really had been trying to help. Did I owe Morley the truth? Did he need to know that our son had been destined to die in 2024 and that Collette had been instrumental in saving him from that fate?

My bleary eyes drifted over to the rose garden where I could almost imagine Collette standing in wistful repose, her sleek hair blowing across her face in the wind. I let out a stifled moan, remembering all the vitriol I'd launched at her during our brief acquaintance.

The answer was 'yes.'

Yes, Morley deserved to know.

And yes, Collette deserved vindication.

Downcast and exhausted, I crawled into the back seat and, behind the privacy of the tinted windows, timeblinked away to Sandalwood Lake.

I was still teary a few minutes later as Morley wrapped his strong, reliable arms around me. The crackling fire and the rhythmic patter of the rain on the roof were comforting, though they did little to ease the pain in my tortured heart.

"Here," Morley said, handing me a tissue. He still hadn't asked what had upset me so much or why I'd come back so soon after we'd agreed to part ways. He probably sensed it would be too awful to hear. He wouldn't be wrong.

I took the tissue, dabbing at my eyes and debating how to

break my news to him. He already knew Collette had taken our son, much to his disbelief, but now came the part where I'd have to admit I'd been completely wrong about Collette.

"Thank you," I croaked, my voice raw, reminding me of Collette's. It sent a fresh rush of guilt straight to my heart. "I need a minute."

"Alright, love. Take your time."

While my breathing slowed and the tears tapered off, I rehearsed my speech inside my head, though it wasn't easy. My mind was running off in a thousand directions.

Morley shifted closer and took my hand. "I don't want to push you, love, but you're making me nervous. I've never seen you so upset. Not even yesterday when you laid the news on me about Collette kidnapping Christopher."

I gave my nose an ungraceful blow, still snuggled against his chest, still unable to speak. The heaviness in my body persisted, as if the weight of the world was pressing down on it. In a way, I supposed it was.

He stroked my shoulder. "I'm sorry I doubted you about that. I just never saw her as the jealous type, much less someone who could abduct a child. She'd dedicated her life to studying the tiny things that hold the world together, always looking to bring clarity, not chaos."

The waterworks almost started again, but I kept them in check. I pushed myself upright and peered into his eyes, choking back a lump in my throat. "Oh, Morley. You were right. She wouldn't have done such a horrible thing without a good reason."

Morley's hand tightened around mine. "Do I dare ask?"

"You wouldn't believe the shit I've been through with her."

"Well, now you *must* tell me."

I took a breath and jumped right in. Told him about punching Collette in the face, her head injury, my brief incarceration, and the shocking news about my involvement in Christopher's abduction. He was only moderately surprised to learn that Collette's mystery illness had indeed been time-blinking-induced. He went quiet at the news of Christopher's fate and how the Novikov principle meant that the only way I could save him was by leaving him in the 2014 timeline...and how I'd begged Collette never to disclose his location to me.

"He's nine years old in this timeline, Morley. Maybe living a few miles from here with people we don't even know. How messed up is that?"

He swallowed thickly. "You prevented Christopher's death. That's all that matters. He's safe now."

"I want to believe that so badly."

"From what you've said, it sounds like Collette's pretty convinced."

"What do *you* think? Would she have any reason to fabricate any of this?"

He frowned and rubbed his chin. "How would kidnapping our son benefit her? The only thing I can think of is what you suggested earlier...that she did it out of spite. It would be odd, though. As I said, that woman didn't have a jealous bone in her body."

"Not true. She flat-out admitted she was salty about our relationship. It's why I'm tempted to believe her story. If she'd denied being jealous, I would have suspected she was lying about everything else."

Morley pulled me in for a hug and rubbed my back. "I can't imagine it was easy turning to her for help."

I could only nod into the crook of his neck, my words stuck behind the giant lump in my throat.

"I honestly thought this visit was going to be about your friend Jarett," Morley said, nonchalantly.

I pushed myself off his chest at the mention of Jarett's name. "No, it's...Wait. What about Jarett?"

Morley folded his arms. "Uh, his visit yesterday, after you'd left?"

"What the fuck?"

"You mean he didn't tell you?"

"He sure as hell did not!" I said, jumping to my feet, glaring down at him.

"Oh boy. I just assumed the two of you were pretty tight, considering he knew how to use the talisman."

My mind was spinning.

"He visited me here," Morley said when I could only stare at him in disbelief. "Introduced himself and politely asked me to break things off with you."

Rage flared up inside me. "*He what?*" I screeched.

How dare he? After everything we'd been through together, after all the trust I'd placed in him, he'd had the audacity to poke his nose into my relationship with Morley? And he'd stolen the talisman to do it!

"Don't be angry with him. It sounded like he was just trying to protect you."

"Protect me?" I yelled. "By interfering in my life? And telling you to dump me?"

"Listen to me, love," Morley said, grasping my hands and standing up to look me in the eye. "This guy obviously cares about you. A lot. Or he wouldn't have risked coming here to warn me off. He was just trying to do what he thinks is best for you."

"Unbelievable. He doesn't get to decide what's best for me! And neither do you!"

To think that Jarett had snuck around behind my back while I grappled with Christopher's abduction. In addition to being insensitive, it was totally unforgivable.

"I'm sorry," Morley said, his brow furrowing. "That came out wrong. I'm just saying the guy has a point. I just...I happen to agree with him. I'm holding you back."

My jaw was clenched so tight I thought my molars might crack. "No. This is *not* your fault. How can you be so calm about it? You should be furious. He stole the talisman and used it for his own gain!"

"Do you have feelings for him?"

I wasn't prepared for the question. "No," I shot back. "Especially not now."

"But you did. Before all this."

My stomach filled with butterflies. I could only shake my head.

"Syd, come on. You know all I want is for you to be happy. And if that means making a life with Jarett the Doofus, then so be it," he joked.

Yesterday, I would have laughed at this. Today? I could barely stand to hear the traitor's name.

"How did he even know when to come?" I mused aloud. "When I wouldn't already be here?"

"He said you keep a calendar. Like the one we have here."

"Yeah, I keep a calendar. In my *phone*." Fuck. As if stealing the talisman wasn't bad enough, he'd also hacked my phone? "I shouldn't have come here."

He took my hands, kissing my knuckles tenderly. "Love. You're going to need some emotional support on the other side, what with everything going on with Christopher, and it seems this guy genuinely wants to help. I think you should cut him some slack."

His words coaxed another tear out of me. It fell on our clasped hands. "I'll think about it." Which felt like a lie. Jarett had crossed a line—several, in fact—that he could never step back behind. How could I ever forgive him?

"Did you tell him about us?" I asked.

"What, that we broke things off already? No. I figured it was your news to tell."

I huffed. "Good. He doesn't need to know."

Morley bounced our hands energetically between us. "Again, my dear, don't be too hard on him. All he wants is your love, even if his methods are a little clumsy."

"I wish I shared your faith in humanity."

He laughed. "I prefer to give people the benefit of the doubt than waste my time looking for their flaws."

"You're amazing, you know that?"

"You're pretty spectacular yourself."

I shook my head. "I gotta hand it to you. When I show up here in three months with my motley crew of plane crash survivors, you do a great job of pretending you've never met Jarett."

He gave me a mischievous wink. "Why spoil the fun? I can't wait to sit back with a bowl of popcorn and enjoy the spectacle of him making the moves on you."

"Trust me, you won't get much of a show."

"On the contrary. Now that I'm forewarned, I'll bet his attempts will be as plain as day."

"So…is this it, then? For us? For real this time?"

He squeezed my hands. "I've had the most fulfilling life with you, Ms. Brixton, as brief as it was. Unfortunately, the universe has different plans for us."

"Do you really believe that?"

Morley leaned down to the coffee table and plucked another tissue out of the box. He gently wiped my tear-streaked cheeks. "You can't mess with destiny, my dear."

I hugged him tight, and we kissed. It wasn't the normal passionate kiss we'd always parted with, but a tender goodbye filled with promise just the same.

Morley stepped back, and I was saddened to see that his normally bright green eyes had dulled. He cleared his throat softly. "I love you, Syd Brixton."

For him, this was merely a pause until some timeblinking version of me showed up later tonight. Or tomorrow. And then all the tomorrows until that fateful day in September. It's why he could be so at ease.

For me, this ending was final, and if I didn't leave now, I never would.

I clutched the talisman between my fingers as I had so

many times before. But this time, it felt different. Tainted. Jarett's paws had been all over it and he'd used it without my consent. I harnessed my anger, using it to combat the heartache of parting with Morley.

"I love you Morley Scott. Return!"

After my short, fretful drive home from the park, I found Jarett sitting on the couch, all decked out in his official police garb.

"Hey, Sunshine," he said brightly, but seeing the storm raging behind my eyes, his face quickly sobered. "Oh no, what happened?"

Without answering, I stomped into the kitchen and grabbed an apple from a bowl on the island. Took a big bite. I wasn't hungry, but my stomach was empty after spending several hours timeblinking, and I needed to get some food into me.

Jarett slinked up to the island. "Is it something about Christopher?"

Worried I might get violent, I left him in the kitchen and found a spot at the window.

"Can I help?" Jarett asked after a minute or two, wisely keeping his distance behind me. "What's got you so worked up?"

"As if you don't know!" I shouted, spinning around. "How dare you steal the talisman to visit Morley!"

He released his breath gradually. "Ah, he told you."

"Fuck, Jarett, of course he did. His loyalty is to me, not you. But I wouldn't expect you to understand that. Apparently, loyalty isn't a concept you're familiar with."

He took a few tentative steps toward me. "Syd, I..."

"Save it," I said. "I have bigger shit to deal with right now."

"Can I help?" he asked again.

I was about to unleash a list of all the reasons why I would never trust him to help me again when my phone buzzed on the hall table.

"That's been going off every thirty seconds," Jarett said.

I pretended not to hear him as I marched over to my phone.

There were several text messages from Sam as well as one voice message. I didn't bother listening to the voicemail. The texts contained all the information I needed to know.

"Great. It's started."

"What?" Jarett said, approaching me, his earlier trepidation gone.

When I'd read the last of Sam's messages, a wave of understanding washed through me.

"Oh my god. Did you tell the FBI about timeblinking?" I asked, squeezing my phone so tightly I felt it might shatter.

Jarett's eyelids fluttered. He seemed shocked by my accusation. "No! What's happened?"

"Christopher's life was threatened because of *someone's* loose lips," I spat, my voice trembling. "That's why Collette took him. To keep him safe."

Jarett's face paled, but he quickly regained his composure.

"Syd, I swear, I didn't tell anyone anything that could harm Christopher. I would never do that to you," he said, inching closer. "Or him. I care about you both too much."

"Well, someone told this"—I looked at my phone— "Agent Lopez about it, because he's the one who ends up killing Christopher!"

"Woah, woah, hold on," Jarett said. "I thought—"

"And now Christopher has to grow up in a completely different timeline. Without me! All because you couldn't keep your mouth shut!"

Jarett's brows were so squeezed together I almost believed

he was telling the truth, but given his shady activities, I couldn't afford to let my guard down.

I grabbed my purse and keys and flung the door open, holding my phone up between us. "This Lopez guy's gone off the deep end and is looking for me now. And what's worse? He's going public with timeblinking by the end of the day if Sam can't convince him otherwise."

I slammed the door behind me and hurried down the hall. My normal breathing resumed only when the elevator doors bumped shut and Jarett hadn't followed, his insistence that he was blameless still bouncing around in my head. To think, I'd almost fallen for that innocent puppy-dog façade.

I pulled my phone out to read the new flurry of texts from Sam.

"Where are you?"

"Call me ASAP."

"We need to meet."

Collette would be waiting for me in 2014 no matter how long it took me to get there, but Sam was my friend, and I didn't want to brush him off. I tapped out my response. *"On my way to your place. See you soon."*

As I turned into Sam's densely treed neighborhood fifteen minutes later, I'd all but convinced myself Jarett had blabbed to FBI about timeblinking. If that were the case, I couldn't help but wonder if he'd truly ever cared about me. Maybe both things were true. Maybe he thought he could have it both ways.

Well, he couldn't.

All he'd done was strengthen my resolve to uphold my promise to Morley: to keep the truth about timeblinking under wraps. And now, according to Collette, it was more important than ever. If I couldn't stop this rogue agent from exposing my group as time travelers, the world as we knew it might indeed fall to ruin.

Chapter Twenty-Five

SEPTEMBER 11, 2024, 9:57 A.M.

Agent Jimmy Lopez

The dim hallway of The Raincoast Hotel stretched before Lopez with its threadbare carpet muffling his hurried footsteps. As he reached his room and fumbled in his pocket for the keycard—at least *that* had been updated in the last thirty years—a giddying energy pulsed through him. If everything went the way he wanted it to, he'd soon be taking his bride of thirty-five years on lavish trips, staying in only the most expensive hotels, enjoying meals made by world-renowned chefs, and drinking the most expensive bourbons he could order.

His daydreaming was cut short when Agent Jenkins stepped out of the adjacent room, his brows tightly knit at the sight of Lopez's disheveled appearance. "Sir," he said. "Everything good?"

Lopez barely registered the junior agent's presence, his eyes darting around the hallway like those of a cornered animal. His tie was loosened just enough to reveal the first few buttons of his white dress shirt. Sweat gathered at his hairline.

"Never better, Jenkins," he replied, the words coming out

snappier than he would've liked. His knuckles were white from gripping the keycard, giving away his current mood.

Jenkins hesitated. He'd never seen his boss so wired. He wondered if Lopez had been out on the town the night before and was hungover. Though that wouldn't line up with the new healthy lifestyle Lopez had been going on about the last few months.

"Need something, son?"

"No, sir. Just grabbing my phone," the younger agent said, holding it up for Lopez to see.

Lopez grunted.

"Got a minute, sir?

"Not really."

"I'll make it quick."

Lopez let out a testy breath, swinging his door ajar. "If you must."

Jenkins followed his boss into the room, closing the door behind him. Lopez tramped to the other side of the room where he snatched his briefcase from a chair and flung it onto the bed.

"What's on your mind, son? I've got a lot to do this afternoon," Lopez said, punching his code into his briefcase lock and flipping it open.

"It's just that...we missed you at the morning briefing and haven't been able to reach you all day. Are you working on a lead?"

"Oh yeah, one helluva lead. A gad-damn doozie. I'll have a full report ready by this time tomorrow, maybe even sooner."

Jenkins stood on the opposite side of the bed, prompting Lopez to stop rifling through his briefcase and look him in the eye. "Care to share the details with me?"

"Soon. I'm just ironing out some final proof."

"Again, sir, I'd appreciate being kept in the loop. Not to mention, protocol states that—"

"Fuck protocol. I can't piss around with formalities right now. This is too big."

"I understand your hesitation, sir, if it's truly as big as you say. But what if you go outside and get hit by a bus and—"

"Yeah, yeah. The old hit-by-the-bus argument." He patted his breast pocket where he kept his trusty notepad. "I've got all the details recorded right here."

"But sir, if they find out you withheld information from your team—"

Lopez clenched his hands into two tight fists and bent over, gently resting them on the bed. "I don't like where you're going with this, son."

"I'm just saying tha—"

"They're gad-damn time travelers!" Lopez shouted, standing upright. He hadn't wanted to spill the beans, but he knew Jenkins loved his damned protocol so much he wouldn't rest until he got at least a morsel of information. Besides, Jenkins would be beholden to keep the story under wraps until they both agreed the case was complete enough to present to the Bureau.

For a moment the two men simply stared at each other. Lopez nearly laughed at the look on the junior agent's face because it was the same one Sam had given him not two hours earlier. He watched Jenkins open his mouth to speak but beat him to the punch.

"I don't need to tell you this is classified intel. It doesn't leave this room. Don't go blabbing a word of this to anyone, son, because like I said, I'll have my proof soon, probably before the day is out. "

"Time travelers?" Jenkins said with a look of amused curiosity.

Lopez's expression remained serious. "Yes, time travelers. You even alluded to it at the lake. Well, it got me thinking maybe you were onto something. Turns out, you were! *The*

444 Five are a bunch of time travelers, and I intend to expose them before someone else does."

Jenkins bit his lip, worry settling in his stomach like a stone. Was this really happening? He knew Lopez had become obsessed with the case lately, but time travel? The guy would be committing professional suicide if he went to the Bureau with such nonsense.

"Sir," Jenkins said, wringing his hands. "Are you sure about this? It all sounds...you know..."

"Utterly bonkers? Yeah, I'm well aware." Lopez turned his focus back to his briefcase, finally laying his hands on the item he'd been looking for. "But I've seen enough evidence to know I'm right. You'll see."

Lopez watched the junior agent's face drop when he brought his hand up from the briefcase. It held a Glock Gen 5, locked, loaded, and ready for the next part of his plan.

"Is that really necessary?" Jenkins asked, eyeing the gun in Lopez's hand.

"It's for show," Lopez replied. "Incentive."

"Look," Jenkins began, taking a few slow steps toward Lopez, his hands raised submissively. "We're partners, right? We should think this through...together."

Lopez narrowed his eyes, considering Jenkins's words for a moment. Then he shook his head, his grip on the gun tightening. "No, there's no more time for thinking. I need answers."

"Of course. This case has been going on for far too long. You're exhausted. We all are," Jenkins said. "Just think about what you're doing. Is it worth putting your career at risk and potentially hurting people?"

"For gad's sake, Jenkins. I'm not going to hurt anyone. I'm just taking the bull by the horns. For the greater good," Lopez said, studying his gun as if it were a fine piece of jewelry. "I was like you once, all bright-eyed and a stickler for rules. But sometimes you gotta bend the rules a little if you're gonna get anywhere."

"With all due respect, sir, you were the one who drilled the rules into me."

"For pity's sake, kid. Of course I did. It's how you build the foundation of a great agent. And when you get to my stage of the career, you'll do it too. You'll take some liberties. For the sake of the mission."

"I highly doubt that."

That's when Lopez noticed Jenkins' hand disappearing into his jacket pocket. A cold thought slid into his mind—was Jenkins carrying, too?

"Stop!" The command sliced through the air, sharp and immediate as he leveled his weapon at his junior agent.

"Easy, sir! It's just my phone," Jenkins said, slowly pulling out the device and holding it up between them.

"Hand it over."

Jenkins hesitated for a few moments but ultimately complied, tossing the phone onto the bed next to Lopez's briefcase. "Now go over there. In front of the pillar near the window."

"Sir, please," Jenkins said, his hands in the air, his eyes darting between Lopez and the door. "Think about what you're doing."

"Move," Lopez commanded, gesturing with the gun. Reluctantly, Jenkins edged towards the pillar.

Lopez sensed Jenkins's fear, but he couldn't let that sway him. He had come too far in his pursuit of *The 444 Five*. If what he believed was true—that they possessed unimaginable power—then risking the final year of his career was worth it.

Once Jenkins had his back against the pillar, Lopez said, "Don't you get it? With this power, we'll be able to stop terrorists before they detonate bombs. Before they fly planes into buildings! I know you were barely knee-high to a grasshopper when that atrocity happened twenty-three years ago today, but I'm sure you've heard about it."

Jenkins nodded gravely.

"And that's just the tip of the iceberg. We could prevent mass murders, plane crashes, deaths from natural disasters. We could catch serial killers before they'd managed to off their first victim. This is huge, Jenkins. I need to get on with my job."

Jenkins beseeched Lopez silently with his eyes. The older agent knew the line he was about to cross, but he'd made his choice. He had chosen to put his mission before everything else.

He leaned over his briefcase once more and produced a set of handcuffs, throwing them to Jenkins. "On your left wrist," he ordered, and Jenkins complied. "Good. Now put your arms back. Around the column. No sudden movements, kid. I won't hesitate to shoot you in the foot."

Again, Jenkins did as he was told. "You're making a mistake."

"Zip it. I know what I'm doing."

Training his gun on his partner's foot, Lopez inched over and secured Jenkins's other hand. He backed away, tucking his gun into his belt.

"I'm sorry it has to be this way. But I can't have you ruining everything now."

"I sincerely hope it works out for you, sir. I've had nothing but respect for you these past few years. All I ask is that you think of your wife before you do anything rash."

"Son, she's the whole reason I'm doing it."

Jenkins tilted his head questioningly.

"Do you know how many times bad people have threatened me with my wife's life? How many times I've worried I'll find her with a bullet in her forehead on the bedroom floor? If you think I'm doing this solely for my own glory, you're mistaken," Lopez said, opening the door. "I'll send someone for you soon."

Chapter Twenty-Six

I made a left onto Sam's street, finding his house just as I'd remembered it, nestled in the shadows of ancient pine, cedar, and arbutus trees. What further news would he have for me that he couldn't include in his texts?

I pulled into his steep driveway and coasted to a stop at the bottom. I didn't see his SUV, but it could've been in the garage. Or he hadn't arrived yet. I dug my phone out of my purse to see if he'd answered my last message. Nope, he hadn't. My stomach tightened at the implications of his silence. What if this Agent Lopez had arrested him? How much had Lopez found out about timeblinking? And worst of all, had Jarett truly leaked everything?

On closer scrutiny of Sam's latest few messages, I noticed he hadn't said to meet him at his house, only that he wanted to meet and to call him ASAP.

When my call went straight to his voicemail, I leapt out of the car and hurried up the steps of his and Lizzy's expansive craftsman-style home. As I rang the doorbell, I allowed myself to briefly admire the bright orange begonias adorning the porch—a cheerful sight at odds with my dark mood.

"Come on, Sam," I muttered under my breath. Deep

209

down, I knew it wasn't just impatience gnawing at me. It was fear. Fear for Sam's safety, and for mine. And for how all of this would affect our fight to keep timeblinking a secret.

"Please be okay," I whispered as I rang the bell again, my worry intensifying. If anything happened to Sam, I'd never forgive myself. After all, it was because of me—because of timeblinking—that he was involved in this mess in the first place. I just hoped he would be spared the danger that seemed to be closing in around us.

The door finally creaked open, and as much as I would have welcomed seeing Lizzy's friendly face, I prayed it would be Sam.

It was neither.

Instead, I found myself staring into a pair of intense green eyes framed with some funky tortoiseshell glasses—eyes that seemed familiar yet foreign to me at the same time. The boy was perhaps thirteen or fourteen years old, his wild blond curls fluttering languidly in the pre-autumn breeze.

It hit me just then—a memory of the day in the cornfield when we told Sam that he wouldn't be able to see his family again. I was sure he'd said he'd had a teenaged daughter, not a son, but evidently I'd been mistaken. Besides, according to Jarett, Sam's only daughter, Hayley, was nine years old. As I opened my mouth to ask the boy if his father was home, a shockwave of recognition shook me to the core.

I was looking at Christopher.

My knees turned soft. I grabbed at the doorframe for support but missed, and the boy caught my arm before I melted to the ground. When he was sure I could stand independently, he let go of my bicep.

"Are you okay?" he asked, in the croaky, half-child/half-adult voice of puberty, and I was instantly overcome with grief. I'd missed not only his fourth birthday but all the sweet, sweet years in between. My heart felt as if it were clamped in a vise.

As he regarded me curiously, I wondered: Did he recognize me? Did he know his biological mother had abandoned him as a toddler in 2014? If so, he wasn't letting on. I decided to play along.

"I'm fine. Just a little dizzy," I replied, never breaking eye contact.

But the moment he heard my voice, his eyes went wide. He knew. We studied each other intently as the world fell away around us. When he finally spoke, his voice came out in a whisper, as if he wasn't sure whether he should say the word out loud. "M…Mom?"

"Christopher," I whispered, tears welling up in my eyes. "Oh, sweetie."

In that moment, all my fears and doubts about my disjointed life evaporated, replaced by the overwhelming need to hold my son again. I embraced Christopher tightly, feeling his lean adolescent arms wrap around me in return. The pure shock of the moment warred with the elation inside me as I tried to process how my little boy had grown up so quickly, right here in Sam and Lizzy's home. I had missed so much of his life, yet I'd seen him as a sweet, innocent toddler not twenty-four hours ago.

"Mom," he whispered into my shoulder, his voice cracking with emotion. "I never thought I'd see you again."

"Neither did I," I admitted, fighting back tears. It was pointless. They gushed out of me like a tidal wave. "I'm here, sweetie. And I'm so happy to see you."

He laughed stiffly over my shoulder. "You don't sound happy."

I pushed back from him and put both hands on his shoulders. "You listen to me, Christopher—"

"Scott. My name is Scott."

A fresh torrent of tears burst forth. How fitting that Sam had given him Morley's surname. "It's perfect, Scott. You're perfect. And I'm so glad I found you."

I could see a million questions behind his eyes, but they would have to wait. I pulled him into my arms again and clung to him amidst the showy begonias and the gathering wind, grateful for Collette's hand in saving him.

As he surrendered to my embrace, the simple yet profound fact of his existence overwhelmed me, and I found myself yearning for all the lost hugs, the bedtime stories never told, and the laughter that had never reached my ears. With an aching intensity, I wanted to make up for all the years I was absent from his life.

What harm would there be in keeping things status quo? Surely, Sam would grant me full access if not allow me to reclaim my son completely. As for Collette's warning about the world's end, well, what could be more meaningful than spending my last days on Earth proving my love to my son?

Reluctantly, I unwrapped my arms from my baby's shoulders and stood back to bask in the glow of his presence. His *realness*. Yes, he would forever be Christopher in the quiet corners of my memory, but I would honor him as *Scott*, the name he'd grown into, if fate allowed our story to continue.

"Oh, Scott, sweetie. I have so much to tell you, but there's something extremely important I need to take care of, first. Do you know where your dad is?"

"No. I just got home, and no one else is here."

As I reached for my phone to see if Sam had replied, the noise of an approaching vehicle disturbed the silence. Looking over my shoulder, I was relieved to find Sam maneuvering his vehicle down the long driveway and pulling up next to my car. His eyes registered only a hint of alarm when he saw me and Christopher—when he saw me and *Scott* together.

"Ah, here he is now," I said.

Sam hopped out of his SUV and started slowly toward us, no doubt trying to figure out what he was going to tell me.

"Hi Dad."

My heart lurched into my throat at the reference.

"Hey kiddo, shouldn't you be at school?"

"I got to leave right after my Physics exam. It was *so* easy. I was the first one finished."

The irony of this almost made me laugh out loud.

"Good job, buddy. Do you mind heading inside for a bit? I need to take care of some business here."

Christoph—*Scott* nodded and gave me a wistful smile before disappearing inside. God, his new name was going to take some getting used to. Or maybe not. This handsome young man bore little resemblance to my pudgy-cheeked little three-year-old Christopher I'd seen just this morning.

Sam climbed the porch steps and gestured towards the Adirondack chairs tucked among the lush begonia display. The vibrant blooms seemed determined to lighten the serious mood in the air.

Once we were seated, Sam said, "I'm guessing I don't have to tell you who the boy is."

I shook my head. "He has Morley's eyes. I almost missed it with the glasses."

"I've always imagined what this day would be like. And to be honest, I'm a little surprised. I expected you to be angry," he said, leaning forward in his seat. "But you seem pretty level-headed."

"I've already cried about him so much. Besides, how can I be angry when I know he's safe, and that he's grown up in a loving home?"

"Can't argue with that. We've made sure to treat him as one of our own."

"This is crazy. All of it. I have so many questions."

"Bet I know the first one: Why didn't I tell you sooner?"

"And?"

"I wanted to," he admitted, running a hand through his hair. "But Collette warned me and Lizzy not to tell anyone...even you if you ever came asking. It was our best shot at keeping his identity hidden."

"And I'm grateful for that. But I'm trying to understand how it all happened. Collette said she'd chosen a family through a friend of hers." And then I realized: "Ohhh...that friend was me."

Sam nodded. "She came to me and Lizzy in October of 2014. Told us a little boy was in danger and that she needed my help to protect him. Obviously, when she told us about the time travel thing, we thought we were on some prank show."

"I know the feeling."

"But the more she explained the situation, the more intrigued we became. We decided to hear her out, fully expecting that we'd be reporting her to Mental Health Services by the end of it. But then she disappeared right in front of us, returning about five minutes later wearing completely different clothes. It was clear she was telling the truth. That's when she asked us to take Scott—*Christopher*—into our family. How could we say no?"

"It's okay, Sam. Please go ahead and call him by the name he's grown up with, and I'll do the same if I'm fortunate enough to spend more time with him."

"I appreciate that, Syd. And Scott will, too."

"So how did it all go down?" I asked. "How did you explain his sudden presence to your family and friends? Medical professionals? Teachers?"

"Between my experience in law enforcement and Collette's access to Morley's pediatric clinic, we were able to set him up as a whole new person in no time. It was scary how easy it was to pull off. And as far as our friends and family were concerned, we told them that I'd heard of his circumstances through work, and we felt so bad for him that we wanted to adopt him."

"Well, I must say you're quite the talented actor. When we encountered each other in the 2019 timeline, you genuinely appeared not to know me."

"That's because I *didn't*. Collette purposely withheld any

details about who you were or where you lived to protect Scott. I'd been tempted several times over the years to put my investigative skills to the test and find you, but Collette was so adamant that it would only put Scott in danger that I let things be."

"Surely you put two and two together when you piggy-backed on my return timeblink."

"Oh, yeah. Immediately. The piggyback was an accident. No one was more surprised than me when I ended up on that flight with you guys. But that's why Lizzy accepted my five-year absence so easily. She knew about the power. So, when I disappeared that day without a trace and without leaving a note, she knew it must've had something to do with time travel. She managed to convince everyone we knew that she didn't believe I'd been kidnapped or killed but that I'd run off with a lover. Knew it was the only way to keep my law-enforcement buddies at bay."

"Poor Lizzy. Raising three kids by herself for five years...one of whom wasn't even hers."

"She's a keeper, that one," Sam said, winking. He sighed. "You can't imagine the guilt we felt when your little guy went missing. We'd known that day was coming, though, given Scott's age when he came to live with us."

"And you still didn't crack when you saw how devastated I was."

"I'm sorry, Syd. Truly. Lizzy pushed me so hard to let you in on the whole thing, but I couldn't risk it."

"Well, it doesn't matter now, not with timeblinking at risk of being exposed."

"No thanks to Lopez."

"That asshole is the whole reason Scott came to live with you."

He tilted his head. "Oh?"

I didn't want to get into the horrific details. "Let's just say Collette wasn't lying when she said Scott's life was in danger…

this Lopez character became completely unhinged in another timeline, but thanks to Collette's intervention, that all changed. It's why I can't be mad at you, Sam. Scott's safe now."

He reached over and patted my hand.

"There is one thing that's been bugging me, though," I said.

"What's that?"

"Well, I've spent many hours with Collette in 2014 the last day or so, and during that time, she repeatedly accused me of being careless by telling too many people about the power. She even went as far as to say that because of my negligence, the world now stands to self-destruct. Yet she told you and Lizzy about timeblinking ten years ago!"

He exhaled wearily. "Yeah. She admitted it was a huge risk, but she never told us how it worked. In fact, we still don't know."

"It's probably for the best."

"I agree. Interestingly, she did tell us the same story she told you...that if the power were ever to fall into the wrong hands, we might as well kiss our quaint little existence good-bye. She refused to give us the details about what the hell *that* meant. Said it would make us crazy if we knew, especially since we had children to think about. In the end, we decided it wouldn't hurt to put our faith in a quantum physicist who'd been to the future so many—oh, shit."

"What?" I tracked his line of sight to the top of the driveway where we watched a champagne-colored sedan skid to the curb. "Who's that?"

Sam got up, moving to stand between me and the driveway. "It's Agent Lopez. This'll be interesting."

Peeking around Sam's shoulder, I watched Lopez practically explode out of his car, his eyes locking onto Sam with an intensity that made me shudder.

"Don't bother protecting her, Douglas," he shouted as he

marched down the hill toward us. "It's over. I can see your friend."

"Look," Sam said, attempting to diffuse the situation. "There's no need for hostility. Please stand down."

"Hostility?" Lopez scoffed, coming to a stop at the bottom of the porch stairs. "I've been chasing ghosts for months trying to understand what happened on Flight 444, and now I find you in a tête-à-tête with one of the people I've been investigating? I have no choice *but* to be hostile!"

"It's not what it looks like, Jimmy. I'm just trying to get to the bottom of this mystery," Sam replied. "Same as you."

Lopez ignored him. "Ms. Brixton, I'll need you to come with me."

I stepped out from the cover of Sam's body. "I've done nothing wrong," I said, trying to keep my voice steady despite the panic threatening to devour me whole. "We're just talking."

"Cut the bullshit. Do you think I'm an idiot?"

I leaned close to Sam. "Come on," I whispered. "We should go talk to him. Quietly. Before Scott hears things he shouldn't."

Sam nodded, resuming his protective stance between me and Lopez as we descended the porch stairs.

Lopez's face brightened as we approached. "Thanks for your cooperation. Right this way, Ms. Brixton." He started toward his vehicle, expecting me to follow.

"Oh, no, no. I'm not going anywhere. You can ask me your questions right here."

He glared at me before briefly lifting his eyes to the sky. "All right. We'll start here. But we're still going into the station."

"What do you want to know?"

"How did you get off that plane?"

"I really wish I could tell you," I said, trying to sound sincere. "But I can promise you one thing: I'm not a terrorist."

"I know that!" Lopez shouted. "But it would be very easy for me to convince my superiors otherwise."

Sam opened his mouth to defend me, but I put my hand on his forearm to stop him. "Agent Lopez, sir. I know it's hard to believe, but I'm not the enemy here," I said. "I'm just trying to protect my son."

"Your son?" Lopez looked almost amused. "You mean Christopher? The boy who disappeared into thin air with Collette Scott, the quantum physicist who's been dead for ten gad-damn years?"

Before I could respond, I heard the sound of Sam's front door unlatching behind us and we both turned around to find Scott standing in the doorway, his eyes wide with concern. "Is everything okay?" he asked, starting toward us.

"Get back inside!" Sam shouted. "And lock the door!"

But Scott just stood there, transfixed by the situation unfolding in front of him.

"Please, sweetheart," I said. "Do as your dad tells you."

"No! Dad!" he yelled, not at us but at a spot over Sam's shoulder.

When Sam and I turned around, Lopez had backed up perhaps ten or twelve feet, and was now standing halfway up the driveway, his gun pointed straight at us.

I raised my hands in surrender. Sam followed suit, inching back in front of me, his protective instincts still on high alert. He took a couple of tentative steps toward Lopez. "You don't want to do this, friend."

Lopez waved his weapon. "We are *not* friends."

I'd never seen a gun in real life before, at least not this close. And never one that was pointed right at me. I hoped Sam knew what to do.

"Dad!" came Scott's panicked voice behind us. We both startled but held firm, never taking our eyes off the deranged agent.

"Get in the goddamned house!" Sam yelled without moving.

Scott must have realized Sam meant business because I heard the door close and the bolt slide into place. One tragedy averted. And Lopez had no idea he'd just seen my time-traveling son.

Just then, a sleek black BMW coasted to a stop at the top of the driveway.

Jarett. Fucking great.

Here was the moment my former friend (almost lover!) revealed himself as a collaborator in Lopez's crazy campaign to expose us. I prepared myself for the smug smile he would inevitably flash me while Lopez patted him on the back, commending him for a job well done.

Lopez glanced over his shoulder. "Who's that now?"

I almost laughed—something I do when I'm extra nervous —at the agent's convincing performance. Fortunately, I was able to maintain a stoic front.

Behind Lopez, I watched Jarett emerge from his driver's seat, still decked out in his pressed blue uniform, minus his gun belt—a detail that wasn't lost on me. After all, why would he bring a gun to a theatre performance? I had to hand it to him, though. He was putting on quite a show, what with the look of concern plastered across his face. As he descended the hill, his eyes shifted between me and the car, as if he was weighing the option of retreating into his vehicle and driving off or staying and braving the storm of my wrath.

Lopez briefly looked over his shoulder, then back to me and Sam. "Well, isn't this a nice surprise? Officer Jarett Cooper. The gang's all here!"

Jarett's eyes darted back and forth between Lopez and us, finally directing a question at Sam. "Everything okay here?"

I nearly blurted, *What do you think? There's a crazed FBI agent pointing a gun at us!* But I stifled myself.

Sam was the next to speak. "Jare, this is Agent Jimmy

Lopez from the Anti-Terrorism Division of the FBI. He's here to find out how you and Syd and the rest of *The 444 Five* got off that plane before it crashed."

A light appeared to go on behind Jarett's eyes as if realizing the man wielding the gun wasn't quite the danger he'd initially assumed. As if this wasn't some random freak threatening his friends.

Did this mean Jarett really wasn't working with the FBI?

He took a few careful steps closer, stopping a car's length away from Lopez.

"Agent Lopez," he said calmly. "Let's talk about—"

"Quiet!" Lopez swung his weapon around, pointing it at Jarett's face. I gasped as Jarett raised both hands in submission. Somehow, it felt scarier seeing the gun trained on Jarett than when it was pointed at me.

If Jarett was fearful, he wasn't showing it. He didn't advance any further, but he also didn't back down. Seconds felt like minutes while we waited in a holding pattern.

"Agent Lopez," Jarett began cautiously, "I understand your frustration. Hell, I'd be banging my head against the wall, too. But I can assure you, *The 444 Five* are no more terrorists than you are."

"For fuck's sake! I know that!" Lopez snarled, his grip on the gun tightening as he waved it between Sam and Jarett, attempting to keep the two cops at bay. "What I'm here to find out is how you time traveled off the gad-damned plane!"

Jarett shot me a surprised look. And in that moment, I finally believed him. He'd been telling the truth. He wasn't the leak. But who was?

"Seriously?" I said to Lopez. "Time travel? That's what you're on about?"

"Listen up, missy," he said, turning his attention fully on me. "You're gonna—"

Before he could finish uttering his threat, Jarett was on him. After that, everything happened in a blur.

Sam pushed me behind my car and then disappeared around the back of his own.

I could hear Jarett and Lopez wrestling with each other, their stiff grunts punctuating the otherwise quiet neighborhood. My car rocked with their repeated thuds against it.

A moment later, their bodies crashed to the ground inches in front of me.

I watched helplessly as Lopez climbed on top of Jarett, pinning him face-down on the ground. The gun was still in Lopez's hand. He hadn't yet seen me. I stood up and aimed a kick at the weapon, making contact. The gun went flying thanks to the muscles in my strong runner's legs.

Lopez cursed and scrambled for the firearm.

Winded, Jarett struggled to his feet and tackled Lopez right as he was scooping up his gun.

A deafening crack rang out, and I hurled myself behind my car. A body hit the ground.

I clamped my hand over my mouth, trying not to betray my location with a scream.

The maniacal agent's voice pierced the ensuing silence. "Gad-damnit! Look what you made me do!"

Oh my god. Oh my god. He shot Jarett.

I wasn't thinking when I leapt up and ran to Jarett's side, collapsing over his still body. "No, no, no!" I cried, wrapping my arms around his warm shoulders as Sam emerged from behind his car, brandishing a gun of his own. He had it trained on the rogue agent.

"Stand down, Agent Lopez," he said. "No need to make this any worse for yourself."

Sam's composure was astounding. Didn't he know his best friend had just been shot?

"I'll put my weapon down when *she* comes clean," Lopez said jerking his head in my direction. "I've got all the evidence I need, except for one extremely important detail. How she does it."

As I looked between the two men facing off, my eyes drifted to Sam's house, where I spotted Scott in an upper-floor window. He had a cell phone pressed to his ear—presumably he was describing the situation to 911. His glasses were clenched in his free hand. It was obvious he'd been crying. Through my own tears, I mouthed *I love you*. He nodded and burst into a fresh fit of crying. It broke my heart that I couldn't hold him and tell him everything was going to be okay. In a way, it was better. I didn't want to lie to him.

I nodded and smiled, silently urging Scott to retreat into the house, away from the horrors occurring in his front yard. As if reading my thoughts, he backed away and disappeared. I swallowed a lump in my throat and was preparing to get up when an arm slid around my neck and jerked me upright.

"As I said, I've nothing to lose now Detective Douglas." Lopez said, his hot breath on my ear and the gun wedged into my side.

"Let her go!" Sam yelled, keeping his own weapon steady.

"Stay back!" Lopez's arm tightened around my neck while I searched hopelessly for a way out of this impossible predicament. I was aware of my hands clutching his forearm...conveniently close to the talisman. I would keep that in mind as a last resort. I didn't want to abandon Sam and Scott.

Lopez jerked me forward. "Stand aside, Sam, or I'll put a bullet in you, too."

Sam's eyes flicked back and forth between Lopez's face and the gun pressed to my side. "You don't have to do this, Jimmy," he said placatingly, using the agent's first name. Probably some kind of police tactic. "This isn't who you are."

"Shut up!" Lopez snapped. "I'm done with this bullshit. Now, get out of my way."

"I can't allow it, Jimmy."

I implored Sam with my eyes to please let us go—to let Lopez take me away before anyone else got hurt...maybe even Scott. But Sam wasn't budging.

"Damnit," Lopez muttered, leveling his weapon straight at Sam. My eyes clamped shut.

More gunfire erupted.

At once, Lopez and I were careening backward, tumbling apart when we hit the ground.

I rolled to one side and curled up into a tight ball, shielding my face with my shaking hands. A hot rush of adrenaline shot through my veins. The fear of death was over-whelming, but strangely, I didn't feel any pain. Relief washed through me as I realized I was unharmed and free of that horrible man.

Seconds ticked by. I strained to hear something—anything. But the only sound was the shrill ringing in my ears, a disori-enting remnant of the shot that had freed me from Lopez' grasp.

To get my bearings, I cautiously ventured to open one eye. A knot of dread tightened in my stomach as the reality of the situation sank in. If it wasn't bad enough that Jarett was dead, Sam might be too...and it would be all my fault. I never should have dragged either of them into the dangerous world of timeblinking.

As I teetered on the edge of despair, an encouraging sight pulled me back. Sam, a few feet away, unharmed, his gun still drawn.

My head swiveled left and right. Where was Lopez? Had Sam killed him?

I scrambled to a crouched position in front of my car, ready to bolt if necessary. With one arm leaning against my bumper, I turned my head, following the line of Sam's gun over my shoulder, noticing, somewhat unnervingly, that we were alone. Lopez had obviously not been shot—at least not fatally—and had probably taken cover behind one of the vehicles. I turned back to Sam, eyes wide, silently asking him what to do. He put one hand up, warning me to stay down.

As the ringing in my ears dwindled to a faint buzz, I heard a dog bark in the distance. There were no other sounds. Not a car engine. Not the squawk of a crow. Not a rustle of leaves.

Consequently, I nearly jumped out of my shoes when a voice shattered the silence from behind me. Lopez. And he was close enough that I could feel his warm breath on my neck.

"Again, Sam," he said, eerily composed. "I have nothing to lose."

There was a faint metallic *click* before I felt the barrel of his gun jab into the back of my head.

My first thought? *I hope Scott isn't watching.*

My second? *The talisman.*

"What good will that do?" Sam asked him. "You kill her, and you'll never prove time travel exists. With Syd alive, at least you'll still have a chance. Right Syd?" he said, grasping at straws.

Slowly—so as not to alert Lopez—I reached up to my neckline for the talisman but froze partway when I remembered something. Collette's heartbeat trick. I could timeblink to any destination I wanted without even holding the talisman and without saying a word, simply by slowing my heart rate to sixty beats a minute or less. What was more, Collette had said in this calmed state, I could simply envision my destination and end up there, even if I'd only seen pictures of it. I'd been to the university earlier today—*god, was that only this morning?*— so I had a clear image of where I needed to be. I hoped Collette was right.

Sam's eyes widened briefly at my hand's movement, as if worried I might try to overpower the agent. It would have been a reasonable assumption since Sam still didn't know the talisman was at the root of my power. Unless Jarett had told him. My heart clenched. Oh, Jarett. I glanced at his still form on the driveway, feeling wobbly on my crouched feet, fighting the urge to vomit.

Lopez's gun shifted in his hand. He was getting impatient. It was now or never.

I closed my eyes tight, the weight of my guilt settling in my gut. I was leaving Sam to face the aftermath of what would be my hasty and no doubt shocking departure, but if there was another way, I couldn't think of it. Fighting a wave of panic, I forced myself to focus on my heartbeat.

With Lopez's gun still pushed threateningly against the back of my head, I reached deep into my memory, to the calming exercises I'd learned all those years ago to help me cope with Isla's disappearance. I pictured myself on a white sandy beach, the ebb and flow of the waves mimicking the beat my heart needed to match. I took a deep breath in for four counts, holding it for seven before releasing it to a slow and steady count of eight.

In for four. Hold for seven. Out for eight.

In the background, I could make out a conversation taking place. Male voices. One comforting, one combative. My body tensed, threatening to turn on me, but my mind wouldn't allow it. I was already drifting free.

As my heartbeat began to sync with the rhythm of the lapping waves, I held the image of my destination firmly in my mind. The back entrance to Collette's lab at the university. Ten-thirty p.m. October 14, 2014.

Chapter Twenty-Seven

OCTOBER 14, 2014, 10:30 P.M.

Nothing in my timeblinking career thus far could've prepared me for what happened next.

Darkness swallowed me. I was falling. *Tumbling.* Over and over, as if I'd been tossed into a pitch-black mineshaft with no bottom. My arms flailed, searching for something tangible to grasp. It was no use. Down, down I went, my mind going to Collette and her clever lies. How could I have been so stupid? She'd duped me. She'd abused my trust and lured me into this pit of death where she could be rid of me forever.

As I descended deeper and deeper, my mind snapped to my life before I'd boarded that doomed flight. How much simpler things had been back when I could enjoy quiet days at the beach with my little boy, his tiny hand in mine as we splashed in the surf. I'd have given anything to turn back the clock and steal one more day like that, my boy's laughter filling my ears like a love song. But it was too late for impossible wishes like that—all that remained was this plunge into darkness and whatever new horror awaited me at its end.

If there *was* an end. Would I be stuck in this freefall for eternity, or perhaps turned to dust and scattered in the wind?

Then, without warning, my back slammed down on an

unforgivingly hard surface, emptying my lungs of air. I gasped for breath and scrambled to my feet, dizzy and still night-blind. Slowly, ever so slowly, my vision returned.

As I teetered on my feet, I surveyed my surroundings. There was little doubt I'd landed in the right spot: a narrow alley between two imposing brick buildings. Several dull barn lights hung over each of the half-dozen doors, exactly as I'd seen them this morning. My eyes did a double take when a thin, shadowy figure standing beneath one of the lights raised a hand and waved me over. In ordinary times, I would've turned around and run like hell in the other direction, but these were not ordinary times.

I staggered toward the willowy figure with the sleek, shoulder-length hair, recalling everything that had happened in the last half hour. *Thirty minutes.* It seemed like a lifetime ago I'd come face to face with my little boy who wasn't so little anymore. The confrontation with Lopez. The crack of the gunshot that had cut Jarett down. Sam trying desperately to reason with the psychotic agent. Another shot piercing the silence, fortuitously missing its target. And then the final crazy freefall that had put me at the mercy of Collette's dubious trustworthiness. A twinge of guilt tugged at me as I limped up to her, thankful she had not condemned me to eternal darkness—or death—when she'd revealed a way to use the talisman without touching it.

"Are you okay?" She was clearly worried about my weakened state.

"Barely. What the hell was that?"

"What was what?"

"Your cardio-telepathic method. It nearly killed me. Is it always that hazardous?"

"Oh dear. I didn't think you would ever use it. Otherwise, I would've warned you more explicitly of the potential dangers." She pulled the metal door open with a creak and held out her hand, which I gladly took.

227

"I had no choice but to use it."

She drew me through the door and let it bang shut behind us. I had to stop and lean on the cool cinderblock wall in the hallway to stop my head spins. Collette pulled out her phone and shone its flashlight into my eyes.

"Judging by your pupil dilation and your unsteadiness, I'm assuming you've experienced the temporocausal drift anomaly."

"Of course you have a name for it."

"It happens randomly due to fluctuations in the space-time continuum at the time of displacement. Don't worry, the woozy feeling will wear off lickety-split."

I found myself smiling at her use of Morley's favorite word.

"Come on," she said, grabbing my arm and slinging it over her shoulder. "We've got lots to do."

As we walked through a maze of hallways, I spilled the story about how I'd left things in 2024, tripping over my words the more I rattled on. By the time I finished, Collette was swiping her keycard in a reader next to another heavy metal door. I was mentally exhausted but lighter in heart. Just telling someone else about my ordeal helped to relieve my panic.

"I suppose it was inevitable that you would find Christopher —or rather, *Scott*—one day, all things considered," she said, leading me inside the lab. The door sealed shut behind us with a hiss. I blinked against the harsh fluorescent lights, taking in the oddly comforting chemical smell and the soft hum of machines.

"I'm glad you picked Sam and Lizzy," I said.

She chuckled under her breath. "You picked them yourself."

"What? I thought you said I didn't want to know where Christopher was."

"You didn't. But we talked about how that other timeline would collapse once I shuffled Christopher off to 2014, meaning you wouldn't, in theory, remember our conversation. It was a risk, but one you were willing to take to ensure Christopher ended up in Sam and Lizzy's care."

As crazy as it was, I'm glad we took the chance.

Collette tossed her keycard onto the counter and guided me over to a stool. "And I'm sorry about your friend Jarett. He sounded like a great guy."

"Yes. He was a great guy," I said, sitting down heavily on a stool next to a counter, grief threatening to consume me. "But I realized it too late. Fuck. I accused him of some terrible things."

"You couldn't have known."

"I think I was looking for a way out."

"Of what?"

"Coming to terms with my feelings for him. I was just so conflicted, you know? I cared about him, but my love for Morl —" I stopped myself short, feeling ashamed to be talking about my feelings for another woman's widower when the woman in question was standing right in front of me and had done so much to help me.

"It's okay. You love Morley too. I can't blame you for that. He's practically irresistible."

I smiled. "He is. *Was.* Wait, where are we now?"

"Ahh, yes, a classic example of temporal displacement disorientation. Not remembering where or *when* you are."

"I've never really had that problem before. Mind you, I've mostly only visited 2019."

"That is truly astonishing to me when there are so many eras to visit. So many things to learn…even if all it got *me* was a ticket to an early grave."

"That's just awful. Do you think you would've done the same thing, had you known about the health risks?"

"Probably," she said. "Ha, who am I kidding? Of course I would've."

"I'm glad you warned me about the dangers. I won't be taking risks like that anytime soon."

"You won't have the choice, anyway. It's why I've asked you to meet me tonight."

"Right. This big fix-the-world mission you've been so vague about."

She leaned her backside on the counter and crossed her arms. "Remember when you tried to change the past, and the events played out the same way regardless?"

"You mean the Novikov thing?"

"Precisely."

"I think I'm starting to understand it better. I did try time-blinking back to the day my twin was abducted, but I couldn't stop it from happening." The memory sent an icy shiver down the back of my neck. "I tried, even though Morley had already warned me not to bother. I should've known it was a waste of time. He himself tried over and over to avoid getting hit by that truck outside the pub, but the accident kept occurring, no matter what intervention he tried."

"Did you know that *intention* is a factor when it comes to changing the past?"

I nodded. Morley and I had experienced that many times. "Why is that, do you think?"

"That's a puzzle I have yet to solve. What I do know is that if you go back with the conscious desire to tamper with events, the timeline pushes back and won't allow it. However, that's not to say your actions in a past timeline can't change the future. They certainly can. Even the most innocuous action in the past can ripple outward and effect big changes in the future...changes that may or may not be favorable."

I shrugged. "I've never noticed anything like that."

She hopped onto the stool next to me and opened her laptop. "You wouldn't because those actions overwrite the original event."

"The way the universe wants it to happen."

"Yes. And now we need to sort out how you're going to pull off this timeline reset."

My gut sank. "Reset?"

"It's how you're going to undo all the damage you've caused."

"I don't understand why it's my fault. You've been time traveling all over the place for twenty-five years. Why haven't your actions caused any ripples?"

"Because I'm a scientist, and I generally take careful, calculated risks. You, on the other hand, are a novice, and you've unwittingly revealed the talisman's power to this scoundrel from the FBI. Given his ties to various government bodies—and thus whole *teams* of physicists—it's inevitable that someone smarter than me will eventually unravel the mystery. And resetting the timeline is how you're going to prevent the resulting chaos. At least temporarily."

"You were serious."

"I rarely joke. Especially about things this important."

My shoulders slumped. "Fuck me."

Collette turned to face me. "Good. You understand the gravity of the situation. It *is* pretty daunting, and I don't envy you for what you're about to do. But if you don't stop Morley from discovering the talisman's power, it will be disastrous for the world."

"You've never said what this big disaster is. Shouldn't you tell me so I can decide for myself if I need to take this massive risk?"

"I've been vague for good reason. You can't even fathom what's coming if you fail to fix the issue."

I pictured rampant consumerism, mountains of waste, hellish wildfires wiping out billions of acres of forest, the devastating loss of life to COVID-19, the war between Russia and Ukraine, and the ongoing conflicts in the Middle East. "I can't imagine how the world could get any worse. Unless another pandemic comes along and turns us all into zombies."

231

"No zombies. But let's just say that if you let this thing go any further, it will result in an entirely new world order. One that makes your 2020 pandemic look like a cakewalk by comparison."

"When?" I said, my chewing on my thumb. "When will all this chaos happen if I decide not to go through with it?"

She crossed her arms. "That's something I can't tell you."

"You said you saw it happen."

"Not exactly. I saw the beginnings of it before my health began to fail and I couldn't go to the future anymore. This FBI agent is the trigger. He's going to turn the talisman over to a team of the most talented physicists in the world and arm them with the knowledge of what he's learned from his investigation of you and your friends. Trust me, at some point they *will* figure out how to make it work—and how to permanently change events in the past—and the consequences are going to be catastrophic."

She pointed at my thumb where it was wedged between my teeth. "You'll chew that right off if you're not careful." I pulled my gnawed finger out of my mouth and shoved it under my arm.

"Can't I just kill the asshole and be done with it?"

She paused, as if she hadn't thought of this idea before, but I knew she was smarter than that. "You could."

I thought about the actual act of taking someone's life. "But I never would."

"That's right, because even with the fate of the world hanging in the balance, murder isn't in your makeup—especially since you know there's a much more humane solution."

The information tumbled around in my head. "What if I just throw the talisman into the ocean where no one can find it?"

Collette sighed. "You can't escape destiny by discarding it, Syd. The talisman's power is *meant* to be found, even at the bottom of the sea."

"So, what's the point of the reset, then?" God, my head hurt.

"The point is *time*, Syd. The reset buys time for the world to learn and mature, and to perhaps be better prepared to handle the power of the talisman when it *does* resurface some-day. It's about giving humanity a fighting chance to weather the storm."

"Ohhh. The reset just delays the inevitable."

"Yes. At least long enough to not be a problem in your lifetime, or even your children's."

"*Children?*"

"I'm speaking hypothetically."

"Oh, yeah. Of course."

"And it all starts with the ruinous day you just left behind. The one where an FBI agent has gone off the rails and is shooting innocent people."

"Maybe I should've let him finish the job...on me. I deserve it."

"That's no way to talk."

"Why not? I've already lost so many important people— my son. Jarett. Maybe Sam. Morley," I said. "And with me gone, timeblinking dies, too."

"Not necessarily. Do you really think the FBI will simply walk away from Agent Lopez's allegations, no matter how absurd they sound? Plus, the rest of *The 444 Five* will still be around."

With Jarett dead and young Eli of no use, that would leave Rose and Lainie to be hounded forever. Could I do that to them?

I thought of something just then. "With the timeline reset, does that mean there's a chance Jarett will live?"

"Possibly."

For the first time in many, many days, I felt a spark of hope.

233

"It's also possible he'll die in the line of duty or from cancer or..."

"Or what?" I said.

"Or in the crash of Flight 444."

My lungs hitched. "Because there will be no talisman to save him."

"I'm sure you realize what this means for you as well."

Everything went quiet, as if the room itself was holding its breath. "I'll be on that plane too."

Collette squeezed her lips together. She didn't have to say another word.

My thoughts went to Christopher—now Scott. I pictured him as a toddler throwing one of his prized rocks into the ocean and triggering ripples like the ones Collette had talked about. Thanks to my interference with the natural order of things, those small ripples now carried the potential to gather momentum and crash down on humanity like a tsunami.

I slid off my stool and paced to the end of the counter, grateful for Collette's silence. I didn't want to hear anything more. I needed time to work out the implications of what she was asking me to do. Of what I was coming to understand *must* be done.

At the end of it, I had a sobering thought. I turned and faced her. "If I do pull off this reset, that means Scott won't even exist."

"I'm afraid so." Her voice sounded miles away.

"Well, that just turned a bad situation worse."

"Don't torture yourself. If fate dictates that you don't end up perishing on that flight, there's a strong chance you'll simply awaken in a whole new timeline, which means you'll be living an entirely different life with no memory of any of this." She gestured vaguely in the air.

"Still without my son."

She nodded.

"Either way, I'll never get to see him again."

"I know it's hard to think about, but please know that whatever happens, you'll have no memory of his existence."

I took another minute to collect my thoughts while Collette punched keys on her computer. She was asking a lot of a simple, everyday mom… who also happened to be a time traveler. A time traveler who really fucked up.

"Okay, so how do you propose I keep Morley from discovering the talisman's power? You've already said we can't change the past on purpose."

"Therein lies the key. We can't do it *on purpose*." She swiveled her stool to face me. "But we *can* outwit destiny, so to speak. I've developed a compound to help with this."

"Compound? What, like Kryptonite?" I was only half-joking. "Do I use it on Morley to make him powerless against me?"

"Not quite. We'll be using it on you. It works by inducing a temporary amnesic state, removing any conscious thought about changing the past. At least, that's how it's *supposed* to work."

"Great. What do you mean by that?"

"It's only experimental at this point. I was about to commence testing when I had to rescue your little boy. It's our best shot, I'm afraid."

As if my life wasn't messed up enough. Now I was about to become a human lab rat. Returning to Collette's side, I squinted at her screen, seeing only a string of meaningless numbers. "What is it exactly?"

"It's called a cortical quantum modifier, or CQM. It's designed to put you into a hypnotic, hyper-suggestible state in which you'll have no conscious intent to change the past."

I was skeptical. My father had tried to have me hypnotized as a last-ditch attempt to "straighten" me out as a teenager. "Hypnosis doesn't work on me."

"This is a drug-induced hypnotic state. Much different than traditional hypnotherapy."

235

"How does it work?"

Collette bit her bottom lip. "It's a little scary, but I think you'll do fine. After all, you jumped out of a crashing plane not too long ago."

"I don't like the sound of this."

"Relax. It's just me trying to prepare you for the worst. Better that than going into it blindly, right?"

"I suppose."

She snapped her laptop shut, making me jump. "First, I'll administer the CQM and suggest a trigger. Then you'll enter a trance-like state which will allow you to access the planted trigger."

"I'll be in a trance? Won't Morley think that's weird?"

"It's an internal thing. You'll act completely normally throughout the process."

"You seem quite sure about all this."

"I'm sure about this part, yes. And you'll have to mind the time. The CQM will activate at the twenty-minute mark and will wear off ten minutes later."

"I have ten minutes to get this deed done?"

"Yes. Timing is crucial. Which reminds me…" Hurrying to the other end of the counter, she dug into her designer bag and pulled out a vintage gold watch with a burgundy leather strap. On her way back, she popped out a tiny, ridged button on the side of the watch, rotating it several times until it wouldn't turn anymore and then compared the time with that of her FitWatch and made an adjustment. "Trusty old thing."

She fastened it on my wrist. "It's beautiful," I said, studying it closely. The face was adorned with gold numerals and delicate hands, and there was a single small sapphire nestled directly beneath the twelve.

"I'm sure you know only analog watches work during time travel."

I shook my head. "I don't own an analog watch. I never really thought about it."

"Well, it will be important for this trip. The watch will remain in 2014 time, but it doesn't matter. You'll just need it to keep track of your ten-minute window."

"So how do I get Morley to give me the talisman?"

"Patience. I'm getting there. It involves 'accidentally' bumping into him at The Bold & Bean, and during your conversation with him, the trigger will prompt you to ask him a question that you'll have no awareness of."

"How can you be sure Morley will say this trigger word?"

"It's not a word. It's the talisman itself," she said. "You're going to ask Morley to see it, and when he pulls it out of his shirt, you'll fall into the hypnotic state. That's when you're going to say you've been admiring it and would like to borrow it because you want to have one made for yourself."

I nearly laughed. "He barely knew me in January 2019. Why would he hand it over to me?"

Collette smiled. "Don't kid yourself. Morley had his eyes on you well before January 2019. He'll lend it to you in a heartbeat."

I thought back to my casual pre-timeblinking relationship with Morley and looked at Collette doubtfully. "But what if he doesn't?"

"Well then, we'll have to try something else."

This was so overwhelming. All of it. The experimental drug so perfectly tailored to our needs that it sounded like nothing more than snake oil. The mess I'd left back in 2024. Having to put every ounce of trust in this woman who—less than twenty-four hours ago—had been a complete stranger. A woman I'd fantasized about killing.

"There's a slight hiccup in all of this," she said.

"Why am I not shocked?"

She rushed over to a metal cabinet and punched a code into the lock. The door, which bore her name, popped open. "So far, I've only tested CQM on rats. It's been approximately ninety-eight percent effective, but whether or not it works on humans is a bit of a question mark."

She paused, letting that sink in, yet the first question that came to my mind was *how can you tell if a rat has been hypnotized?* I was too tired to hear another scientific explanation and let it go.

"And there's one more thing," she added, bringing a futuristic-looking acrylic case back to the counter. She set it down and withdrew a small vial of glowing, yellowish-green liquid that reminded me of disinfectant bathroom cleaner. Positively toxic.

"It takes months to produce a single dose of CQM. This is all I have." She held it up between us. "Enough for a hundred rats. Or one human."

Collette must have sensed my anxiety. She put the vial back in the case, clasped her hands, and looked me square in the eye. "I know we've just met, but you need to trust me, Syd. I wouldn't suggest any of this if I thought it was unsafe."

Once again, I was mesmerized by the stunning mosaic in her eyes. The longer she held my gaze, the more convinced I became of her sincerity, and thus, of Morley's conviction that she wanted to help people, not hurt them. "Are there any side effects?"

"Most of the rats were a bit sluggish afterward, but it wore off pretty quickly. They were otherwise fine."

I gave her a tired smile. "I'm sorry I messed this up so bad."

"You didn't do it intentionally. Besides, I should really be thanking you for being the first—and likely the last—human CQM recipient. If I hadn't compromised my cellular structure so terribly, I would have tested it on myself."

"I suppose this is where I should say I'm honored to serve as your lab rat."

She chuckled. "I won't pretend to be humble. This *is* a pretty big deal. I'm just disappointed I'll never be able to share this or any of my time-travel studies with my peers. Never mind. In light of recent events, I obviously made the right choice keeping the power to myself all these years."

Lopez's face popped into my head. "Humans are such assholes."

She laughed again. "Anyway, we should get started." She slid a drawer open and selected a giant syringe from a tray.

I reeled backward. "What the hell is that?"

"The administration route for the compound. Don't worry. It just looks ominous. It's really no big deal."

"No big deal if you don't mind needles."

"You'll be fine."

She filled the syringe with the entire vial of CQM, tapping out the air bubbles with her finger and slipping a protective sheath over the end.

"Good God. I can't believe you're going to jab me with that."

"It's okay to be scared. You'll just have to do your best."

Her words catapulted me right back to my childhood, to the day my mother had taken me for my first swimming lesson. Only back then I'd been learning how to save myself. Not all of humanity.

"You have a lot of faith in a person you barely know."

"On the contrary. I've been following you for some time now. I know your strengths as well as your weaknesses, and I have no doubt you'll slay this particular dragon."

It was no secret that she'd been watching me, and at this point, I didn't care. I was broken and exhausted, and I just wanted this nightmare to be over.

She allowed me to take the syringe for a closer look. I turned it over several times in my grasp. "You sure I can't just drink the stuff?"

"Sure, if you want to dissolve your stomach from the inside out."

I handed it back. "That's reassuring."

"Will you know what you have to do when you land back in 2024?"

"Honestly, I have no idea what's waiting for me there. Maybe Sam is dead. Or he finally subdued Lopez. I just hope the rest of Sam's family hasn't shown up in the meantime."

"Yes, let's hope everything goes smoothly. Are you ready?"

I drew in a deep breath. "Can a person ever be ready for something like this?"

"Why don't you give me a step-by-step rundown of what you're going to do when you get there? It will help solidify the mission in your mind."

I closed my eyes and took several deep breaths, picturing myself at the moment of my return where Lopez had gone bonkers. When I opened my eyes again, I had only one comment. "Immediately get my butt to 2019."

"That's step one. What's next?"

"Find Morley at The Bold & Bean."

"When?"

"January twelfth. He always walks there on Saturday mornings, right?"

"Yes. A creature of habit, my husband is. What time?"

"I'm going to say nine fifteen?"

"That's about right. He always leaves after the BBC News. Worst case you may have to wait for five minutes, but that still gives you plenty of time. It's too bad I can't go on a reconnaissance mission to confirm this for you."

"I wouldn't even think of asking."

She smiled. "Next?"

"Strike up a conversation with him. Try my best to sound natural when I ask to see the talisman." I glanced at the hypodermic needle in her hand. "You're sure I won't experience any weird behavior with that radioactive goop?"

"A thousand percent. I was able to ascertain *that* much in my experimentation."

"I guess I'll have to trust you. As for what comes next, I'm a little hazy."

"Well, if all goes according to plan—and I'd be willing to bet my life that it will—you'll switch to autopilot, as it were, and ask Morley to lend you the talisman. But you won't have any awareness of doing it."

"And then?"

"I'd *almost* bet my life that you'll simply continue to exist in a whole new timeline."

"Or?"

She shook her head gently. "Don't think about that."

"How can I not?" A few tears started to trickle down my face. I had to know. "If my fate is to die on Flight 444, will I feel pain?"

"That, I suppose, is the only benefit of this endeavor. You'll just cease to exist."

"But what about Lainie? And Jarett and Rose? They'll still die horrifically."

"You mustn't agonize over this." She reached over and stroked my arm. "Think about your sisters and their families."

"What happened to you betting your life I'll wake up in another timeline?"

"I said *almost*. In my heart, I believe that's what will happen…but since I wasn't able to test it, I can't guarantee it."

"You shouldn't have told me. You should've said everything would be cool. I wouldn't have known the difference, right?"

"It's not ethical. I wouldn't do that to anyone, even my husband's mistress."

I swiped my tears away in a quick, dismissing motion, bracing myself. "Let's do this."

"I admire your bravery, Syd. You're a true pioneer in the field of quantum physics. I just wish you could be recognized for your sacrifice."

"I don't want recognition. I want to live. I want to save the world. I want to hold my child in my arms again."

Collette flashed me a sorrowful look. She knew it was impossible for me to have all three things without sacrificing so many more.

"Oh, I almost forgot," Collette said, going back to her purse. She produced a mid-sized Swiss Army knife and flipped it open. "For protection. It sounds like you're going into a volatile situation."

She spun the knife around and handed it to me, its blade still extended. Though solid and secure in my grasp, it would be no match for Lopez's gun.

"Ready?"

"Ready."

"I'll need you to remove your sleeve."

My whole body tensed as I shrugged out of my hoodie. "I can't believe I'm doing this."

"You'll do fine. Now, take two deep breaths and hold the third one," she said, hovering the needle over my upper arm. On my third inhale, there was a small sting, then nothing. I pushed all the air out of my lungs as Collette applied a bandage to my arm. Phase one complete.

"Don't forget to note the time," she said, pointing to my wrist.

I glanced at the watch. "Eleven sixteen," I said, then slipped my arm back into my sleeve.

"Which means?"

"The CQM will be active at eleven thirty-six."

"Then what?"

"Any time after eleven thirty-six, I'll ask Morley to show me the talisman."

"Correct. But before eleven forty-six."

I nodded.

"All right. Off you go," she said breezily but with a disquieted look behind her eyes. "Good luck, Syd."

"I'll do my best."

I clutched the knife a bit harder and took the talisman into my free hand. "Return."

Chapter Twenty-Eight

I n the blink of an eye, I was back in 2024 crouched next to
my car. In my hand was the pocketknife with its small but
sturdy blade extended, ready for anything. I slid it into my
pocket, within easy reach, hoping like hell I wouldn't be forced
to use it.

Suddenly, Lopez's voice boomed amid the quiet weekday
afternoon. "Consequences? I don't give a rat's ass about
consequences!"

I peered out from around my car, and by a stroke of luck,
Lopez's back was turned. Perfect. He hadn't seen me arrive.
He was gesticulating wildly with his gun, his frenzied eyes
fixed on the ground a few feet in front of him. It could only
mean that Sam had fallen…or had been shot.

Remembering with sudden alarm that I was on a strict
schedule, I pulled my sleeve back to glance at Collette's watch.
She'd been right. It was still showing 2014 time—now eleven
seventeen—with the second-hand chugging along reliably,
proving it was still functioning properly.

Gathering my courage, I scrambled to my feet and crept
out from the cover of the car, believing with all my heart that
Lopez would not harm me. He needed me alive.

Finally, I spotted Sam, and what I saw wasn't good. He was curled in a ball on the driveway, grimacing in pain, a crimson splotch blooming across his thigh and his hand pressed against the wound. His eyes burned with defiance. "You don't mean that," he croaked out, clenching his jaw against the pain. "You're so close to...mmph...getting all the evidence you need. Having two dead bodies won't win you any...leniency with the Bureau."

"On the contrary, my friend. The Bureau will turn a blind eye to collateral damage when they find out what I know." Lopez leaned over, his finger poised on the trigger. "Now I'm going to ask you one last time. When will she be back?"

"Hey!" I called out, thrusting my hands into the air as his head whipped around, eyes wild. Sam caught my eye. I couldn't tell if he was relieved that I'd shown up or worried for my safety. Perhaps it was a bit of both.

"Please don't hurt Sam. I'll do whatever you want."

Lopez's shock morphed into a victorious grin. "Well, well. I knew you'd be back, despite what our friend here kept insisting."

"Leave him out of it. He's not involved."

"The fuck he's not involved! He's been trying to gaslight me from the beginning. Not that it matters, now. You've just said you'll do anything. Let's start with the truth."

I laughed bitterly. "How's this for the truth? You're right! I'm a time traveler." I took another step closer to him. He swung his gun away from Sam and aimed it directly at my heart. "In fact, I've been time traveling for five whole years now. Hundreds of times. My fiancé in 2019 and I call it time-blinking. And guess what? *The 444 Five* are in on it. All of them. Well, you can't count Jarett anymore, you fucking barbarian."

"I gad-damn knew it."

Through gritted teeth, Sam yelled, "Syd! Don't tell him anything more. He'll never be able to prove it."

I let out a tired breath. "It doesn't matter, Sam, because you know what? All of this," I said, spreading my hands in the air. "Everything we know to be real right now...It's all about to change." If my mission was successful, that was. If not? I'd have a dogged FBI agent nipping at my heels for my entire future...whatever grim future that might be.

Lopez squinted. "What the hell does that mean? What's about to change?"

I checked Collette's watch. Eleven nineteen. That meant there were seventeen minutes to go before the CQM kicked in. Still plenty of time.

"You were right. I'm the grand poohbah of this whole operation."

I pulled the talisman out of my shirt fully intending to tell Lopez everything. But when he leaned forward and practically salivated, I decided to keep that detail to myself. At least for now. I dropped the pendant back to my chest and carried on with the abbreviated version of the story.

"I had the power to zap my friends off that crashing plane right into September 2019. Rose outfitted us with skydiving gear and taught us how to use it. When we returned to 2024, we ended up back on the plane and the five of us jumped to safety before it crashed. I'm sure you've heard the rest of the story, the part where we were discovered safe and sound in that Iowan cornfield. Oh, but here's something you don't know: Sam was with us."

"Syd! That's enough!" Sam barked.

But I wasn't looking at him. I was completely focused on Lopez, and judging by the agent's glazed-over expression and now lax stance, he hadn't been expecting the truth to be so shocking. He'd even lowered his gun.

"That's right. Sam is here on a timeblink from 2019. He didn't run off with a secret lover for five years as everyone believed. He took a surprise ride to 2024 with my group when he caught us timeblinking out of a hospital room." I turned my head. "Right, Sam? You've known about timeblinking since 2014 when Collette asked you to raise Christopher— *Scott* now—as your own."

Sam shook his head incredulously, begging me with his eyes to keep quiet.

"It's okay, Sam. As I said, it doesn't matter. I've met with Collette several times in the last few hours, and she's filled me in on the devastation this jackass was about to cause," I said, tilting my head to Lopez. "And I'm about to fix it."

"What do you mean?" Sam asked, still trying to stem the flow of blood from his leg.

Lopez finally spoke. "I knew it. I bloody well knew your kid was part of this whole crazy thing when he disappeared with the physicist." He swung his head back around to Sam. "And I damn well knew you were involved, too, considering the necklace was at your house."

My stomach dropped.

"Necklace?" I said, trying to feign ignorance.

"Come on, Ms. Brixton. Do you seriously think you can keep secrets from the FBI? I mean, it's what we *do*. The coffee meeting with your recently fallen comrade told me everything I needed to know."

My memory flashed back to Monday afternoon at The Bold & Bean when Jarett had given me the talisman. Apparently, we hadn't been careful enough. "I don't know what you're talking about."

"There was no sound on our video surveillance, of course," Lopez said. "But that doesn't matter. I bet you didn't know one of my talents is lip reading."

I bristled.

"It comes in handy every decade or two. The footage was pretty rough, but I got all the information I needed when Officer Cooper handed you the necklace and you mentioned going back to 2014 to rescue your kid—a kid who's a gad-damn teenager now! It all makes perfect sense!" He pointed to the talisman now on full display on the outside of my t-shirt. "You'll be turning that in *tout suite*."

My hand flew up to the talisman, shielding it from his view, while Sam issued a terse warning. "Syd! Don't say another word. That video surveillance of you and Jarett wasn't recorded. Lopez even admit—"

"Shut your face," Lopez snapped, never taking his eyes off me. "It doesn't matter anyway because I have all the proof I need. That piece is how you time travel. Or as you say, time *blink*."

Until this moment, I'd been harboring doubt about Collette's warning. How, I'd wondered, would the FBI know about the talisman's power if the only person I'd told was Jarett? I glanced at his still form. How wrong I'd been to accuse him. How wrong I'd been about his loyalty.

"Well, the joke's on you, asshole," I spat. "My next time-blink will be to reset everything that's happened since January 2019. Timeblinking will never be discovered. It'll go to Dr. Scott's grave with her."

"Why would you do that?" Lopez said. He sounded like a kid whose mother had just taken away his Xbox.

"What's that saying? Oh yes…*this is why we can't have nice things*. There'll always be people like you who can't keep themselves from ruining something special. And in the case of timeblinking, if I don't prevent you from getting your dirty little meat hooks on the power, humanity itself will go to ruins."

"You're bluffing," Lopez said, his hand tightening on his gun.

"I'm not." I looked at my watch. Eleven twenty-four. Twelve minutes until activation. "And I'm about to prove it." I took up the talisman once again and opened my mouth to recite my destination when a blur of movement caught my eye over Lopez's shoulder. It was the front door swinging open. Scott came barreling out.

"No!" I shrieked.

But Scott didn't even glance my way. He flew to Sam's side.

"Dad!" he cried, collapsing to his knees, his slight but sturdy shoulders shaking in despair.

Sam put on a brave face. "It's okay, buddy. Just a flesh wound." His pallor and volume of blood loss said otherwise. I wondered if the bullet had hit an artery.

I gasped when Lopez swung the gun toward them. "Well, there's a mind-blowing sight. Two time travelers from different eras converging in a whole different timeline. The wonder of it all!"

Scott glowered at Lopez, opening his mouth, but no words came out. He was in complete shock, and it was anyone's guess what he might do next.

I rushed over, hands raised, positioning myself between Scott and Lopez. My thoughts went to the knife in my pocket, but it might as well have been a wet noodle for all the good it would do against the agent's weapon. I briefly considered timeblinking my way out of there and returning with a gun of my own four and a half minutes later, but I couldn't bear the thought of leaving Scott and my wounded friend to fend off this madman by themselves…even if none of this would be an issue in a few short minutes.

There was only one option.

"Take me," I said to Lopez. "Take me to the station, and I'll tell you everything. I'll even demonstrate how the talisman works." It was a brilliant plan. I figured once he got me into the car and far away from Sam and Scott, I would timeblink my ass out of there.

He glanced down at Sam, nodding once. "You hear that, Sammy? She's finally come to her senses."

Sam could only grunt his disapproval.

Lopez turned to me. "But the boy comes with us."

"What? Hell no. Do you want my cooperation or not?"

"I don't think you have a choice in the matter, Ms. Brixton."

Damn it. This is not how I envisioned things going, but time was running out. I would have to pivot.

As I turned to help Scott up, he was already on his feet, shooting past me, throwing all his weight into Lopez's gut. The two of them slammed to the ground. Sam cried out for Scott to stop. The gun discharged, shattering my car's left headlight before twirling through the air and landing a couple of feet away. I ran for it, but Lopez was closer. Faster. He swiped the gun off the ground, simultaneously wrapping his arm around Scott's neck, securing him in a chokehold. I couldn't believe the guy's agility; he had to be at least twenty years older than me.

Out of breath, Lopez hauled Scott to his feet, jabbing his gun into the side of my baby's ribcage. "Cut the bullshit, kid," he said.

Scott struggled in Lopez's grasp, ramming his elbow deep into the man's stomach. The agent barely flinched. He was too big. Too strong.

"Don't, sweetie," I said, keeping my tears at bay. "Everything will be okay if we do what he tells us."

When Scott stopped squirming, Lopez swung the gun toward me and nodded toward his sedan where it was parked up the hill at the curb. "Move."

I trudged up to his car, overcome with worry when he didn't follow with Scott. Did he mean to hurt him? What was worse, when I got to the vehicle, I noticed that two of the tires were flat.

"Open the trunk," he shouted up at me, his arm still wrapped around Scott's neck. "There's a box of hand restraints under a blanket. Bring me two of them."

When I returned to where they stood, Lopez instructed me to fasten Scott's hands with one of the plastic ties. As I worked, I peered deep into my son's eyes, doing my best to reassure him; the unwavering trust reflected back nearly broke me. In a matter of minutes, I'd be erasing his presence from this world. My knees buckled momentarily. I was no better a human than Lopez. What mother would do this to her child?

A mother who was trying to save the world.

Finishing up with Scott's restraint, I noticed movement over Lopez's shoulder and was horrified to see Sam commando-crawling toward us. There was no way he was going to make it, and even if he got to us, what could he do? I shook my head at him. *Stay back. I've got this.*

Lopez pushed Scott into the space between us. "Kneel."

When Scott hesitated, Lopez shouted, "I'm not gonna say it twice!"

"Do it, sweetie," I said. "Please."

Scott glared at Lopez. "Fucking asshole."

I was so shocked I almost laughed out loud. My sweet little boy was so grown up.

Lopez did laugh. "I've been called worse. Here. Put this around your mom's wrists," he ordered, handing the plastic tie to Scott. "You do know she's your mom, right?"

Scott just scowled.

As I held out my hands, Lopez muttered, "Uh-uh. Turn around. Yours go behind."

I realized with dread that that would leave me unable to access the talisman. "Seriously? What am I going to do with my hands tied together?"

"Turn around!"

"Fine!"

Once my hands were secured at my back, Lopez got me to kneel next to Scott. I don't know what hurt more: the jagged gravel biting at my knees through my leggings or the feeling of complete and utter helplessness. I trembled. This was how they executed people.

Lopez briefly inspected his gun and plodded around behind us. I turned to Scott, hoping to comfort him but failing to conceal my own terror. Scott looked away and closed his eyes. This could be it for us. Maybe it was for the best. We would die together.

"I'll need the key to your SUV, Sammy," came Lopez's voice at our backs. "Now!"

Sam didn't reply. After a few muffled grunts, I heard the faint *thunk* of Sam's fob landing on the ground. "Sorry I gotta use your wheels, buddy. It's whatcha get for shooting my tires out."

"Syd, you don't have to...mmph...say another word," I heard Sam grunt out.

"Shut up!" Lopez yelled.

The gun fired.

Scott screamed.

I whirled around on my knees, losing my balance and crashing to the ground. My ear struck the gravel and ignited a white-hot flash of pain that radiated through my skull. As I lay there—by some grace still conscious—I had an unobstructed view of Sam. *Oh, Sam. You've done so much for me. And this is how you're rewarded?*

But he wasn't limp and lifeless as I'd expected. He was very much alert, and his hand was still pressed to his wound. My lungs deflated. It had been a warning shot. That was all.

"Not another word, or next time I won't miss," Lopez growled.

I gave my friend a defeated smile and mouthed *I'm sorry*. What he didn't know was that I'd come here with a plan. Yes, that plan was a bit off the rails at the moment, but if Lopez was about to do what I expected him to, I could get it back on track.

I turned my attention to Scott who was curled into a tight ball next to me with his hands covering his face. He was no longer screaming but whimpering softly, still not aware his dad was safe.

"Scott, sweetie," I said, powerless to hug him, but at least I could offer reassuring words. "Your dad's fine. He's going to be okay."

"Get up," Lopez ordered. "Both of you."

I did as Lopez asked, and to my relief, Scott followed. His eyes were vacant, his cheeks smudged with dirt and streaked with tears. He stole a glance in Sam's direction and, learning his dad was indeed still alive, let out a barking sob of joy.

Lopez opened the Suburban's back door. "In you go. Back seat, both of you."

"Asshole," Scott said again, climbing into his dad's vehicle, turning to help me up.

"The far back," Lopez said. "Where you can't bother me."

And where you can't control me, I thought. By some crazy miracle, he hadn't confiscated the talisman. There was still a chance to salvage this mission.

Lopez went around and hopped into the driver's seat and caught my eye in the rearview mirror. "No funny business." He held up his gun to remind us he wasn't beyond using it again.

"Don't worry about us. I'm well aware it's over."

"Well, fancy that. This is just the beginning for me. I've got a timeblinking momma and her teenage mutant time-blinking son to prove I'm not crazy. And the bonus? It'll justify Officer Cooper's death. Poor guy just had to get in the way, didn't he?"

"You're sick," I said as Lopez slammed the SUV into reverse and rocketed backwards up the driveway. As we neared the top, I spotted three cop cars parked a short distance down the road with an ambulance just beyond. I nudged Scott's shoulder, nodding in the direction of the cavalry.

"HA!" he blurted, much to my alarm. "You're so busted! The cops are here, and I told them you killed Jarett!"

"I *am* the cops, son. They're here to escort us to the station."

A police escort? Was he delusional? They were only here because a terrified kid had reported a lunatic with a gun.

We skidded backward into the road, screeching to a stop before Lopez thrust the gearstick into drive and punched the gas. Scott and I hit the back of our seats with bone-jarring force.

"Hold on, kids!" Lopez shouted. "This ride's about to get rough."

I ventured a glance out the back window where two of the police cars were scrambling into action, their sirens howling to life as they approached. The third one pulled into Sam's driveway followed closely by an ambulance. Scott caught my attention with fear plastered across his face. *What do we do?* he mouthed.

Pushing my rattled nerves away, I leaned into his ear and spoke as calmly as possible. "There's a knife in my right pocket. Get it and cut my hands loose."

As he fished around clumsily in my pocket, my focus went back to the rearview mirror. It was important to reassure Lopez that we were behaving ourselves should he check on us. Fortunately, he had bigger problems to deal with, like the police car pulling up next to us, trying to get his attention. I caught the officer's eye, trying to silently alert him that there were innocent passengers on board, but when a bus rounded the corner coming in the opposite direction, he had to drop back behind us.

Once Scott finally got a hold of the knife, I angled my body away from him. While he sawed through the stubborn plastic, I fretted over the possibility that he might not succeed, leaving me to resort to the heartbeat trick—a daunting prospect given my heightened state of anxiety. And even if I succeeded, I'd arrive at Bold & Bean's back door in a complete brain fog with precious time slipping away as I struggled to escape my hand restraints.

So, it was back to plan A.

I could feel Scott working diligently behind me, determined to cut me loose. A tear slid down my cheek. This child was my heart. My soul. My everything. And once he finished this task, I would be free to wipe him from existence—the worst betrayal a mother could imagine.

"I can't do it!" Scott whispered, though never ceasing his work. "It's too thick."

I turned slightly over my shoulder, hoping he couldn't see the tears streaking my face. "Keep trying, baby. You're so strong."

"Hey!" I heard Lopez scream as he wrenched the wheel to the right, knocking us off balance. The knife fell from Scott's grasp and bounced on the floor a couple of times, making a tinging sound as it hit something metal. I prayed Lopez couldn't hear it over the wail of the sirens and the Suburban's roaring engine.

When I looked up, Lopez was glaring at us in the rearview mirror. "What are you doing, son?"

I answered for him. "My wrists are burning. He's trying to help."

"Well, stop it!" Lopez ordered.

I noticed Scott scanning the floor for the knife, and when he was sure Lopez's attention was back on the road, he bent down to get a better look. I could feel my heart hammering against my ribs. *Come on, baby. Come on.*

With my focus alternating between the rearview mirror and Scott's frantic search for the knife, a chilling possibility took hold. Was Novikov's principle manifesting in this very moment? What if, after everything I'd done to keep my baby safe, his destiny was still to die at the hands of this horrible man?

As I swiped my teary cheeks over one shoulder and then the other, Scott sat back up, showing me the knife in his grasp. I gave him a quick smile and leaned forward slightly, trying not to turn my body too much. Scott seemed to understand

that this new position—though more challenging for him—
was necessary to conceal our activities. He resumed his
sawing.

"When you were little," I said, Lopez hearing me but
letting me speak, "you collected rocks. All sorts of them. Big,
small, round, jagged, barnacle-covered, moss-coated. It captivated me, your fascination with something so simple."

He stopped sawing to rub my arm, then resumed with
what felt like even more determination.

"But it taught me that the simplest things in life carry the
most meaning."

There was a sharp snap, and the restraint fell off. Lopez
hadn't heard it over the cacophony of blaring sirens.

I rubbed my wrists and stole a glance at my watch. *Oh my
god.* It was eleven thirty-three. That meant there were only
three minutes until the CQM activated—and I hadn't even
gotten to 2019 yet.

Come what may, I took the knife from Scott, and with
unexpected ease, cut through his restraint. Then I gathered
his sweet face in my hands and pressed my forehead to his.
"Sweetheart. Whatever happens, I want you to know that I—"
Sorrow strangled the words in my throat. I swallowed hard.
This needed to be said. "I have never loved anyone or
anything the way I love you." I leaned back to get a good look
at him. To look him in the eye. "Letting you go was the
hardest thing I've ever done, but I had no choice."

"I know, Mom," he said, choking back tears of his own. "I
always knew."

"Hey!" Lopez yelled, jerking the wheel again, throwing us
crashing into each other. I pushed myself up and pulled my
baby into my arms, squeezing him so tightly it felt like he'd
melded into my core. I buried my face in his hair, lingering
there for a moment before pulling myself away, barely regis-
tering Lopez's shouting.

Instinctively, I reached past Scott and pulled his seatbelt

around his torso, buckling him in. Yes, it was fruitless, but what mother wouldn't do the same thing, knowing what was to come?

"I'm so sorry, sweetheart. I wish things could be different for us."

He nodded despondently, as if he understood I was about to vanish from his life a second time.

Collette had insisted I would have no memory of my sweet boy after the reset, but I knew that couldn't be true. It just couldn't. He would exist in my soul forever.

When Scott reached over and gently patted the back of my hand, just as his Morley used to do, it almost shattered my heart.

Lopez took a corner fast, sending the hulking vehicle up on two wheels before it thudded back to the pavement. We were about two blocks from Blackfin Cove. The metal guardrail. The bluff.

I took the talisman between my fingers, waiting until the last possible moment to timeblink away from Scott forever.

One block.

Twenty feet.

I wrapped my free arm around Scott's shoulder, hugging him tight.

The SUV fishtailed. Tilted. And the moment its tires left the road and smashed through the guardrail, I released my son and called out my destination.

Chapter Twenty-Nine

My momentum came to a jarring halt when I collided with a big green garbage bin and thudded to the ground. Pain radiated through my shoulder to my elbow from the impact, but it couldn't compare to the grief swirling inside me. Scott's face flashed before my eyes, his terrified scream echoing in my ears as I abandoned him in his time of need. *Again.*

As I lay in a crumpled heap whimpering in the foggy January morning, I had only one thought: *Oh, sweetheart. How could I have done this to you?*

Then I imagined Collette's voice drifting on the breeze. *It wasn't your fault. It was his destiny.*

But all of it was the stuff of fairy tales, wasn't it? Scott's existence? Morley's love? My ability to timeblink? If it wasn't imaginary before, it certainly would be soon.

There was no time to waste.

I pulled myself up with a grunt, steeling myself against the eddying fog and damp wind, regretting my recent habit of picking the most impractical clothing for my timeblinks. Shivering, I tucked the talisman into my t-shirt and zipped my hoodie up to my neck. It would do me no favors if Morley spotted wife's precious necklace now. My mission would be over before it even started.

The Bold & Bean stood predictably before me, a painful reminder of the happy times I'd spent there surrounded by people I cared about…some of whom would no longer be a part of my life after this was all over.

If I even *had* a life after this was over.

Clutching my throbbing arm against my shattered heart, I shuffled to the front entrance of the café. As I reached for the handle, a fit young woman in yoga gear burst out with a latte in each hand, propping the door open with her hip. I thanked her and stepped inside, grateful for the instant warmth, ready for the next phase of my plan. According to Collette's watch, it was eleven thirty-five. I gasped. One minute until the CQM kicked in. Eleven minutes before it wore off. I prayed Morley was already there.

As I scoured the busy café for his face, the first soulful chords of Joni Mitchell's *Both Sides Now* floated down and wrapped my heart in sorrow as thick as the fog outside. I sank despondently into a scruffy velvet armchair, allowing the haunting melody to consume me.

I had undeniably seen life from two sides.

Indeed, for a brief, magical spell, one side had been brightened by the glow of Morley's love. With lazy mornings tangled in bed, his smooth fingertips trailing over my skin. With afternoons snuggled behind him on one of his motorbikes, exploring nature and restaurants and shops up and down the coast. And with moonlit walks around the lake or nights curled on the couch together, crying at sappy movies.

On the other side, of course, had been my beautiful life with Christopher in my natural timeline.

Now, both of those realities—and possibly my very life— were about to end.

By the time the song launched into the enchanting parallels between love and the whimsy of Ferris wheels and summer nights, my tears were flowing freely. I picked up a paper napkin from a small table next to my chair and blotted my tears, willing Morley to walk through the door and end my misery. It was time. I was ready.

But it wasn't meant to be.

In an aggravating twist, I spotted Stuart, one of my regulars at the pub, waiting to pay for his order at the cash register. Miraculously, he hadn't seen me yet.

I rose carefully to my feet to attract as little attention as possible—though my tears had already elicited some concerned looks—and scooted back outside. It would've been disastrous if Stuart had ever brushed skin with me in my natural timeline and observed Morley talking into thin air. Even more disastrous would've been if Stuart *could* see me and wanted to chat. I couldn't afford to sit through one of his long-winded stories.

Clearly, Morley wasn't inside anyway, so I hurried to a park bench across from the café to watch for his arrival. With the damp morning fog seeping through every pore in my clothing, I spread out my pilfered napkin and sat down, cursing Stuart for buggering up my plan. The guy had no clue he might be the reason civilization went sideways today.

"Come on, Morley," I muttered through chattering teeth, scanning the fog-cloaked Fourth Avenue—Morley's likely route of approach. But the street was eerily devoid of activity.

Behind me, one street away, lay one of three marinas in the area. It was the biggest one, and the most prestigious. Listening carefully, I could hear heavy ropes brushing against masts, sailboats bumping the dock, and the ever-present lonely squawk of seagulls. My nerves settled instantly. The familiar sounds were my anchor in this moment of uncertainty, empowering me to stay calm in the face of my difficult task.

Just then, a woman in a long, puffy coat appeared out of the mist, her tiny poodle trotting confidently alongside her.

Mildly concerned that I'd screwed up my arrival, I asked her what time it was.

She whipped her phone out of her pocket. "It's nine thirteen," she said with a pitying eye, no doubt noticing my hunched-over posture and insufficient clothing. She probably thought I was homeless. "God bless you," she said.

As she left, I attempted a smile with my numb lips. What did I have to smile about though? At least I could find solace in the fact that I'd timeblinked to the correct time. And if all went well, Morley would be arriving any moment.

But two minutes later when he still hadn't shown up, I pictured the last traces of the CQM escaping from my bloodstream, stopping this operation in its tracks.

"Damn it, Morley. Where are you?"

I contemplated running over to the condo to see if I could catch him there, but it would take me too long, especially in my flimsy black flats.

I hazarded another glance at the watch. My stomach tightened with panic. Eleven thirty-nine. That meant the CQM had already been active for three minutes and I only had seven minutes of its effect left.

Just as I was about to get up—to do what, I didn't know—another figure appeared out of the fog across the street, scattering my thoughts. I straightened up, squinting, trying to discern if it was Morley, and as I watched the person stride crisply toward The Bold & Bean, I nearly screamed for joy. It was unmistakably Morley, the man who, in another timeline, held the other half of my soul.

I leapt up, waving to catch his attention. "Morley!"

Through the swirling fog, I could see his eyes narrowing as he looked around, trying to find the source of my voice. Would he recognize me? In this timeline, he would be used to seeing me five years younger...mind you, it was always in the darkness of The Merryp—

"Syd?"

"Hi!" I yelled, trying to keep my composure, failing miserably. This was it, the world's fate hinged on this moment.

Morley's face lit up when he indeed recognized me, checking the street before hopping off the sidewalk to jog over. He flashed his charming, dimpled smile that would never fail to make my heart flutter, even now. For him, we were but casual acquaintances, with none of the history or heartbreak that our intertwined—yet completely separate—lives had accrued over time.

"What a pleasant surprise," he said as I gestured for him to join me.

He pulled out a handkerchief, spread it on the bench, and made himself comfortable. I barely heard a word of his polite small talk after that. My mind was buzzing, searching for the most natural way to steer the conversation toward the talisman. With mounting panic, I imagined resorting to desperate measures, simply asking him to show it to me out of the blue.

When Morley's lips stopped moving, I realized he'd just asked me a question.

"Pardon me?" I said.

His face scrunched into a look of concern. "Forgive me, but is everything okay?"

"Yes!" I blurted. "The brain's just a little scattered today. Listen, I—"

"Well, you look absolutely frozen." He nodded toward The Bold & Bean. "Would you like to join me for coffee?"

I shook my head. "I'm meeting a friend any minute now, thanks. But there is someth—"

"Just a sec." Before I could finish, Morley stood and shrugged out of his leather jacket and draped it gently over my shoulders. The lingering warmth comforted me immediately while the traces of his cologne, a soothing blend of cedar and bergamot, stirred a bittersweet longing deep in my soul. I closed my eyes for a moment, letting the spicy scent transport me back to simpler times—evenings spent curled in his embrace, my face buried in the nape of his neck. I used to tease him for spritzing on too much of that cologne, but now the scent only sharpened the pain of everything I was about to lose.

"Just until your friend arrives," he said, winking. "Can't have you catching your death out here."

I smiled cheerlessly, drawing my arm from under the jacket to steal another look at Collette's watch. Three and a half minutes left.

"Well, that's interesting," Morley said, eyeing my wrist. "May I?" he asked, reaching for my hand. I nodded, sensing I'd goofed.

He pulled my sleeve back. "Your watch. It looks strikingly similar to one that belonged to Collette." He turned my wrist back and forth in his grasp, shaking his head. "The burgundy strap. The sapphire. It's uncanny. If I didn't know better, I'd say this was the exact one. Come to think of it, I don't remember seeing it in her possessions after she died. I'll have to look again. I've been meaning to let go of some of her things…"

He seemed to want to say more but stopped himself and released my wrist. I could only nod as the second hand raced ever closer to my deadline.

"Anyway," he said, coming back to himself, "Collette inherited hers from her father who'd bought it in Peru. Did I ever tell you her family was from Peru?"

"Yes, I think so."

"Anyway, it's astonishing, the similarity. Where did you get it?"

That was my *in*. And I wasted no time jumping all over it.

"At one of the little shops on Antique Row. I have a weakness for vintage jewelry, and this one particularly interested me. Just like your dragonfly necklace…the one you inherited from Collette."

His hand went up to his shirt. "Of course, I remember you admiring it at the pub. Beautiful piece, isn't it?"

"Yes, particularly because I'm also a sucker for dragonflies. As a matter of fact," I said, willing myself not to lunge at him and grab it myself, "I'd love to see it again."

"Oh, of course," he said, obviously flattered as he fiddled with the top button of his cozy grey waffle shirt. I held my breath, torn between celebrating my victory or fearing for my life.

As Morley continued fumbling with his button, he sighed. "I must've told you I rarely take it off. One of these days, I'll have to say goodbye to it—along with all the other items I've been hanging onto the last four years."

I hated to rush him in his time of reflection, but there was less than a minute to go. "Maybe it's for the best," I said, practically vibrating with panic. "I'm sure Collette wouldn't want you to—"

His eyes narrowed. "Are you okay, Syd? You've suddenly gone very pale."

"I'm fine," I said, despite being on the verge of fainting, wondering if the CQM was partly to blame. *Oh God, don't let me pass out now.* "But I'd still love to see your—"

"Are you sure? No dizziness or nausea?" Morley pressed, clearly worried about my state.

Resisting another peek at the watch, I estimated there were less than thirty seconds to go. I leapt to my feet. "Please, Morley. The necklace. I need to s—"

He stood and gently took hold of my elbow. "Come on. You're trembling. Please sit down a minute."

"I don't have a minute," I said, my gaze darting around wildly, seeking a means to salvage this mission. It was no use. I would have to resort to brass tacks. "The thing is…I've had lifelong anxiety, and I'm at level ten right now," I sputtered, pulling my arm out of Morley's grasp, and taking another panicked glance at my watch. Nine seconds. I had to see that talisman. "And for reasons I'll never understand, the image of a dragonfly has always calmed me."

Without having to explain myself further, Morley undid another button on his shirt and pulled out the piece, holding it up for me to see. It twirled hypnotically between us for several seconds, and I felt a small shift in the air. I braced myself.

But there was nothing more. No blackout. No waking up in another realm. No falling into a fiery pit of hell.

I wobbled on my feet.

"Syd?" Morley grabbed my elbow again. "I'm worried about you."

I pulled my sleeve back. Five seconds past the deadline.

"No, no, no," I murmured, sinking to the bench.

Morley joined me and rubbed my shoulder tenderly. I stared at the talisman resting innocently on his shirt, willing myself to feel something—*anything*—that would set off the trigger. But the earth was still spinning as usual. And I was still breathing.

I'd failed.

I'd failed Collette. And my son. And the whole fucking world.

"You're trembling. Are you sure you won't at least join me for a nice, hot drink?"

"I—I don't think so. But thank you."

Despite his relaxed manner, worry lingered in his eyes. I wished he would gather me up in his arms and tell me everything would be okay, but we were just friends in this timeline. Virtual strangers whose union would someday spark worldwide chaos.

"Another time, then?"

I nodded, getting to my feet. I slid out of his warm jacket and handed it to him as he stood to face me.

"Thank you," I said, not knowing what I meant by it. Thanks for the coat? Thanks for being a friend? Thanks for possibly saving my life? Maybe I should have said *sorry* instead.

For whatever bedlam was about to be unleashed on him and the rest of the world.

"Glad to help, Syd. Enjoy your visit with your friend."

I already have, I thought.

After we said goodbye and Morley had disappeared into the café, I set off on a walk to clear my head. The implications of not resetting the timeline had my mind spiraling. I hadn't even considered the possibility that I would be returning four minutes and forty-four seconds after Lopez's car had left the road and plummeted over the bluff at Blackfin Cove.

Did it mean that I, too, would die in the fiery crash alongside Scott?

Maybe I deserved everything that was coming to me. Penance for exposing timeblinking. For interfering with the natural order of things. For abandoning my child.

Before I knew it, I found myself standing before the rose garden at Lighthouse Park, the mist casting an ethereal cloak over the scraggly, now dormant vines. Not another soul was in sight—helpful for my return timeblink.

I stepped through the archway and traced a path to the middle of the maze where the sundial offered no hint of the hour under the swirling fog—a cruel reminder that my time had run out.

I lowered myself despondently to a nearby wooden bench, not caring about the dampness seeping through my leggings. Not caring much about anything.

Four and a half minutes would have passed in the time that I'd left the doomed SUV. There wasn't a thing I could do to change it. Even if I opted *not* to go back—if I opted to stay here—the elasticity thing would boomerang me back to 2024, right into the burning vehicle...now or in two weeks. Why wait like a felon on death row?

I pulled my hoodie zipper down.

Took a breath.

Reached inside my shirt.

Another breath.

Grasped the talisman.

Turned my head left and right, hoping for someone to show up. Hoping for fate to intervene.

But no one came.

If I had to die today—whether because of Novikov or the stars or something bigger—it might as well be next to my son.

"Return."

Chapter Thirty

In the next instant, I was back inside the SUV.

To my utter astonishment, it wasn't engulfed in a raging inferno. The vehicle had come to rest intact and upside down, with me curled up on the cabin's ceiling. The space was unnervingly dark and cramped, with only a blade of afternoon sun slicing through the smashed front window. Lopez was still in his seat, his head bent at a horrific angle, the side of his face a gruesome mess of torn flesh and shattered bone. He wasn't moving.

I could hear ticking, hissing. Waves crashing against rock. Sirens in the distance. My stomach heaved at the stench of rotting seaweed and something else much more alarming: gas. It would only be a matter of moments before the vehicle erupted into flames.

From my curled position amongst a pile of shattered glass, I turned my attention to Scott. He was unconscious, dangling from the confines of his seatbelt. Blood dripped from a gash on his forehead and his glasses hung haphazardly on his face, one lens cracked. I reached over and removed them, managing in the tight space to tuck them into my pocket.

I had to release Scott from his seatbelt, but due to the

angle of the overturned vehicle and his slumped over position, the buckle was impossible to reach. I had to get him off that buckle.

"Come on," I pleaded.

With broken glass mercilessly grinding into my back, I uncurled my body and pressed my feet up against his shoulder, pushing with every ounce of strength left in my legs. But my window had been blown out, and I couldn't get leverage in the squished space. He wasn't budging.

The sirens had stopped. Maybe the police had parked and were on their way down the path at the south end of the cove. "Help!" I shouted. "Oh, please, anyone!"

As I shouted, I kept pushing, letting out an agonizing shriek when something sharp pierced my lower back. I felt it lodge itself in there, digging through skin, through muscle. I imagined it as a broken shard from the rear-view mirror, which was nowhere in sight. I stopped pushing. The pain was too extreme.

It was no use, anyway. I would never get him free.

"Oh, please don't take my baby this way."

With the growing reek of gas fueling my fear, I curled my arm behind me to pull the shard from my back, shuddering when it sunk even deeper. The world tilted. My vision dimmed. Oh, God. I could *not* pass out now.

I took a deep breath, my fingers closing around the shard.

I yanked it out of my spine.

Exhaled.

Commended myself for staying conscious.

Then I discovered that it wasn't a chunk of mirror at all; it was Collette's pocketknife.

And now I had a means to set Scott free.

With newfound hope, I began sawing frantically at the seatbelt. The knife was small but viciously sharp, and if I'd had sufficient room, I'd have severed the restraint in an instant. But the tight quarters rendered my efforts nearly useless and only triggered my lifelong fear of confined spaces. My back protested with each movement, agony radiating from where the knife had pierced my flesh, but I wouldn't give up now.

"Hang on, baby," I choked out, sawing, sawing, my stomach roiling from the stench of rotting kelp, body odor, and gasoline.

With a few more desperate strokes of the knife, the belt finally snapped. Scott collapsed to the debris field next to me with a thud but remained motionless. At least now I had a chance of getting him out. Of getting us both out. A stab of pain ripped through my back as I stretched to grab his shoulders, refusing to give up. I heaved him toward me, screaming until I was hoarse.

Just as I was making some progress and had moved Scott a few inches, his shirt ripped in my grip. I flew backward, my head knocking out the remaining glass in the window. Scott slumped away from me. Back to where he'd started.

"FUUUCK!"

I slammed the seat back with my fist repeatedly.

"HELP! SOMEONE, PLEASE!"

I wiggled out of my hoodie in the small space, meaning to hook it under Scott's armpits and try to drag him out that way, but his left shoulder was pinned beneath him. I screamed again.

My screams were so loud in fact, that I almost missed the sound of hurried footsteps crunching on glass outside the vehicle. Legs, a torso, and then a face appeared in the window —a police officer on his hands and knees surveying the situation. His embroidered name tag read *J. McCall*.

"It's going to explode!" I shrieked. "Please! You have to get us out."

"It's okay, miss. We've got you."

"My son! He's unconscious." The truth was, he might have been dead. But I didn't want to say it out loud.

"We'll get him. Come on, you need to come out first, though. Just relax, and I'll do the rest."

Why was he being so fucking calm? Wasn't it obvious the vehicle was about to blow?

"Oh, hurry," I begged. "Please, please, please. He can't die this way."

Officer McCall had me spin around with my head out the window. He linked his hands under my armpits and told me to relax again.

"I'm trying!"

"The sooner you do, the quicker we can get your boy out."

That did it. I went as limp as a dead fish.

The moment the officer had pulled me out of the wreck, there was an ominous whooshing sound. Sure enough, flames began crawling along the exposed undercarriage, small at first and spreading quickly. The officer's eyes went wide. He dragged me away from the vehicle as another cop arrived and took over Scott's rescue. "Please hurry!" I screeched, clawing the ground in terror until my nails began to bleed. "Please, please, it's going to blow!"

"I got the kid!" the new cop shouted. "Go grab the driver!"

McCall disappeared around the other side of the vehicle to pull Lopez out. It was probably a waste of time, judging by the asshole's injuries.

Bringing my attention back to what mattered, I allowed myself the faintest hope that Scott might survive, despite Collette's insistence he would not. But wait. She'd never said for sure that Scott had perished in the crash—just that it was his destiny to be in it.

And what if...*oh my god*...what if, because my boy had grown bigger and stronger in the meantime, it meant he would be more likely to survive the crash?

I leapt to my feet with renewed optimism, pacing as I waited.

As the second police officer worked quickly to extract Scott, I heard a commotion behind me. Half a dozen firefighters had appeared at the top of the steep bluff and were making their way down to the beach with armloads of rescue equipment and a hose. I turned back to the wreck, its undercarriage now a spectacle of flame and smoke. With a final tug, the officer pulled Scott's limp body out of the window and slung him over his shoulder.

A moment later, flames consumed the entire vehicle, shooting thirty feet in the air.

"Get back!" one of the firefighters yelled. "NOW!"

Everyone but the two firefighters carrying the hose scattered across the rocky shoreline, desperate to escape the unfolding disaster. I couldn't be sure if Officer McCall had succeeded in dragging Lopez from the wreck, but a small part of me hoped he hadn't.

Once we were a safe distance away, we all turned and stood in awe of the blazing vehicle—now just a vague outline within the consuming flames, barely recognizable as a car at all.

There was one more sinister whoosh.

Then it blew apart.

Chapter Thirty-One

The sliding glass doors of the Morley C. Scott Children's Pavilion whispered open, and I hurried through, my fingers burning from the cup of hot cocoa I was holding. A nurse at the reception desk looked up and offered a friendly hello, which I returned with a nod. Behind her, a framed photo of Morley caught my eye, and I smiled inwardly, knowing that this entire wing was a tribute to my long-lost soulmate.

At the end of the cheerily decorated corridor, I pushed through the door of Scott's room, expecting to see four occupied beds. Instead, I was surprised to find Lizzy and her other two kids chatting with Scott, the remaining beds empty. It shouldn't have surprised me to see Lizzy there. She was Scott's mother, after all, and these were Scott's siblings, both of whom I had yet to meet. All eyes were on me as I moved slowly into the room.

Scott was the first to speak. "Hi, Auntie." He winked mischievously, the bulky bandage on his forehead shifting.

"Hey, kiddo."

"My gosh, it's so good to see you," Lizzy said, rushing over to meet me at the end of Scott's bed, and giving me a warm

273

hug. I flinched and sipped air through my teeth, the small wound in my lower back stabbing me without warning.

"Oh! I'm sorry. You're still in pain."

"It's fine. I'm getting better. Though my fingers are on fire," I said, nodding to the cocoa in my hand. I hurried to the head of Scott's bed and deposited the cup on his side table.

"Kyle, Hayley…say hi to your Auntie Syd."

The boy, Kyle—a dark-haired cutie bearing a striking resemblance to his father—was quick to object. "She's not my auntie!"

Hayley rolled her eyes and gave me a shy wave. "Hi, Auntie Syd. Nice to meet you. Don't worry about Kyle. He's too young to know what manners are."

"Am not too young! I'm nine!"

Lizzy put her hand on Kyle's head. "Hey, hey. Enough, mister."

"That's okay," I laughed. "It's going to take some time for us to get to know each other."

Lizzy picked up a pile of jackets at the end of the bed. "Anyway, we were just about to leave. What do you say, munchkins? Shall we let Scott and Auntie Syd visit now?"

"Aw, can't we stay?" Kyle again.

"No. Hayley has to get ready for her soccer game this afternoon."

"Booooooring."

Lizzy shook her head as she distributed the jackets then slipped into hers. "Have a nice visit." She kissed Scott's temple and gave him a brief, tender look that I felt in every pore. It was the relieved look of a mother who understood how close she'd come to losing her child.

"Bye, Mom. See you tomorrow."

His reference to Lizzy as *Mom* still stung a little, but it was getting easier by the day. My greater struggle was adapting to *his* new name. It had been easy for the most part, but occasionally, a familiar gesture would flash me back to his toddler years, and I'd inadvertently blurt out his former name. He knew I was trying and never corrected me when I flubbed, opting instead to give me a wry smile or a knowing wink. Besides, he'd had his own lapses, referring to me as *Mom* a few times, especially that first day when he was drugged up with painkillers. Now? The *Auntie* label was flowing naturally off his tongue.

Once the family had left the room, I said, "So, I finally meet your siblings."

"Don't worry about Kyle. He's weird with all new people."

"I'll take that into consideration." I swept my eyes around the room at the empty beds. "Where are all your roomies?"

"Some kind of dance show on the main floor. I couldn't go because I had visitors."

"That's too bad."

He laughed. "I really didn't want to go. Sounded like it was for little kids anyway."

I tilted my head to the cup I'd left on his table. "I brought that for you. It's hot chocolate."

His face went solemn.

"You don't like hot chocolate."

He pushed his glasses up his nose and shook his head apologetically. "I don't like chocolate, period."

"Goodness," I said, sitting on the bed next to him. "Maybe we're not related, after all."

He laughed and rested the unbandaged side of his head on my shoulder. "You can't get rid of me that easily."

"Trust me. If you knew what I've been through the last three weeks, you'd know it was the last thing I wanted to do."

He lifted his head. "Thanks for visiting me every day. Will we still get to see each other after I get outta here?"

I ruffled his hair. "You can't get rid of me that easily."

"Very funny."

"But seriously, your mom and dad and I have worked it out. You're probably going to get sick of my mug."

"I don't think so. I still have so many questions about... *you-know-what.*"

His discretion was admirable, but it wasn't necessary in the confines of his hospital room. "And I can't wait to tell you all about it."

He beamed me the most charming smile that made my heart skip a beat. His resemblance to Morley was uncanny, dimples and all.

"Listen, this is just going to be a quick visit today. I'm off to see your dad right after this. Apparently he has some news about this Lopez fellow."

"What an ass that guy was."

"Now, now. The poor man was at the end of his rope. He got stuck with an unsolvable case, and his frustration got the best of him."

"*Poor man?* It's no excuse. He shot people."

Jarett's face popped into my thoughts, and a tear crested my bottom lid. "I'm so sorry you had to go through that, sweetie. It was awful. For all of us."

"It's all so unbelievable."

Sam and Lizzy had filled Scott in on his origin story two days ago, and he'd apparently taken the news in stride. What they hadn't been expecting was rapid-fire questions about the physics of timeblinking that neither of them had any way to answer. One day I intended to recount my dealings with Scott's former guardian and partial namesake, Dr. Collette Scott, but not today. Today was for being thankful.

"Before I go, I have something for you," I said, rummaging through my purse. "Don't worry, it's not chocolate."

He chuckled, and his eyes narrowed when I produced a small blue velvet box.

"I talked to your folks, and they agreed you should have this."

I popped the lid open. Nestled in the middle was Morley's

chunky white-gold ring, which I pried out and held up between us.

"It belonged to your biological father."

His face lit up. "Really? I can have it?"

"Really. I gave it to him when I proposed."

He studied it with awe without taking it from me. "Wait… *you* proposed to *him*?"

"A woman can't ask a man to marry her?"

"I'm just surprised. It's usually the other way around." He leaned in for a closer look. "What does it say inside?"

"That's the best part. It says *To live in hearts we leave behind is not to die.*"

He looked past the ring into my eyes. "How can my father live in my heart if I barely remember him?"

"Oh, Chris—*Scott*. The eight months you spent with him were some of the happiest of his life. He is most definitely in there," I said, placing my hand on his chest.

He nodded solemnly. I took his hand and slipped the ring onto his thumb, not surprised to find that it matched my own in size.

"He would've been so proud of your bravery the other day, kiddo, trying to take Lopez down like a boss," I said, attempting to bring some levity to the moment. "But, for goodness' sake, promise me you'll never do that again."

He cracked a self-conscious smile then went back to studying the ring. "I'll wear it forever."

I hoped I was doing the right thing giving a fourteen-year-old boy a precious keepsake like that. If he ever lost it, I would have to remind myself that it was just how things went.

"Well, sweetie, I'm off to see your dad in the other wing. I wish you could come along, but I need to speak with him privately this time around."

"That's okay, he came and saw me this morning already. Besides, I'm going to try to read for a bit—before all the rug rats get back from the show. See you tomorrow?"

My heart.

"Yes, and all the tomorrows after that. I love you."

"Love you too, *Mom*." he said, winking for the second time today, just like Morley used to do.

Sam wasn't in his room, so I checked the next obvious place: the other private room right next door.

"Well, well," I said, finding him seated in a wheelchair next to Jarett's bed with a handful of playing cards fanned out in his grasp. "If it isn't my two favorite cops."

"And if it isn't our friendly world savior. Come on in and join the party," Sam said, collapsing his cards and sliding them back into their box.

Jarett flashed me a wide smile. "Ah, yes, there she is. Our hero."

He looked much healthier compared to yesterday's visit when his face had still been the color of raw shrimp. He was still connected to several monitoring devices, though his oxygen cannula had been removed. He was improving by the day.

"You two are hilarious. I'm no hero. I failed to reset the timeline, remember?"

For two days after the crash at Blackfin Cove, I'd been consumed with dread about my botched mission. I'd spent every possible moment with my son, convinced that sometime in the near future, apocalyptic-style chaos would rain down on humanity, all because of my failure to set things right.

That is, until I woke up with a start in the wee hours of yesterday morning, remembering my last conversation with Collette. She'd said that the talisman *had always been meant to be found*. I'd been too overwhelmed at the time, but in a moment of complete clarity at three a.m., I'd recalled that she'd said that the purpose of the reset was to buy us bumbling mortals extra time so that when the talisman *did* resurface, we'd be much better equipped to handle its power. Maybe I hadn't bought as much time as I could've, but I *had* kept the talisman away from Lopez in the end. I'd shared the encouraging news with Sam and Jarett yesterday.

"So what if you failed your impossible mission?" Sam said, gathering up the rest of the cards. "Lopez is dead. He never got his hands on the talisman. Everyone lives happily ever after."

I dragged an ugly green armchair over and sat next to Sam. "But what happens when the FBI reads his reports?"

"That's what I wanted to talk to you about."

"Oh no."

"Don't worry. It's good news." He lowered his voice, even though it was unnecessary. "Apparently, the only record of Lopez's time-travel theory got incinerated in the explosion."

I looked at him sideways. "How does that work? What about *the cloud?*"

"Lucky for us, the guy was anti-tech. He'd submit only his basic findings electronically to keep his higher-ups from breathing down his neck, but if he was sitting on something big, he'd wait until the last minute to file his reports. Didn't trust computers as far as he could throw them." Sam repositioned his wounded leg with a grunt. "When Agent Jenkins came to see me yesterday, he let it slip that Lopez had been formally reprimanded several times for it over the last couple of years but still refused to follow protocol."

"So, what did he use? A typewriter?" I asked, incredulous.

Sam gave a satisfied shake of the head. "Even better. A silly little notepad that he kept with him at all times. It never stood a chance in the explosion. Apparently his clothes melted to his body."

"Ugh." The thought of it was horrible, even for a man who'd nearly killed my child.

"What's more, Jenkins intimated that the Bureau's having

a bit of a meltdown about Lopez's unwarranted aggression toward you and Jarett. They're hoping the whole thing can quietly go away."

"Does this mean they're going to finally leave us alone?"

"That's the impression Jenkins gave me."

Wow. The world wasn't going to end anytime soon *and* the FBI was going to back down. I wondered if I'd been destined to fail my mission all along. And if so, had Collette known?

I supposed it would have to remain a mystery; there was no way I was ever going to timeblink again. In fact, as soon as I'd been released from the hospital on Wednesday night, I'd driven out to the cabin and stashed the talisman in a spice jar at the back of a kitchen cupboard. I was still trying to decide what to do with it.

"Anyhoo," Sam said, tossing the deck of cards into his lap. "I gotta make tracks."

"Where are you off to in such a hurry, buddy?"

Sam released his brakes and rolled himself back from the bed. "Never liked being a third wheel," he said with a chuckle, giving his wheelchair an ironic pat.

I rolled my eyes. "Oh my god. Are you on about *that* again?"

"Oh yeah, again. And again. And again. Until you both realize what's under your damned noses."

I got up to open the door for him.

"See ya later, *Ross*," Sam said on his way out.

The door bumped shut. "Ross?" I asked, heading over to Jarett's tray table to grab his empty glass.

"Ha. You don't wanna know."

"I sure do."

"Okay, then. He's been calling me Ross for weeks. As in Ross Geller."

I furrowed my brows. The name sounded vaguely familiar.

"Ross and Rachel? *Friends*?"

"Oh my god. Seriously?"

"We're spitting images of them, don't you think?"

I shook my head in mock disgust as I stalked over to the tap to fill his glass with water. Inside, I relished every minute of it.

"Here. Drink up, before you get dehydrated."

"That would be impossible," he said, holding up his arm to show me his IV line. He took the water anyway.

As I sat back down, my lower back twinged, an enduring reminder of what I'd been through four days earlier. Though I didn't think I deserved the good fortune, I'd been spared the worst of the injuries of the group.

Scott had suffered two broken ribs, a head laceration, and a serious concussion, yet he bounced back surprisingly quickly and was scheduled to be released tomorrow. Sam had had a rougher time and required surgery thanks to Lopez's bullet tearing through his left thigh. It had missed his femoral artery by millimeters, so the outcome could've been much worse. He would need a few weeks to recover.

And then there was Jarett. Oh, Jarett.

He'd gotten the worst of Lopez's rampage, no doubt about that.

The Kevlar vest he'd been wearing under his uniform had provided no protection from the 9mm Luger round discharged from Lopez's gun. The bullet had hit him in the hip, dropping him to the ground like a sack of potatoes where he'd gone into a rare form of shock that I'd mistaken for his death.

"Any updates from your doctor?"

"Same old stuff. I'm going to need weeks —maybe months —of intensive therapy."

I patted his hand. "As I keep saying, you're going to kick ass."

"Hell yeah. I'm looking forward to the challenge." He waited a beat then looked me in the eye. "Listen, I have a confession."

"Oh boy."

He reached over to his night table and pulled out an item that made my breath catch.

The talisman.

"What the *fuck?*" I cried.

He tried to hand it to me, but when I recoiled, he lowered it to the bed.

"How did you get it? I hid the wretched thing at the cabin."

He bit his bottom lip tentatively, and then sighed with resignation. "Right after I stole it from Lizzy, I paid a silversmith an obscene amount of money to have a replica made on a rush basis. My plan had been to replace it like we'd talked about, but when I picked it up the next day, it was such an excellent copy that I got an idea."

My eyes narrowed. "What idea?"

"That I would switch it with the real one on your bedside table while you were asleep…and then pay Morley a visit."

My jaw fell open. I'd known about his trip to see Morley, of course, but this was a whole new level of sneakery.

"Why bother switching them? The original would've only been missing for five minutes while I was asleep."

"Like I said, I already had the copy. It was free insurance."

Where Jarett's deceit had once consumed me with rage, I'd come to recognize his actions as a misguided act of love, an attempt to clear a path to my heart by asking Morley to step aside. It was a shame it had taken me so long to see it.

I eyed the duplicate talisman on the bed, its likeness to the original uncanny.

When I looked up, Jarett's face had grown troubled. "There's something you need to know about it."

A wave of foreboding swept down my spine. Jarett shifted uncomfortably in his bed.

"After I visited Morley," he began, "I was sitting on my bed in your spare room, mesmerized by the talisman's power. I kept thinking about the possibilities, and before I knew it, I'd gone on four more timeblinks to various points in my life."

"Oh my god, you didn't go to the future, did you?"

He shook his head. "Why do you ask?"

"Long story," I sighed. "I'm just glad you didn't."

"I remembered it was how Morley found out his death date and didn't want to take that chance. Thought it was safer to go to the past."

It was hard to be angry with him. He looked as fragile as a baby bird. I could only shake my head in disappointment amidst the gentle whir of machines.

"I'm sorry," he said. "I couldn't help myself. The power was right there in my hands."

"I know the feeling."

"But something crazy happened after my final timeblink."

My jaw tensed.

"I was sitting on the bed, thinking about where to go next, when I totally crashed."

"You mean you fell asleep?"

"Yeah. Out cold."

"That's nothing out of the ordinary. I warned you about blink-lag."

"That's not the crazy part. The thing is, when I woke up several hours later, you were already up, and you were wearing the replica."

"So, when did you switch them back?"

"That's just it. I *didn't.*"

"Wait, what?"

He picked up the talisman by the chain and dangled it in front of me. "This is the original, Syd. I never got a chance to replace it."

My mind raced. "So that means…"

"You've been using the duplicate to timeblink ever since."

I stared at Jarett, the talisman twirling menacingly between us. He shrugged his shoulders apologetically.

"Are you sure?"

"Yeah. I was baffled. I wondered if maybe I'd sleepwalked and switched them back, but I checked. As identical as they were, the jeweler didn't get that little nick at the top quite right." He turned the talisman over in his hand to show me. Sure enough, the imperfection was there, like always. "The nick in the copy isn't as pronounced."

"H...how is it possible?"

"I've been banging my head against the wall trying to figure it out."

Indeed. How could a copy made from modern material possess the same power as an ancient piece that Collette's ancestors found in a cave? And if there were two talismans with the same power floating around, surely there would be more. I would never be rid of the curse.

"How?" I asked again.

"Maybe it's the dragonfly design."

"Maybe."

Or maybe I had the power forever now that I'd used the original one so long. Perhaps I didn't even need the talisman to timeblink anymore.

And that was a troubling thought.

Chapter Thirty-Two

OCTOBER 13, 2024, 11:40 A.M.

Vibrant splashes of green, gold, and scarlet stretched over Sandalwood Lake, its surface rippling gently under a mild breeze. Scott and I sat on the dock bundled tightly against the chill—me in a thick wool coat and Scott in a long-sleeved waffle shirt and down vest. Our breath escaped in faint clouds that dissipated over the shimmering water as the natural splendor of the lake calmed my soul. Out here, it was easy to let the troubles of the world slip away and enjoy the miracle of my son's survival.

Scott took a sip of his mint tea with honey—his favorite hot drink. Two peas in a pod, we were. "I've been meaning to ask you," he said. "Did Dad tell you about Dr. Scott's files?"

I'd been wondering when he would bring this up. "Yes, he did. Apparently he's had her trunk in his possession for some time."

"Yeah, Since 2015. Dr. Scott gave it to him a few weeks before she died. She said she trusted him to keep it hidden and that it wasn't to be opened until sometime in 2024."

"*Sometime?* She didn't tell him a date?"

"Nope. Just gave him an envelope that said '*Do not open until*

2024. You'll know when.' So when I got abducted from the lake that day, Dad figured it was the sign he'd been waiting for."

I wondered again if Collette had known all along that I would fail my mission. If so, what had been the point of it in the first place? The truth was, I didn't honestly care. Scott was safe, Lopez never got his hands on the talisman, and world chaos had been prevented (at least temporarily). And given what we were about to do today, it would be a very long time before anyone else stumbled on the talisman—or the replica—and reawakened its powers. That outcome was good enough for me.

"Your dad mentioned he's rifled through Dr. Scott's papers several times since that day, but he can't make head nor tails of her notes. What about you? Is it all gobbledygook to you, too?"

He chuckled. "Some of it, yeah. But I'm actually surprised at how much of it makes sense. I just finished reading her journals. Pretty interesting to hear her side of the story. You were so brave taking that CQR."

"CQM."

"Right!" He smacked his forehead where only a faint scar remained. "Cortical quantum modifier, not reviser."

"I barely remember what it stands for myself. You're way ahead of the game."

Scott plucked a flat oval-shaped stone from a pile next to him on the dock and weighed it thoughtfully in his palm. "It was cool reading about you from her point of view and why you were forced to give me up."

"I clearly made the right decision. Your folks love you very much."

In fact, I couldn't have asked for more exemplary adoptive parents for my boy, and now we were all getting into the groove of shared custody. Off the books, of course.

"Dad figured I should have full access to the trunk, since

Dr. Scott's work was about..." he lowered his voice to a whisper, "time travel."

I rubbed his back. "It's okay, kiddo. No need to be so cautious anymore. It's over."

"I know, Mom—er, *Auntie*," he chuckled. "I just know how important it is to keep the talisman's power a secret. I'll never tell anyone about it. Not even Hayley or Kyle."

"You're amazing, you know that?"

"Yep." He chuckled again. "I'm just glad you don't have to deal with the FBI watching you anymore."

I nodded vigorously. Indeed, the Feds had formally dropped their investigation of *The 444 Five* shortly after Lopez's funeral. They'd concluded that the agent and his protégé, Jenkins, had failed to prove beyond a doubt that my group had had anything to do with the plane crash. Granted, they were still scratching their heads about the other matter— how we got off that plane unscathed—but since we'd committed no crime, they had no grounds to continue their investigation. And Agent Jenkins was happy to let what he called "the bizarre theories of a man unhinged" die with him.

Scott went on. "It doesn't mean I won't try to learn all I can about time travel now that I have Dr. Scott's notes. I'll just do it behind the scenes."

I smiled, pride rising in my belly. My boy would sadly need to hide the secret of his origins in time and space forever. Perhaps exploring the relics of Collette's brilliance would be enough of a consolation.

I patted his knee. "Dr. Scott would be happy to hear that. Keeping the power a secret is all she talked about during our short time together."

"Her theories and trials are fascinating, but I've only just begun to explore them," he said. "She studied it all; time manipulation, biomechanics, mythology, chemistry, precious metals, you name it. All I gotta say is, wow. She's given me a lot to think about."

With a deft flick of his wrist, he sent his stone flying. It skipped across the water four times before vanishing into the depths. We watched the ripples spread and disappear.

"A new record," I said. "Five skips next time."

When Scott turned back to me, his boyish smile had faded into a more contemplative look. "My teacher says I have a natural talent for physics. We've been learning about space-time, dark matter, and Schrödinger's Cat."

"How about the Novikov principle?"

His pushed his glasses up his nose. "Not in class, but since it was such a big part of Dr. Scott's research, I've been studying it on my own. It's this idea that if time travel really existed, you couldn't change the past no matter how hard you tried."

I laughed. "That definitely sounds like something she would've said."

"According to Novikov," he continued, excited to explain the concept in more detail, "the universe kind of corrects itself. Events still play out how they're supposed to, they just unfold in a way where the time travel was already part of the sequence of events. Does that make sense?"

"Hell no," I laughed. "But I imagine it's partly why you're sitting here with me today."

"Yep," he beamed.

"I love that it makes sense to you."

"Thanks to the way Dr. Scott described it in her writing. She made it so easy to understand. The basic idea is that the timeline protects itself."

He shook his head, seemingly in awe of his words, much like a comedian might laugh at his own jokes. "Do you think human beings will ever know the whole truth about time and space and reality?"

"Oh boy, there's a question." After pondering it a few seconds, I said, "It's hard to say. Perhaps we were never meant to fully comprehend those mysteries, but I do think pursuing understanding is meaningful. In fact, it's one of the things Dr. Scott was passionate about. She believed it was important to explore life's deeper mysteries, especially as a means to help others."

Scott nodded, turning this idea over in his mind as he surveyed the tranquil lake. "Yeah, I want to figure that stuff out," he said. "I want to be a famous physicist and invent something that makes the world a better place for us."

I smiled and smoothed back a stray curl that had fallen across his forehead. My little boy who'd once taken apart a TV remote just to see what was inside was already dreaming big. I drew him close, kissing the top of his head. He lingered there a moment, comfortable in my embrace. I hoped he would never grow tired of this closeness.

Behind us, the faint crunch of tires on gravel broke the silence as a vehicle made its way down the driveway toward the cabin.

"Dad's here!" Scott shouted, jumping up and sending a few of his collected stones splashing into the water. I couldn't help but chuckle. After all this time, he was still fascinated with rocks, though now with a physics twist, experimenting with how many times he could bounce them across the water.

I followed Scott, attempting to keep up but failing miserably. Even as a dedicated runner, I was no match for the stamina of a fourteen-year-old boy—a boy who, besides being a science genius, was a star soccer player.

By the time I'd scooted through the house and arrived at the front door, Sam was already in the foyer getting the rundown of Scott's visit. The highlight, it seemed, was the project from yesterday afternoon—sanding and waxing the hull of my old canoe, a relic we'd pulled from the rafters in the garage and hauled down to the dock together.

Yes, it had been a great twenty-four hours, just the two of us.

Sam was smiling from ear to ear. "That sounds fantastic, buddy. Is she seaworthy?"

"Dad, we're just going out on the lake with it. But yeah. Look," Scott said, pulling up 'before' pictures on his phone. "Wait till you see it now. Looks straight out of a showroom!"

I chuckled. "I wouldn't say that, but you sure did make her sparkle."

Sam turned his attention to me, tilting his head toward his shiny new Suburban. "Where do you want our guest of honor?"

"How about you take him straight to the dock? We've cleared the path."

Sam's mouth fell open when he saw all the work we'd done on the previously overgrown jungle leading down to the lake. "You two really have been busy today."

"We did that yesterday," Scott volunteered. "Also, we moved my cherry tree to a different spot. Did you notice when you drove in? It's in the front yard now, next to the giant hydrangea bush. I hope it survives. We found out that you shouldn't transplant trees this late in the season, but not until after we already moved it. Auntie says it doesn't matter if it survives or not, since I'm alive."

"Hear, hear," Sam said, before Scott had a chance to ramble on any longer.

"Do you need help with Jarett?" I asked.

"Nope, I think we're good. Give me a minute."

I lingered in the doorway to watch Sam pull a wheelchair out of the cargo area of his vehicle and whisk it around to the passenger's side door where Jarett was expertly mounting a pair of crutches. I waved. He gave me a smile that matched the warmth of the midday sun. He steadied himself against the SUV while Sam engaged the wheelchair's brakes.

"Your chariot, sir," Sam joked.

"Thanks, buddy. I'll remember you if I ever need to choose a best man," he said, emitting short grunts through clenched teeth as he lowered himself into the chair. When he was safely seated, Sam patted his friend on the shoulder with a tenderness that gripped my heart.

"Good morning, Sunshine," Jarett chimed as Sam wheeled him over. He reached for my hand, and a tingle went up my spine when his lips brushed my knuckles.

"Good morning to you," I said. "Glad you could join us."

Our short relationship had once been burdened with extraordinary complications, and in no way had I expected him to forgive me for the shitty way I'd treated him. However, his gaze continued to hold only love and kindness, not judgment, and I found myself letting go of my guilt, little by little every day.

"Shall we?" Sam suggested, pointing toward the path to the lake.

"You guys go ahead. I'll meet you on the dock in a few minutes. I hope you're hungry."

"Do you need help, Auntie?" Scott asked.

"No, I just have to pull the brie out of the oven and put the finishing touches on the charcuterie board. But you could grab a couple of side tables off the deck for the food."

"I'm on it."

Gosh, I had a good kid.

In the kitchen, I spread a dollop of spicy tomato jam on top of the brie before sliding it back into the oven, and while I waited for it to heat, I watched my little entourage setting themselves up on the dock. Jarett had jumped at the chance to get away from rehab for the afternoon and take part in today's ceremony—a symbolic letting go. By the end of the day, time-blinking would be a distant memory, only to be dredged up years, decades, or perhaps even centuries from now when some unsuspecting soul stumbled on the talisman and the strange and dangerous power it possessed.

As Scott and I carried the food down to the dock and I caught sight of Jarett trying to get comfortable in his chair, I felt an overwhelming need to look after him. Forever, if necessary. The idea, I discovered, didn't scare me at all.

After I'd set the hot cheese on a cork trivet, Jarett caught my hand and drew me down, planting a kiss on my lips that made me quiver with pleasure. If I hadn't sworn off using the talisman ever again, I would've been tempted to transport myself to a time in the future where his wounds had healed, and he'd regained full bodily function. His specialists had insisted that would happen sooner rather than later at the rate he was tackling his therapy, and I couldn't wait.

"Go on, eat before it gets cold. It's your favorite."

"You're too good to me."

I winked at him. "Isn't that the truth."

"You two are the ding-dang cutest," Sam said. "And to think how you insisted there was nothing going on."

Jarett popped an olive into his mouth. "I said nothing of the sort."

"That was aimed at you, Syd."

I gave Scott a look of mock annoyance. "These two just can't help themselves."

"It means they like you."

"Wise words from the young'un," Jarett said, raising his can of soda. The other two clinked their cans against his, and they all erupted into laughter.

Twenty minutes later, I had Scott and Sam overturn the canoe and lower it into the water, tethering it to a boat cleat on the dock. The mood had gone down a few notches as we began our ceremony, but not enough that it could be called somber. In fact, we were all looking forward to getting it over with as quickly as possible.

"Any objections before we do this?"

Scott raised his hand.

"Let's hear it, then."

"I've seen what that necklace can do. Don't you want me to study it and become a famous scientist someday?"

I walked over to him. Placed my cool palms on his rosy cheeks. "Sweetheart, you're going to blow the socks off the scientific community on your own merit someday. You don't need this silly necklace to do it."

"But…"

"No buts."

"You asked if anyone had any objections."

"True, but I didn't say it would change my mind."

He groaned. "I'll just have to get my diving certificate and go looking for it someday."

I glared at him. "You wouldn't dare."

"He wouldn't," Sam said, putting his hand on Scott's shoulder. "He's terrified of the water."

Scott scowled at his dad, and before he could open his mouth to protest, I pulled two glass spice jars out of my pocket. "Well, it's now or never," I said, holding up the jars and giving both talismans a quick rattle.

Scott's eyes narrowed. "Wait. Why are there two?"

"I'll fill you in later," I promised. "Come on. Let's do this."

"No way, Auntie. You're not getting off that easy. Seriously, where did the second one come from?"

When it was clear he wasn't going to let me off the hook, I explained how Jarett had had a duplicate made and how, for reasons beyond my comprehension, I'd been able to timeblink using the copy. I finished with my suspicion that having utilized the original one for so long, I could now timeblink without any talisman at all.

"But I still want to get rid of the vile things."

Scott wore a pensive look. "Have you tried timeblinking without them?"

"Not on your life. I'd rather not know that I'm cursed for all of eternity, thank you very much."

He was staring at me with such focus, I could almost envision the gears in his brain spinning. And then his eyes went wide. "No, no. You won't have the power forever! You can dump the talismans in the lake and be free."

"How?" I asked wearily, not really believing a fourteen-year-old boy held the solution to this problem.

"Dr. Scott's experiments," he said, absently spinning Morley's ring on his thumb. "She'd been testing her theories on temporal energies being absorbed through skin contact."

"Can you say that again in plain English, please?"

"Sure. Dr. Scott had tons of notes explaining how she herself had experimented with duplicate talismans. They would work at first, but after a while, they would lose their power."

"I'm sorry, but you've lost me."

He began pacing the dock. "Wow. This all makes so much sense now."

We all stared at him, waiting for the punchline.

And then he delivered it. "Dr. Scott realized that the original talisman was giving off this residual energy that could be absorbed by the wearer's skin, and that the duplicate talismans would in turn absorb that energy. Then, after about a week, their power would naturally wear off. Kind of like sunscreen. Like, it's only on your skin for a while, then it washes off or gets absorbed into the bloodstream and filtered out of the body."

Nobody spoke.

Scott pointed to the jar labeled '*copy*' in my left hand. "When's the last time you touched that one?"

"Oh, several weeks ago now. I wanted nothing to do with either of them after that crazy day last month."

Scott smiled matter-of-factly. "I'll bet you a million bucks that if you tried the fake now, it won't work. Any residual energy from the original talisman has already worn off of your skin."

I eyed the replica, hesitant, but curious to know if Scott's theory held any weight.

"I mean, it's worth a try, right?" Jarett said.

I handed the original talisman to Scott then spilled the fake out of its jar and fastened it around my neck. It settled comfortably on my chest, midway between my collarbones and cleavage. "I hope you're right about this, sweetie."

"I *know* I am. It's all in her notes."

I took the piece between my thumb and forefinger and then recited a location, time, and date: the night of my first timeblink. "Chapman Falls, April 20, 2019."

I closed my eyes and braced myself.

To my utter astonishment, when my eyes flicked open a moment later, I was still rooted to the dock, surrounded by my special people.

"Told ya!" Scott shouted.

"You sure did." Sam patted him on the shoulder.

I shook my head, relief spreading through my entire body.

Scott pulled the other spice jar out of his pocket and jingled the real talisman in front of me. "Do we really have to get rid of it? Can't we just keep it in the jar forever?"

I threw Sam a look of dismay. "Does he insist on keeping spiders and snakes, too? You know, other scary things that can hurt you?"

Sam only laughed.

"Come on. Let's get this show on the road." I was desperate to end this chapter of my life and get on with a new one.

Scott and I boarded my newly polished canoe and we paddled out to the middle of the lake.

"Here?" he asked when I stopped rowing.

"It's as good a spot as any."

He looked around. "Yeah, I think I'll be able to remember where we dumped it."

"Come here so I can whip your butt," I joked.

He laughed, unscrewing the lid from the jar while I removed Jarett's fake talisman from around my neck.

Once I had the replica grasped firmly in my hand, Scott asked, "Why're you getting rid of that one, too? It doesn't work anyway."

"Because it makes me anxious."

The explanation seemed to satisfy him.

"All right," I said, looking him in the eye. "Ready?"

He tipped the talisman into his palm and studied it longingly. "If we must."

We held our fists face-down over the placid water.

Exchanged a final nod.

Opened our fingers.

And let go.

As the artifacts plunked gently into the water, Scott and I leaned over the side of the boat to watch their descent. A shaft of sunlight struck both dragonflies as they twirled around each other like mischievous fairies before vanishing into the depths.

"Well, that's that," Scott said, sighing. "Now what?"

I picked up an oar and waved it enthusiastically at the two men on the dock. Their hoots and hollers carried across the water and filled my heart with joy.

"We go live our best lives, my dear, just like the universe always planned."

Acknowledgments

As this grand timeblinking journey draws to a close, I'm profoundly grateful to those who have come along on this big, crazy ride with me. Your presence transformed the solitude of writing into a shared adventure, and together, we've brought Syd's universe to life.

To Alistair, my partner in all things practical and fantastical, your grounded support is my secret weapon.

To my cherished circle of friends, mentors, and beta readers: Dawn Dugle, Jessica Cantwell, Janet Rau, Ginny Martin, Stephanie Dunham, Patrick Zulinov, Lee Gabel, Alison Cairns, Erin Fischer, and Dorothy Mumford. Your encouragement and insights have helped guide this story along its destined path.

A special nod to the clever minds behind the scenes: Amanda Peters, whose editorial acumen is unmatched; Elizabeth Mackey, for cover art that captures the essence of my stories; and Alison Cairns, for managing all the digital frippery backstage like the Great and Powerful Oz—oh, and also for your exceptional beta reading skills to boot! Without your passionate views on *Dragonfly*'s original ending, this story may not have reached its full potential.

And to you, dear reader, for finding your way to the Time-Blink trilogy. Attracting a readership for this unique mix of time travel, thriller, and love story has been a strange and wonderful endeavor. But clearly you get it. Thanks for investing in Syd, her friends, and her ensemble of handsome leading men—even the dastardly Viktor way back in book one.

As we part ways in this timeline, I'm excited at the prospect of meeting again in future stories, which will promise the same engaging twists and turns you've come to enjoy. Until then, hold your talismans close—and should you wish to revisit Syd's world someday, you need only whisper, "Return."

MJ's Cabin Crew

AN INVITATION

Join MJ's Cabin Crew to ensure your future includes new release updates, sneak peeks, book deals, surveys, and a dash of time-traveling fun to brighten your inbox.

Plus: Get *Dragonfly: RESET*, a **free** downloadable **alternate ending** to *Dragonfly* and discover an entirely different destiny for Syd…one you may or may not have wished for.

Sign up at **mjmumford.com**
or scan this QR code to access the bonus ending.

About the Author

MJ Mumford's first novel, *TimeBlink*, debuted in 2020 amidst a worldwide health crisis. It wasn't the worst timing for a book launch. At a time when many of us were scared, anxious, or bored to tears, books provided the perfect escape to less precarious worlds.

As a huge fan of time-travel thrillers, suspense novels, and simmering love stories, MJ created The Syd Brixton Time-Blink Series to blend all three genres into one narrative.

When she's not dreaming up devious ways in which to torment her characters, MJ enjoys tap dancing, practicing yoga, and traveling to faraway places with her husband. Curiously, MJ never leaves home without her own trusty dragonfly talisman—an object rumored to be more than just decorative.

Hang out with MJ in the following places:
mjmumford.com

Before You Go...

If *Dragonfly* has entertained you, please consider leaving a review on your favorite reading platform. Besides being a meaningful way to show your enjoyment, it helps new readers discover the TimeBlink series.

With heartfelt thanks,

MJ Mumford

Made in the USA
Middletown, DE
14 October 2024

62576911R00187